Praise for *The Principles of Love*

"Love Bukowski lives up to her first name as a sweet and charming character whose trials and tribulations, seen through her witty and keen perspective, will have you rooting for her all the way to the last page. A delightful novel and journey that Franklin's writing makes feel like your own."

—Giselle Zado Wasfie, author of *So Fly*

"Both funny and moving, *The Principles of Love* is a wild ride that gives a fresh perspective on what really goes on at boarding school. I couldn't help but get sucked into Love Bukowski's life, and look forward to her next adventures."

—Angie Day, producer of MTV's *Made* and author of *The Way to Somewhere*

"Whether you're sixteen and looking forward or thirty-six and looking back, the first book in the Love Bukowski series will pull your heartstrings with comic, poignant, and perspective takes on the teenage tribulations of lust, life, and long-lost mothers."

—Heather Swain, author of *Luscious Lemon* and *Eliot's Banana*

"It's easy to fall in love with Love Bukowski. Emily Franklin's novel is fun, funny, and wise—a great book for readers of all ages."

—M. E. Rabb, author of *The Rose Queen* and *Missing Persons Mystery Series*

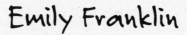

the PRINCIPLES of L♥VE

Piece, Love, & Happiness

Emily Franklin

nal jam books

NAL Jam
Published by New American Library, a division of
Penguin Group (USA) Inc., 375 Hudson Street,
New York, New York 10014, USA
Penguin Group (Canada), 90 Eglinton Avenue East, Suite 700, Toronto,
Ontario M4P 2Y3, Canada (a division of Pearson Penguin Canada Inc.)
Penguin Books Ltd., 80 Strand, London WC2R 0RL, England
Penguin Ireland, 25 St. Stephen's Green, Dublin 2,
Ireland (a division of Penguin Books Ltd.)
Penguin Group (Australia), 250 Camberwell Road, Camberwell, Victoria 3124,
Australia (a division of Pearson Australia Group Pty. Ltd.)
Penguin Books India Pvt. Ltd., 11 Community Centre, Panchsheel Park,
New Delhi - 110 017, India
Penguin Group (NZ), cnr Airborne and Rosedale Roads, Albany,
Auckland 1310, New Zealand (a division of Pearson New Zealand Ltd.)
Penguin Books (South Africa) (Pty.) Ltd., 24 Sturdee Avenue,
Rosebank, Johannesburg 2196, South Africa

Penguin Books Ltd., Registered Offices:
80 Strand, London WC2R 0RL, England

First published by NAL Jam, an imprint of New American Library,
a division of Penguin Group (USA) Inc.

First Printing, November 2005
10 9 8 7 6 5 4 3 2

Copyright © Emily Franklin, 2005
All rights reserved

NAL JAM and logo are trademarks of Penguin Group (USA) Inc.

LIBRARY OF CONGRESS CATALOGING-IN-PUBLICATION DATA:

Franklin, Emily.
    Piece, Love, and happiness : the principles of Love / by Emily Franklin.
       p. cm.
    Summary: As summer vacation comes to an end, Love Bukoski faces her junior year at
Hadley Hall with some trepidation as she tries to cope with her favorite aunt's struggle
with cancer, her father's continuing remoteness, lost friendships, a faded romance, and
being responsible for hosting the new exchange student from London.
    ISBN 0-451-21666-0
    [1. Interpersonal relations—Fiction. 2. Aunts—Fiction. 3. Fathers and daughters—Fiction.
4. Coming of age—Fiction. 5. Boarding schools—Fiction. 6. Schools—Fiction.]   I. Title.
PZ7.F8583Pie 2006
[Fic]—dc22   2005014383

Set in Bembo
Designed by Ginger Legato

Printed in the United States of America

For Jules, my transatlantic sister

ACKNOWLEDGMENTS

Thank you: Faye, Anne, Jenn, and Adrian for all the enthusiasm and help. And, as always, love and appreciation to: Adam, Ellie, Sam, and Nathan, and the rest of my wonderful family.

CHAPTER ONE

♡

End of summer

With a name like mine, signing letters has never been easy. If I write *Love,* Love, I sound either redundant or drunk, and if I go with *From,* Love, I feel like I'm passing out third-grade Valentine's Day cards (and not in that ironic way), and *sincerely* sounds neither sincere nor friendly. So, though I've gotten only as far as scripting a letter to Jacob in my head, I haven't committed the words (or anything else, for that matter) onto paper. I'm using not knowing how to sign it as my excuse. Besides, Jacob's still in Europe, pouting in France, or doing whatever it is people do in Belgium—and I'm here.

Here being a train en route from Boston to Providence to visit Brown University–attending Lila Lawrence (aka Shiny Perfect Blond Girl). After summering in Newport, I'm sure Lila's a tan ten, and probably she's been granted an enormous suite with other freshmen of her ilk (emphasis on ill). But I have to say, I'm psyched to see her. Since I pretty much lived in the editorial offices of *Music* magazine this summer, staring out at a New York City I hardly ever got to experience, I've been missing actual human contact. Sure, there were other people in the office with me, but they were mainly of the tank-topped and toned hip set (of which, despite my internship, I was not considered one) and forty-year-old editors who never knew who I was. One of them actually called me *Thingy* (i.e., "You there—Thingy—could you just run out and get me a soy macchiato?") or, even better, to the infamously cool guy rock star from northern England whose wallet wound up lost in an uptown cab, "Don't worry about canceling the cards—just have Thingy do it."

"Hi, I'm Thingy," I wanted to say when I came back to Boston with my crumpled clothing. (Can I just say how much doing laundry is *not* like in those sexy ads where hot boys always seem to lurk by the fabric softener machines?) Back at my house, Dad was as remote as I'd ever seen him, tucked in his study filing papers or just sitting there at his desk.

"Hello?" I'd tried standing in the doorway, shifting my weight and scuffing the hardwood floors to get him to turn around, but he hadn't. Finally, I went over to him and hugged his shoulders.

He tipped his head back to face me. "Hi, Love." I've lived with my father and no one else for all of my nearly seventeen years, and I can honestly say that I'd never heard his voice so drained. Not even last year when I'd been in trouble at school, not even when I'd pissed him off by repeatedly wanting information abut my mother, not even in our early years before his somewhat cushy position as headmaster at Hadley Hall.

"Want to tell me about it?" I asked, trying to be the parent in an after-school special. (Worst title ever = *Is Jenny Smoking the Dope? No, Jenny, Don't Do It!* Lila and I found the grainy video from 1981 in the library last year. This summer, we reenacted it when I'd visited her in Newport, one of her mother's clove cigarettes, in a 1920s Art Deco holder, no less, substituting for "the Pot".

Dad didn't pick up on my light tone. Instead, he turned back to his desk, shuffled through some papers, and—when he saw me snooping over his shoulder—turned whatever he was reading facedown. "Are you going to the Vineyard with Mable?" he asked. "It's so nice there this time of year." His face had that look of remembering something, but he didn't offer to share whatever was mulling around in his mind.

I shook my head. "I was going to, but Lila's got her second weekend at Brown—classes don't start until Tuesday, so I thought it'd be—"

He cut me off, which—being a principal and convinced students and teenagers will spill their guts without being asked if they're just allowed to ramble—he hardly ever does. "Well, have fun."

"So I can go?" He didn't even mention the lack of supervision, the fact that I'm a soon-to-be junior heading off for a college weekend. I didn't wait for him to reconsider.

Outside my Amtrak train's window, Providence is in view. I don't mean providence, like some divine intervention, but I'm not ruling that out. I mean the little city south of Boston, population 173,618 (10.34 percent in the fifteen-to-nineteen-year-old age bracket—yes, I do spend far too much time online with my God of choice, Google, but what can you do)?

It's weird, those choices you make in life that usually end up making the differences; I could've gone to Martha's Vineyard with Aunt Mable and had a whole group of experiences that I'll never know now, but I made the decision to come here. Just like my decision this past June to go to the infamous Crescent Beach grad party where—amidst the sand, sweat, and seniors, I managed to alienate Jacob. Jacob, one of the highlights of my sophomore year. Jacob with the tousled ringlets and green eyes. Jacob with the extensive knowledge of lyrics from every decade, who actually cared about what I had to say and wanted to travel around Europe with me.

Jacob who somehow thought he saw me making out with someone in the dunes at said infamous Crescent Beach party. Lila said shit like that happens every year; someone gets dumped, or throws up, or confesses four years of love or lust. And every year, someone goes home heartbroken. This year, I was that person.

"It's the *end of something* emotions," Mable explained to me when I met her for coffee at Slave to the Grind after the party's fallout. She'd cut back on her hours there on Sundays (even after calling off her engagement in the spring, which I still don't fully understand) claiming fatigue (fatigue=boredom?)—to bake caramel grahams and oversized krispy treats.

"Huh?" I wasn't particularly eloquent that afternoon, having been up virtually the entire night, dealing with a frantic Lila at Crescent Beach (Frantic = *Will I make friends at Brown? How the hell can I cope with my crazy mother this summer? Oh my God—I loved my years at Hadley Hall—I can't believe I'm done with high school! Will I make friends at Brown?* Um, you already asked that, Lila. And so on, in a vicious cycle of questions and reassurances).

Then, right when I'd calmed Lila down, I'd gone for a quick walk with Chris the MLUT (male slut) and was enjoying actually conversing with said slut in the quiet dark of the dunes (we were hunched over, shielding our eyes from the massive wind and sand gusts) when I spotted Jacob, who hadn't even planned on showing up for the festivities, claiming they were lame/for drunk seniors/too far away. He marched over to us in a state of total guy-pissed-offness (could I be any less grammatical?). He had that look like he'd caught me in the act of something terrible, and put his hands on his hips, twisted his mouth, and raised his voice (okay, probably this was due to anger *and* the fact that he had to in order to be heard over the wind, blaring music, and shrieks).

"I don't believe you," Jacob said. He looked around the tiny cove as if there'd be evidence—a ripped condom wrapper, mussed sheets, or smeared lipstick—none, none, and none. (I don't even like lipstick, and I can attest to never having ripped a condom open except in sex class, which, at Hadley Hall, is called Options and Information: A Health Journey—um, yeah, sex—and the second part of it—what the students call "Advanced Sex"—is coming up—heh—next year. How thoughtful of the academic planning committee to save that choice morsel for senior year).

Chris the MLUT stood up, somehow totally in tune with the situation, and tried to calm Jacob down. (Chris is English and always sounds calm—or debonair, which I admit wasn't helpful in this scenario.)

"Listen, Jake," Chris said. He brushed the sand off of his shorts and raked his hand through his floppy hair (floppy = sexy British, not Viagra-esque).

"Jacob. Not Jake," Jacob the Agitated corrected.

"Jacob," I said and went to hug him. "I didn't think you were coming."

"I'm sure you didn't," he said. He backed off from my hug and swiped my hand away when I tried to clasp his.

"Look," Chris said, "I don't know what you thought you stumbled upon here, but I assure you—"

"You look," Jacob said to both me and Chris. "Save the bullshit for someone else. Clearly, I misread you this year, Love." My heart was racing, I opened my mouth to talk, but Chris spoke first.

"Dude, you're totally overreacting. We were talking."

"Oh," Jacob said, TV-sarcastic. "You were talking." He stretched out the word and pointed his finger dangerously close to my chest. I looked down. The top two buttons of my button-down had popped open. So much for shopping cheap in the boys' section.

I laughed. "Oops. Sorry." I quickly did the buttons up, but then the top one popped again. "Guess it's a little . . ."

Jacob stuck his hands in his pockets. "Forgive me, then, if you were just talking. I hope you remembered a condom for the *conversation*." I'd never heard this kind of tone from Jacob. He always spoke in a mellow, hushed way. Part of me was annoyed about how annoyed he was, but part of me—I don't know—is it weird that I was attracted to him being bothered? To his credit, he didn't bring up the internship at *Music* magazine, or my choice to accept that rather than his invite to Europe. (I believe his exact words were, "I'll always be here for you, and so will Europe—

except the parts like Venice that are sinking—but you might never get a chance to work at that kind of place again.")

And just like that, he stormed off. Of course, I chased after him; he was too much a part of me to just act cool and let him, but he didn't want to hear my explanation. Chris the MLUT even tried to defend my honor—a bit too frantically, actually—but nothing worked.

So that's where Jacob and I had left things; he'd gone to Europe and I'd frolicked in New York (frolicked = was editorial muffin slave). The best part of the summer had been writing a two-sentence blurb in *Music* magazine (which sadly was cut from the final printing), meeting some big-time music execs whose business cards I still have, and visiting Lila in Newport. Ah, good times.

CHAPTER TWO

♡

From my backpack, I pull out a slightly wrinkled photograph of me and Lila on the beach in front of her palatial waterfront house. You can see Hildgaard, the maid, a speck way in the background. What you can't see is the tray in Hildgaard's hand—a tray thoughtfully prepared with Long Island ice teas à la Lila's mother (read: way sweet but totally alcoholic). We spent the weekend flirting with the double-breasted-blue-blazered set: Edward III this, Petey Duckworth Livingston, Jr., etc. (etc. = bizarre nicknames like Bean, Chucko, Cricket), swimming, and generally goofing around. And never once, despite still feeling a tiny morsel of it inside—did I feel like the ugly stepsister. I felt like I belonged.

I know that the train conductor is announcing our arrival into Providence—right near the Brown University campus—because I recognize the view—and because I can see Lila jumping up and down, flailing her arms like a deranged cheerleader. I crack up. The lady across from me on the train raises her eyebrows, probably thinking I am one of the disturbed teenagers she's reading about in her *Time* magazine. This just makes me laugh harder.

I sling my bag over my shoulder, pick up my mini duffel, and clumsily make my way off the Amtrak and over to Lila. She whips off her hat and shows me her newly cropped head. Her hair is short at the back, and blond bangs cover the side of her face.

"You are the only person besides Gwyneth Paltrow who can pull off that cut. You look amazing!"

"Oh my God, I'm so glad you're here!" She throws her arms around me before I've dropped my bags, and this knocks me so off-balance I fall over, pulling her with me. We're collapsed in a heap, Lila kind of lying sideways on my legs, me toppled onto the cushion of my duffel. Two guys walk by and shout "Girl fight! Yeah!" like we're topless or squelching in a pudding product or something.

"You wish!" Lila says back to them, laughing.

"Could we be any dorkier?" I ask. We don't even bother to stand up until one of the train station porters tries to get by us with a massive cart and can't.

"We should go," Lila says. We start walking toward the exit, and she takes one of the handles of the duffel so it swings between our hands, lighter for each of us.

"I can't wait to see your room," I say. "And meet your friends. And see the campus. The only time I ever really spent in Providence was that day last year . . ."

She finishes my thought. "The day with Jacob, you mean?"

"Yeah." We dodge the oncoming passengers, swaying together so we don't drop the bag or bump anyone.

"Do you miss him?" Lila adjusts her baseball cap. It's a pink one with the Boston Red Sox logo on the front. Of course, she looks sporty and adorable at the same time.

"I do." I stop for a minute. I can picture his face so clearly, the way his mouth turns down at the sides. How his hands felt on my face. And I didn't even get to feel them that much. But everything about him is so easy to recall. "I wonder what he's doing right now."

"Probably getting ready to go back to Hadley."

"Maybe." I picture him in Paris, or Rome, and wonder about all the amazing landmarks he's seen. If he's seen them with someone else.

"God, that's really far off," Lila sighs. We keep moving.

"What is?"

"The whole high school thing. Hadley Hall." This doesn't come out wistfully, more snooty.

"It's not like it was that long ago, Lila," I say and semi-snort. Pretty. "You graduated only three months ago."

She shrugs. And then, just as I'm about to make a joke about her being *so* much more mature than I am—just a soon-to-be-lowly-junior—two amazon-tall women (blur of dark denim, tweed, flowing hair) come by and say, *"Bonjour"*. Ah, Euros. (Euros = the titled and the wealthy wannabes. The kind of people who keep their passports in their pockets every day—never know when you'll be invited to someone's château or decide to do a day trip to Brugge.) Seeing the two women makes Lila immediately drop her side of the duffel, which sends me flying to the ground.

"Part two of the Dork Olympics!" I shriek up at Lila. But she's not laughing. She's looking at the Euros and then back at me, and—I don't think I'm imagining this—she looks like she's embarrassed to be seen with me.

"This is my room," Lila says, showing me her digs. She's part of a sextet (and, yes, having seen her other roommates, I think the emphasis is on the sex part. Three gorgeous women and three even better-looking guys—hello, reality show?).

"It's nice," I say. It's fine. Just a bed, a dresser, and a small window. Lila hasn't unpacked yet. Her suitcases and bags are all unzipped, partially undone—clothes everywhere. For some reason, I thought she'd have gotten settled before I visited. Or at least cleared a place for me to sit.

"Just push the clothes onto the floor." I sweep my arm dramatically over the end of her bed, sliding two dresses and a shirt onto the rug in the process.

Lila's pissed. "Not those. I just had those cleaned." She huffs and picks the dresses up, cradling them like a day-old baby, and puts them carefully onto hangers and into the closet.

"Sorry," I say.

"No, I'm sorry," she sighs. "They're just dresses. Never mind." Sheepishly, she takes off her hat and turns to me. I stare at Lila's new haircut. Aunt Mable always said that when women alter their hair—either color or cut, or both—it means there's something brewing emotionally. I've never really done much with mine—it's been stick straight and copper toned forever. But with Lila, I'm seeing Mable's words come true.

Four hours later and we've skipped dinner (since when did Lila eschew a good burger? She didn't even want a handful of Cap'n Crunch that was on offer in the dining hall), and my stomach is making hissing noises while Lila sips her fifth martini-esque drink.

I'm sitting with Lila and Dominic Der Pashmina (I'm making up that last part—she slurred when she introduced herself—but close enough) and a variety of Brown University preps and poshes.

Lila grabs my arm hard enough to leave a mark. "Oh my God, there he is!"

"Who?" I ask. Lila rolls her eyes and Pashmina does the same.

"My plan B," Lila says. "You know, like if I can't get Hans Hecklefranz, my first-choice guy, I'll go for him."

"His name is Giles, I think," Pashmina says. She's talking to us but also into her incredibly small cell phone. "Shut up! Mitin!" This last part she's yelling into the phone. (Mitin = more information than I needed—an oft-used expression by Lila and her suitemates.)

Lila turns to me and smiles, normally, not like the college android she's turned into. "But enough about Giles, I'm so getting Franz." She pronounces Giles in French: *Jeeeluh.*

"I thought you said his name was Hans."

Lila's annoyed. "Yeah, but everyone calls him Franz."

I picture where I could be right now: home in bed watching *My So-Called Life* on DVD, or writing songs I won't sing, or actually finishing an email to Jacob, or just hanging out on Martha's Vineyard with Mable. Then I feel rude, so I try to join in on the fun.

"So, what classes are you guys taking?" It's lame, sure, but it's all I can quickly summon up without cashing in on the bitchfest that Lila and the Moneys are having. No one responds.

"Here she is," Pashmina says. She gestures with her pinky to the door. "The whore d'oeuvre." Lila and the Moneys crack up.

When I don't, Lila begrudgingly explains, "She's the slut who gets to a party first."

Then, just when I think it can't get worse, the infamous Hans or Franz arrives. Granted, the man is hot (hot = movie-star hot, not regular-person hot). And charming. He's got a drink for me, compliments Lila on her scarf-as-belt, and begins to regale us with humorous stories from his summer in the Loire Valley. I know that this is in France, but couldn't really tell you more than that, but I have to nod along with everyone else and shrink back when they turn to me and ask questions like, "Isn't the view from [insert foreign restaurant here] just incredible?"

And suddenly, having been surrounded by the lush-flushed masses (lush flush = liquor rouge) I am totally deserted. Alone on the leather couch, I consider my options. In the corner, Pashmina and her girl gaggle are doing the smoke-drink-laugh-hair-toss combo, and some guys are playing pool, various people drift in and out of the room, but Lila and—yup, say it with me—Hans/Franz are nowhere to be seen.

Nowhere, that is, until I head back to Lila's room and find her door locked. I pound on it.

"Hello?" I whack my palm against the door.

"Go away!" Lila, drunk, says this from inside so it sounds more like *ger-ray*.

"I will not ger-ray!" I shout. "Let me in." Okay, a total little pigs moment. Or, wait, am I the big bad wolf? "Come on!"

Hans/Franz opens the door a crack. With his unidentifiable accent he says, "Sorry to inconvenience you, Lovey, but we're a tad busy at the moment."

Cue the big giggles from Lila. I push past Eurodude and burst in on semi-clad Lila.

"I'll just grab my things," I say, fuming.

Lila's clueless. "See you later?" This isn't so much a question, but rather a *get out* disguised as friendly.

"I don't think so," I say.

"Oh my God, you are so overreacting." Lila sighs and Hans tackles her—the least suave thing he's done yet. I shove my sweater into my duffel, and do a quick scan to see what I've left behind. Only when I'm outside, walking to the train station, do I realize it's the old Lila, my old friendship, that's missing.

CHAPTER THREE

♡

A mere eight hours later, I am sore, exhausted, twenty dollars out from my gasoline purchase on Route 495, and yet still relieved to be waiting at the Wood's Hole ferry terminal for the first boat of the morning to Martha's Vineyard. In forty-five minutes I'll dock at Vineyard Haven, where Mable will be waiting—hopefully with an extra-large latte for me.

With time to contemplate the weird events of the day before, I lean on the railing, looking out at the ocean and the horizon line. I have one of those movie-camera moments where I'm that sullen girl on a boat, soundtrack cuing up in the background. But what's my problem? I feel like I'm floating (yes, I know I am literally floating—that's not what I mean) between people (Jacob, Lila) and places (I wish there were one venue I felt totally connected to). I want a best friend—clearly Lila's not it. And I want the relationship I thought I'd have with Jacob. That's what I feel: all talk, no reality.

My cell phone bleeps to announce a new message, so I punch in my code and hope it's Lila, explaining her actions. But it's not. Instead, I hear in a wildly upper-crust British accent:

"Um, yes, hello! This is Arabella Piece, the exchange student? I'm due to arrive this autumn? From London? Just ringing to check you've got my flights and that you'll send a driver to collect me? Your dad was kind enough to give me this number just in case I needed to reach a Hadley contact? Well, looking forward to it. Bye!"

Her cheerful tone and upturned sentences are too much for me. (Why do so many girls need to make questions out of normal sentences?) Plus, she is a cold reminder of the Euros I just had to deal with at Brown. I can already see Arabella Piece as a label-wearing, jet-setting, posh girl who's sheltered enough to assume she'll be met by a driver at the airport.

Since there are no other messages for me, I gaze out at the steady horizon, wishing for coffee or company, and it's right when I'm thinking this that I feel a tap on my shoulder. "Sarah?" the voice attached to the finger tapper asks me.

I turn around. "Nope. Good guess, though," I say to the guy in front of me. I do a quick check. He's older, maybe college. (I am not destined for a career in forensics;—he's wearing a T-shirt with some insignia on the chest—a rather firm chest, I might add).

But instead of following through with what I thought was his pick-up line, the guy says, "Oh, well, then, I apologize. Go back to your thoughts." He backs away. I watch him and smile. It's so early in the morning we are the only two people on the ferry deck except for a young mother and her toddlers.

"Wait," I say. "I'm Love."

"I'm Henry," he says. Yay, a normal name! Not that I have any problems with the Euro nomenclature, just a relief that I can actually spell it. "I thought only fishermen and families with kids took this ferry." He checks his watch as if to confirm that, yes, it's really only six fifteen a.m. He has that sleepy cute boy thing happening—slightly fuzzy around the edges. Maybe my summer guyatus is ending. (Granted, it didn't start by choice exactly, but with Jacob out of the picture—at least for now—and the hectic pace of life and losership in NYC, it kind of happened.)

"Is this your way of telling me you're a fisherman?" I ask. Hey, I can flirt even with no sleep! The breeze picks up as the ferry moves out into the open water from the Wood's Hole area.

"Lobsterman, actually."

"Trap much?" Jeez, I should sleep deprive myself more often. I am way more relaxed than I usually am. Henry smiles at me and then raises one eyebrow. I can do that, too. (My dad says he's sure it's some recessive gene or something. He can do it, but only because he trained himself—ah, time well spent—but I was born knowing how. It's great for sarcasm or random moments on boats with boys, but that's about it.) So I raise my eyebrow in some sort of weird facial toast and Henry nods.

We go inside to the shelter of the snack bar. Blue plastic seats and tables bolted to the floor make for an atmospheric breakfast. Henry buys a really sticky sticky bun—the kind in a prewrapped cellophane—and we share it. Somehow, the conversation drifts from baked goods to colleges and somehow—and I don't know how—when I say, "I just spent a horrific night at Brown," Henry interprets this to mean that I am an actual attendee of that fine institution.

"Freshman year, huh?" He does the eyebrow thing again. "Don't worry, it gets better."

I lick my fingers and take pause. Probably I'll never see the guy again. "Does it?" I ask. Not an outright lie, just a glossing over of the facts. I'm too exhausted to go into the Lila–Euro-trash fiasco anyway. Just thinking about her—and her Stepford Student change—makes me nervous and nauseated. Or maybe that's the sticky bun.

"To be honest," Henry says and crumples up our trash. He arcs the wrapper balls into the trash can. "I'm only guessing—I'll be a sophomore." I calculate on my fingers—give me a break; it's not even seven o'clock in the morning—a three-year-plus age difference. Not insurmountable, I think, aware of my interesting word choice.

The boat's horn sounds. I stand up, and through the windows I can see the island, the dips and curves of the shoreline and wooden houses that dot the bluffs and coves. Henry reaches out a hand to me.

"I have to go," he says. He gestures with his head to a man standing by the doorway. "Dad's here." I look at his father, who gives me a salute.

"Oh," I say. "Well, thanks for the sticky bun." I feel cheesy now, but Henry shrugs.

"No problem. See you around, right? I'll look you up if I'm ever at Brown."

Sure thing, buddy. I'll be the fake freshman. We part ways—with Henry heading downstairs with his father to reclaim their vehicle. (You have to book about a year in advance to get a spot for your car on Labor Day weekend, so I am hoofing it.) I go back to my spot on the deck and get ready to search the crowds for Mable's face. I've been to the island a bunch of times—my father has an enormous affinity for the place, some nostalgic connection—the details of which I am not privy to. But this is the first time I've been here without him. Not that I'll be alone, but I won't be trailing after my father or having to ask if I can have a snack. (Basically, I haven't been here since I was maybe ten years old.) And if I ride the oldest carousel in North America, the one in Oak Bluffs, it will be with my very cool aunt in music-video style.

When the ferry ties up to the dock and the metal bridge clanks onto the concrete, the few passengers traveling by foot make their way down to the land. My scuffed duffel over one shoulder, I take a minute to scan the line of cars for Henry, just in case he's got the window rolled down and is looking for me. That'd be a *no*.

Halfway down the gangplank, I try to spot Mable. She's easy to pick out of a crowd—you just look for the giant pile of blond-and-brown curlicues that bob up and down with her frenetic waving. But I don't see her. In fact, even when I'm on land, scanning the ferry terminal, the parking lot, the clam shack, I don't see her. The cool morning air is enough to make me rummage in my bag for a sweatshirt, which I layer over my long-sleeved blue T-shirt. It's the kind of temperature that announces summer's end; school will start next week—later than public, fashionably allowing for students still on vacation in exotic locales to return home, pack up, and drive or fly to boarding schools. Junior year (or, um, college freshman year?) looms in front of me, and I know I will break up the year according to the weird calendar of events that have nothing to do with the rest of life (Labor Day, beginning of school, Columbus Day, midterm, Thanksgiving break, the netherland between Thanksgiving and Christmas break, and so on). Still no sign of Mable or her hair.

Random families swarm around the Black Dog bakery, pawing muffins, the parents grateful for their coffees, kids clad in the eponymous T-shirts and sweats. Cars are already in line for the return boat back to the mainland. I look behind me at the ferry. It seems huge. It is huge. I feel tiny. And alone. And then I finally see Mable leaning up against the side of the clam shack.

At first, I don't think she sees me. She's hunched over (maybe tying a shoe? But no, even from a distance I can see the bright orange flip-flops we picked out last spring). Then she gives a small wave and motions for me to come over. But not very enthusiastically. She's been acting weird all summer. She never visited me in New York like she'd promised, never really explained why she broke off her engagement last spring to her sweet coffee bean distributor. I haven't actually seen her in two months—the longest I've ever gone in my life, minus the time Mable vanished for four months, galavanting with some guy she met in line at the DMV and sending weekly postcards. This summer, I got only one letter and it basically just asked questions about my life (or lack thereof) in New York.

My bag is getting heavy. Even though it's a duffel, I link the straps around my shoulders as if it's a backpack and head over to Mable. As I get closer, I understand why I couldn't see her hair; she's got an Emilio

Pucci scarf on her head. I remind myself to ask to borrow it later. Then, right in the middle of my superficial thoughts, I come to a standstill. Mable and I lock eyes. Mable reaches for her scarf—but I know what she's going to reveal. My aunt has no hair.

Suddenly, it all makes sense. My dad talked endlessly about "big changes" this summer. I'd assumed he meant he and my bitchy math teacher from last year would be moving in together or something, but they actually broke up. He did go on and on about the nature of life. He wrote me a letter that read like one of his headmaster pep talks: "Loss allows us to grow" and "We learn from the challenges fate throws our way" —and I didn't even think he believed in fate. (Usually he says that fate is an excuse for not making decisions.)

Mable begins to walk toward me, one hand smoothing hair that isn't there, the other gripping the scarf. She's lost weight. I am flooded with fragments from last spring and this summer—how she complained of being so tired, how she had to cut back on her hours at Slave to the Grind. With Mable in front of me, her arms around me in the tightest hug, I burst into tears.

"It's okay, Love," Mable whispers.

But I know it isn't. I don't know exactly what's going on, but I am entirely sure that whatever it is will change my life forever.

CHAPTER FOUR

♡

Labor Day

"**L**et me explain," Mable says as she rewraps her bald head with the scarf. Without her hair, Mable's face seems so small, her eyes wide and almost too large. She searches my face to see if I'll beat her to the punch. I stay quiet. She pulls me by the hand and we walk in a lopsided fashion with my bag on my shoulder, my sweatshirt riding up, over to the Black Dog. The place is now fairly crowded. Tourists desperate for T-shirts with that shadowy Labrador are redirected to the Black Dog store (as opposed to the bakery), crumpled-looking dads on morning duty with their kids slurp coffee, kids eat muffins the size of their heads, and pairs of teenagers who look like they belong at Hadley Hall, all frayed khakis and sun-bleached hair, wait in line for cranberry scones and iced coffees.

Mable gets herself an iced tea; an unusual choice for the normally coffee-prone maven. "So I won't have to compare and contrast with the good roast I serve at Slave to the Grind," she explains as she stirs sugar into it. "I always end up preferring my stuff more and having order-regret."

How can she be normal right now? How can she even drink tea or any beverage when clearly she's—Mable interrupts my thoughts. "Come on." She hands me a large coffee and a paper bag. I peer inside, on slo-mo, as if I'll find a genie in there. I could use those three wishes. Mable pokes my ribs with her cold tea. I flinch.

"Just tell me," I say too loudly.

"Fix your coffee first," Mable says. When I am statue still, she pushes me over to the little counter, where cream and sugar sit in squat pitchers and bowls. "Go on." She's insistent.

Mable drifts off to the front of the bakery, outside, presumably to wait for me or to snag a place on the coveted bench. We'll never get a seat now—it's way too crowded. As I dribble cream into my coffee and add what is surely way too much sugar—even for me—I feel myself being watched. Not in that *I'm a teenaged girl and perpetually feel like I am the star of my own movie* kind of being watched, but really being stared at. I look around for something with which to stir my drink. The spoons and stirrers are located on the other side of the room, and I feel like I'm about to lose it. Why can't they be with the cream and sugar? Wouldn't that make more sense? I'm weighted down with the task of having to slalom through chirpy families to get my sugar to dissolve properly. Then— presto—a plastic spoon appears in front of me. I look up.

"Hey . . . Love," Henry says with a big grin. He thinks he's fixed the world's problems by handing me a utensil.

"Hi, Henry," I say quietly as if I've known him for years and this is a regular counter encounter.

"I just wanted to . . ." He raises his eyebrow as I add more sugar to my nearly saturated coffee. Outside the screened window, Mable cups her hand over her forehead and tries to see inside to where I am. She looks lost, helpless.

"I gotta go," I say to Henry, and I just leave him there, with the scone as a *sorry,* and take my coffee and bags outside.

"Well done," I say to Mable on her scorrage of the entire bench in front of the bakery.

"Works like a charm," she says and points to her hairless head. She smiles—and now looks like her regular self. The grin is the same. "So, as you can probably tell, I'm"—she drumrolls on her knees—"bald!"

"Yeah, I gathered that," I say. I can feel the tears welling up again.

"Now, just stop that." She swipes at my eyes with her shirt cuff. I'm suddenly aware of my chest cavity as a pit in which my racing heart just sits, about to get crushed. "I have breast cancer, Love."

"No," I say and then, louder, "No!" A little girl in red shorts and a ponytail nearby thinks I'm yelling at her and starts to wail. The mom shoots me a mean look. Then I start to cry, too. Mable stays totally calm. "How can you be so . . . so . . . so . . ." I can't even think of the word.

"Unemotional?" Mable fills in. I nod. "I've known for a lot longer than you, Love. And it's not easy, but I'm trying."

"So I take it this is why you didn't come see me in New York?"

"The chemo, yeah. It was time-consuming, not to mention the fact that I felt like crap." I look at the bluish circles under her eyes, her pale skin. "I'm still a little under the weather."

Now I'm a whirl of confused emotions myself. "Under the weather? Mable, it's not like you have a cold or something. Jesus. I mean, you have . . ." I don't even want to say it. Too real.

Mable knows me too well. "Say it, Love. Just say *you have breast cancer.*"

I take a deep breath. "You have—" I stop myself.

"Look," Mable says, draining her iced tea and crunching on a cube. "It's not like if you don't say it I'll suddenly be cured. I'd rather just be open about it."

But I can't. We walk to her car in silence and shove my stuff in the trunk. Once she's started the engine, fiddled with radio, and rolled down her window, I find myself unable to contain a shout. "I can't fucking believe you didn't tell me sooner!"

"Don't swear, Love," Mable says, sounding parental instead of her usual cool self. "If I'd told you in June, would you have gone to New York? Can you honestly say you would've taken the internship at *Music* magazine?"

"I have the right to know!" I say. "I should have been allowed to make that decision."

"And you do know, *now*." Mable takes my hand. I'm crying and snotty and gross and tired. My hair is sticky from the sticky bun on the ferry (I somehow wound up with bits of it dotting my head—tasty!) and my eyes are burning. "This isn't the end of anything, Love. This is a challenge. For me, for you, for . . ."

"You sound like my dad," I say. The air gets warmer as we drive past the water toward Edgartown Center. The ferries are tiny specks in the ocean, the beaches flecked with swimmers and sand castle builders.

"I'm going to beat this, really," Mable says, staring straight ahead. For now—right now—I try my best to believe her.

"You better," I say and smile. I wipe my snotty nose on my sweatshirt. (Note to self: Do load of laundry soon.)

"I will—as they say in the treatment room—kick cancer ass."

I turn to her and crinkle my face up. "Do they really say that?"

Mable winks at me and we keep driving.

For some reason, I assumed Mable had a double room at one of the hotels in town. Instead, she's got the sweetest cottage, an open-plan living room/kitchen and two bedrooms on either side of it, each with its own ridiculously small bathroom.

"Hey," I say in the bathroom that's attached to my room. "I can almost wash my hands while sitting on the toilet!"

"That gives a new twist to the word multitasking . . . And you thought you wouldn't have any fun!" Mable shouts back. "Do you want some pancakes? I need to keep eating, you know, keep my weight up—or are you just too tired?"

I wash my hands (not while sitting) and join her in the kitchen. "Do you mind if I take a nap?" I ask. It's nine thirty in the morning, but I feel like the day should be over already. No, wait. I don't want the days to slip by. Mable is okay. I don't want school to start. I just want to stay on pause for a while.

"You look like a cow," Mable says.

"Gee, thanks, you should be a life coach or something," I say. I pick at the chocolate chips Mable's sprinkling into the pancake batter.

"I mean, you're about to fall asleep standing up."

"Huh?" I can feel myself swaying.

"Like. A. Cow." Mable punctuates her words and makes her eyes wide. "Go to bed!" she orders. And I do, but with this haunting feeling of wondering if Mable will still be here when I wake up.

When I do open my eyes a mere three hours later, I have no idea where I am. And for a second it feels kind of good. Until I remember about Mable and cancer and lumpectomy and chemo and all the words she said this morning. Then I feel nauseated and go to find Mable to have her reassurance. Then I feel guilty for needing her to reassure me when she's the one who's—whatever. I get in the shower, even do a deep conditioning mask that promises to hydrate my hair to health (now what can it do for my emotional state?) as an excuse to stand under the warm water until my fingertips are screaming for Botox.

After I'm dressed in slightly fraying khaki shorts (apparently required Vineyard apparel) and an ancient dark green T-shirt of my dad's (ancient = it reads Boston Marathon 1983) that is frighteningly small—at least it would be on him—flip-flops, hair in a messy knot, I go into the kitchen where Mable has left this note:

Love-a-licious,
Gone fishin'. (Not really, but haven't you always wanted to write that?) I'm at a meeting in town. Come find me later around the public docks.

—The Cue (as in bald as a cue ball)

I can't believe Mable's sense of humor. I'm no psych major (um, there *are* no majors in high school—maybe I mean my fake major at fake Brown), but I know she's putting up a brave front for me. But perhaps it's not only for my benefit. Maybe she needs to be funny just to give herself a little distance from the constant plague of physical symptoms and worries.

I grab my iPod (possibly the best gift from my internship—it came fully loaded with a plethora of songs, soundtracks, and studio versions no one but music execs have even heard yet). The iPod slips into my pocket, the headphones go on, and I can flick through the roster of Jacob-reminiscent songs. (I will not—repeat—will *not* be listening to any Nick Drake songs unless I want to wallow in my near-miss relationship with Jacob. But I digress.) So I select one of Mable's favorites, The English Beat's *Special Beat Service,* and am rocking along the cobblestone streets (no, not in that "Feelin' Groovy" way, more in that trying not to wipe out/still unsteady from a long night way), listening to "Spar Wid Me," which I can't really understand because it's ska, but it's cool. Plus, I am agog at the sheer number of fine male specimens (I actually must add that to my journal list of words I can't stand—it makes me think of pee) on the island. On my left, hottie in a hoodie. On my right, beautiful beach bum boy. And so on.

I flit from cute shop to even sweeter one, ogling the merchandise and men (okay, boys) until it's time to meet Mable. Not that I know where the public docks are, but—and I don't have to fake being in college for this knowledge—I'm assuming the docks are by the water.

Mable meets me as I'm dangling my feet over the dock's edge, watching people row boats in from the large yachts that hulk the harbor. Women in expensive straw hats tote bags of organic produce, tanned boys come ashore with their dogs, the catalogue-worthy girls look windswept and lovely. I am as freckled as usual. Maybe one shade darker—in that I'm not translucent.

"Where were you?" I ask Mable. She's got a wad of papers and folders in her arms.

She shakes her head. "Nowhere. What'd you get up to?"

"Wandering. Showering. Looking. Lots of *ings*."

Mable has traded her scarf for a Boston Red Sox baseball cap—just like the one Lila had on when she met me at the train station. Over lunch at the Edgartown Deli, I relate my half night at Brown to Mable.

"That sounds terrible." Mable is sincere.

"It was," I say. Not like breast cancer, I think, but still. Mable totally knows my thoughts.

"You can't compare everything to my illness," she says. "You'll drive yourself nuts if you do . . . Seriously, Love. Life goes on. I'm sick. I'll get better. Let's eat fries."

I nod. "Anyway, I haven't called Lila. I'm sure she's too busy Hanzing or Franzing with her Euros to care."

We walk toward the cottage. Mable points to a sweater she likes in Petunia's.

"Have you seen anything you like?" Mable asks.

"Not really," I say and then pause to look at a pair of sunglasses in the Summer Shades window.

"I don't mean those," Mable smiles. "I meant more like that." She points directly to a guy walking right toward us. Before I can push my aunt's gesture away, the guy is directly face front and grinning.

"Do I know you?" he asks us. He has that summer hair—lighter on top, brown underneath. I fight off images of him doing decidedly non–Main Street things.

"I don't think so," I say, apologizing.

He walks off. Mable shouts to him when he's a block away, "Maybe you should!" And then, in case he doesn't get it, "Her name's Love—look for her!" She points to the top of my head, then holds two fingers over me like she's the prankster in the class photo.

"You suck," I say. It's the first normal thing I've said to Mable since I got here.

"Oh, hello, Love," she says and smiles at me. "So glad you're resurfacing."

"Don't do that again," I warn, and we link arms until we're back at the cottage.

"How'd you even find this place?" I ask. I wander around testing out the plush chair tucked into the bay window, then move to the couch, then flick the brass lamp on and off like I've never seen actual furniture or lighting before. But the place is special—perfect, really.

Mable's thumbing through her papers and making lists of things she has to do. "What do you mean?"

"I mean, is this place part of the Harborview Hotel or what?"

Mable looks a little flustered. "Um, no. No, this is just a cottage."

"Are you in some kind of witness relocation program?" I ask.

Mable laughs. "We've—I've been coming here a long time. I just like this cottage, that's all." She shows me a couple of photos from years before: Mable wearing T-shirts with shoulder pads, standing on the front stoop. My dad painting a red bookcase on the front lawn. He looks so young.

"When did *he* come here?" I ask.

"What should we do for dinner?" Mable wants to know.

"What's the policy on non sequiturs?" I ask. But Mable doesn't budge. She won't divulge any more info about anything, which, of course, makes me assume (assume = know for sure in this instance) that the place is obviously connected somehow to my mother. My mother's mysterious nonpresence in my life seems to be interrupting my existence more and more. I have too many questions, and what once seemed irrelevant now piques my interest. "Did my mom come here?" I try one more time. But Mable's gone into her room for a nap.

*   *   *

After dinner, we walk to Mad Martha's for ice cream. Someone orders this enormous sundae with a scoop of each flavor in it, which causes the staff to yell "Piggie Piggie!" I'm hit with a wash of English class with *Lord of the Flies* and that psycho blond kid character. But Mable and I lick our cones (black raspberry for her, peanut butter cup for me) and do what people do here—walk along, look at the shops, hang out. I should add to my list of preferred activities a fondness for fabricating scenarios with the boy we passed today on Main Street. There've been many an Abercrombie since, but none to equal him.

"This used to be a dive bar," Mable says and gestures to the island's answer to CBGB, Boiling Point.

"When?"

"Back in the day." She crunches on the top circle of her sugar cone. "Your dad came here a lot." She looks at my face. "No, I'm serious. It might be hard for you to believe, but he was pretty progressive. He was—"

"Don't say cool. Principals are not cool. Progressive, political, maybe. But not cool."

"Well," Mable says, licking her mouth for ice cream traces. "He wasn't a principal then. Just a struggling academic with a love for folk-rock. He's different now."

I'm gathering that she means my mother made him cool. Or that they were young enough to pull off whatever coolness or vibe was happening at the time. "Was she?"

Mable meets my gaze. "Yes. Your mother was decidedly very cool. Maybe too much so."

Case closed. And with my father coming tomorrow morning on the Oak Bluffs ferry, doubtful as to whether that case will reopen for the duration of the weekend. Which is only two-plus days. Ugh. Just a weekend until school starts. I should email Jacob. Or write him. Or call. But then, maybe it's better to wait until I see him in person.

Hadley Hall, the dorms, random people like flakey Cordelia, my fellow faculty brat, seem far away. In the recesses (heh) of my mind, I recall with dread that my ex-crush Robinson Hall is sending his friend fuck (i.e., combo of girl that is a friend who then crosses the line) Lindsay Parrish to Hadley Hall.

But these worries will have to wait. I have a weekend left here. I sit at my window, watching the fuzzy moonlight on the water, listening to the locals and the revelers. Mable's asleep. And just when I think I'm headed for bed, I see a group of people clustered around one of the old streetlamps. They're only half a story down and maybe a couple of feet away. I can see them enough to know one of them is Henry (formerly of the ferry, then of Black Dog utensil fame). For a second, I think he sees me. Then I rationalize that he couldn't possibly. I'm like the size of a dime from where he is. So much for a clichéd balcony scene.

I borrow Mable's car the next morning so I can taxi my father from the Oak Bluffs ferry back to the cottage. The extra-large spaces make parking easy, and I sit on the hood of the rusting Volvo watching gulls careen for scraps of pizza crusts and muffin crumbs while the huge boat docks. To my left is the Bluffs green, with its antique bandstand and, farther in, the carousel and gingerbread houses all crammed together in a brightly painted, jumbled architectural heap. One night in August there's a festival in Oak Bluffs where everyone lights lanterns and sits on their tiny porches; I remember going as a kid and now have one of those romantic fantasies about strolling hand in hand with the boyfriend I don't have (cue the violins) amid the glow and charm.

But now it's already September, so there's no chance of that little number coming true. I flip-flop over to where the passengers are disembarking.

"Hi, Dad!" I'm relieved to see him. Now that Mable's condition is out in the open, I'm sure my father will be more relaxed. I want to be all patient and understanding, but what flies out of my mouth is, "How could you have kept it a secret?"

I sound infantile or at the very least, *OC*-dramatic. But it *is* dramatic; my aunt has cancer and my own father never told me!

"Love, this is Viola," he says, glossing over my accusatory tone while introducing me to the random ultra-prep beside him. First I think he said Violent, which proves to be an apt mistake. The woman looks like she stepped out of *The Preppy Handbook* circa 1983—it exists, seriously. Mable has a marked-up copy back in Boston. And I'm not just being judgmental because I had no idea my father had another "friend." (Why do adults insist on calling their flings and dates "friends"? Like that makes the situation any more palatable?)

Cupping her hand so there's hardly any skin-to-skin contact, Viola shakes my hand and makes sure her collar is up. I have no problems with the return of Izod and the like, but I'm all in favor of mixing it up a little. Madras, moccasins, and argyle sweater-vests all together make me want to heave.

My father insists on driving, which puts Viola in the passenger seat, and little old me (emphasis on little) buckled into the backseat. Luckily, I didn't need a car seat (although, if one had been available, perhaps my dad would have snapped me into it). On the way back, my father points out every identifiable restaurant, cove, street name to a clearly disinterested Viola. She and I lock eyes in her side-view mirror once, and it's not pretty.

"I thought we'd be at the Harborview," Viola says when she's given the three-second tour of the cottage. "I liked the way it looked online."

Mable has gone through the trouble of making breakfast for everyone; fresh-squeezed grapefruit juice, crepes with lemon and sugar, a hollowed melon with slices of cantaloupe and strawberries inside.

"Wow," Dad says. "This looks great!" What he means is: Thank God you're alive. He has tears in his eyes looking at his sister. Mable grins at him, and just for a second I can picture them as kids together.

Mable offers some juice to Viola. "I don't care for citrus," she responds. Who the hell says that? Especially to someone who is bald and bruised from an IV line? If I was merely bothered by Viola prior to this, I now officially hate her. Last year, my father made the colossal mistake of dating my horrendous math teacher—and, to be honest (which I was with him), I thought it couldn't get much worse. However, I was clearly in the wrong.

The phone rings and Mable picks up, her face suddenly aglow with news. Maybe she's cured, I think, my heart racing. Dad puts fruit into his crepe and eats half, then wordlessly slides the other half toward me. We share the fork. Viola is disgusted. I am thrilled, not just that we've grossed her out, but that after all the years of living as single dad and daughter, we still have these weird rituals that won't disappear, despite the distance that has sprung up the past couple of months.

"Dad," I say and poke him in the ribs.

He turns to me and puts his hand on my shoulder. "I'm sorry I didn't tell you. I wanted to. I did. But Mable made me promise. She knew you'd feel too guilty going to New York, and we both just . . ."

"It's okay," I say and slide my finger across the plate to swipe up the last of the sugar. Viola taps her foot.

Dad looks around and sighs. "It's good to be back," he says. Then he notices me staring at him.

"On the Vineyard or here, like in this room?" I ask. I narrow my eyes. He's totally been here before. He knew right where the silverware drawer was without checking the obvious place near the sink. "What's the deal with the cottage, Dad?"

He clears his throat like he does before student lectures and faculty meetings. "Oh—uh—no, I meant . . . it's lovely this time of year. Not too crowded."

Viola takes her cue and pipes in with, "I want one of those Black Dog shirts. With the year on it." She'll probably get one of the back-dated ones that says 1989 or something, so when you wear it, it looks as if you've been summering on the Vineyard forever, like you'd been in on the Black Dog before Clinton and the rest of the populace began ordering the damn things online—except you can tell they're fake old since the colors are still bright.

"Well," Dad says. "If we can take the car, let's head on into Vineyard Haven and get you one, shall we?"

They head out the door, arm in arm, and I'm suddenly bummed. Not that I wanted to spend the entire day with my father, but a full five minutes might have been nice. Mable's still gabbing away into the phone. I catch words like *rental agreement, beverage permit* and assume she's chasing down issues with Slave to the Grind's summer shifts. But I should know by now not to assume anything.

Dad runs back in after Viola is safely in the car. "Hey, Love, let's do something this afternoon. Just you and me."

"Sure," I say. "Mini golf?" It's sort of a joke, but I do love those courses. I'm fairly adept at getting the ball into the windmill or a giant shoe. I'm not saying I belong in the LPGA, but if there were a miniversion, maybe. Let's hear it for useless skills!

"I was thinking more like a boat ride," Dad says.

Later, I say to him, "I thought you meant one of the kiddie rides." We're standing on the public docks, waiting for the rental boat to come in so we can head out for a sail.

"What's the fun in that?" Dad says. He's all kitted out for the adventure: Hadley Hall baseball hat, 800 SPF lotion, a bag with water and snacks.

I gesture to his gear. "How long you planning on going for, Gilligan?" I ask.

"Better to plan ahead," he says.

We motor out, and Dad puts me on rudder duty. Once we're past the traffic of the harbor, we raise the sails. Farther out, we zip along and I'm thankful Dad brought along his old Harvard sweatshirt. I put it on.

"You look like . . ." He pauses. He has that Dad look, combination pride and awe. "I can't believe you're going to be a junior." I nod and sigh. "Just think, this time next year, you'll be writing college essays."

"Don't remind me," I say. "What would I even write about?"

"I'm sure you'll think of something," he says. "You always do."

"Are you scared about Mable?" I ask. Dad swallows and lets the sail out more so we go even faster.

"Incredibly," he says. "It's just not something I'd ever given much thought to. You know, I'm always ready for crises in my job, but I never . . . I never thought I'd lose Mable, she's just . . ." His voice trails off and if he completes his sentence, I don't hear it—the words are lost in the wind.

An hour later and I'm glad Dad packed the snack bag. We sit and much on Cape Cod potato chips and swig seltzer while we wait for someone (anyone? hello?) to untangle us from where we've hit a rock ledge and gotten tangled on a mooring. Dad's embarrassed, and more than a little pissed at the thought of paying the damage costs, but I'm glad to avoid shore and Mable and Viola and walking around town, wondering what to do next.

"I don't mind being cast adrift," I say like some heroine in a romance novel. And I mind it even less when we are spotted by a Boston Whaler helmed by none other than the hot guy Mable accosted on Main Street.

But when he motors over to us and uses a black fender as a bumper between our boats, he gives no sign of recognition. Shit. It's one thing to be humiliated in front of a potential crush, but worse not to have even made any sort of lasting impression.

"David Bukowski," Dad says in his full octave-deeper voice—the headmaster tone.

"Charlie," he says and shakes Dad's hand.

"Just Charlie?" I ask. "Like Cher?" Oh my God, clamp my mouth closed right now! Yes, Love, like Cher—the rugged boat boy in front of me is just like wig-wearing prima donna chanteuse. (It's French—that's what a year in prep school has done to me.) He is practically a twin to Cher.

"I'm Love," I say. I look into Charlie's blue eyes for a hint of acknowledgment, but still *nada*. (Yep, that's Spanish. I made it through first year Spanish but can only describe my house, a trip to the greengrocer, and how sad I was that the rain ruined the day with my boyfriend at the beach. Hey, even in other languages I'm lame!)

"How could I forget?" Charlie says and more than redeems himself and my slightly faltered confidence in one breath.

Charlie has me hold the rudder still, wedging it between my knees for firm support (like a good bra I almost say, my near–Tourette's Syndrome verbosity rearing its ugly head) while my dad steadies the mooring ball. Unable to unwrap the lines from their massive tangle, Charlie whips off his shirt (me = breathless, slight drool) and dives into the water with a knife to cut the boat free. In the minute that he's submerged, I allow my Johnny Depp pirate fantasies to run amok in my brain and then shove them into hiding when Charlie, wet, cold, and rather nipply (I have never used that to describe a guy—but seriously, the Atlantic Ocean is cold this time of year) reappears. My dad gives him a towel from the trusty day pack and I hand over my dad's sweatshirt.

"Harvard, huh?" Charlie looks at the top as he wrangles it over his wet body. Yummy.

"Yup," my father says. "Good school."

"For some," Charlie says. He sounds skeptical.

Once we're attached to Charlie's boat (oh to be that vessel!), he tugs our rental back to the docks. We say thanks as he helps us knot the boat to the piling and calls the harbormaster to explain what happened. And Dad settles up the damage with the boat rental people, I stand with a still-dripping Charlie on the dock.

"You here for the weekend?" he asks.

"Yeah, I head back late on Monday." I squelch my feet in my flip-flops, then take them off, leaving footprints on the dock (my clever way of avoiding eye contact). "Back to Boston," I add in case he cares or in case it buys me if not local status, then close to it.

"Well, I hope the island treats you well," he says. He's got a gravely sort of voice, and a slightly off-center nose, which just adds to his incredible appeal. He catches me sneaking a glance at his face and touches his nose. "Rugby," he explains.

I point to the scar on the side of my right eye. "Chicken pox."

Charlie traces a line from the inside of his tanned arm to the outside of his elbow. "Fishing hook."

My turn. I bring my knee up and point to the crescent on the top. "Red rover." Charlie grins. "What? It's a brutal game."

With my knee still up, I begin to wobble and before I land on my ass or in the water, he steadies me with both hands. With more than that, actually. His is just a steadying presence, like nothing could truly be wrong when he's around (or, if it were, he'd arrive with duct tape and wires to fix it).

Dad pops over with his fingers still in his wallet from paying the boat guys. To my horror, he plucks out a ten-dollar bill and hands it to Charlie.

"Thanks for the dive," Dad says, all prep school bravado. Just call him Chester Duckworth the fifth.

"It's not a problem, but thanks anyway," Charlie says and wrinkles his brow at the cash.

"Really, it's the least I can do," Dad says, shoving the money at him. Charlie pushes it back.

"I don't need your money. Really."

My cheeks are aflame at this point, not sunburned, just mortified.

"Dad, it's a gesture of goodwill," I explain. Dad rolls his eyes.

"Well, so's this. Boat guy like you," he says to Charlie. "I'm sure you could use it. Go treat yourself to a pizza or something." Charlie sighs. My tiny moment of hoping he'll say "only if Love comes with me" vanishes when the money is handed back along with the Harvard sweatshirt.

"Just do the same for someone else sometime," Charlie says, his voice tinged with disappointment. I open my mouth to just come out and ask him to meet for coffee later, or a walk, but he's gone.

"Nice, Dad," I say.

"What? Who turns away good money? It was a tip."

"I don't think he works here," I say and gesture to the boat rental place.

"He's probably just an islander getting ready for the off-season. I thought he'd appreciate it. Maybe I should've offered twenty?"

Um, clueless much? I'm left dockside, wishing I had either the guts to go after Charlie or convince my dad of his faux pas, or both. But I stand there, just admiring the view (sea vista = 9.5, Charlie's slow stride, wistful hands in the pockets, wide shoulders = 10).

CHAPTER FIVE

♡

Mable has tied her cancer scarf around my eyes and is leading me, blindfolded, through the streets of Edgartown on a mystery walk.

"Only when we reach our destination will I remove it," Mable says. Her voice sounds extra loud. I can hear children chattering, snippets of conversation. (*Can't we get vanilla, Mom?* And *I think Susan would like the red ones,* and then a familiar voice saying *Dude, I totally know that girl*). But then Mable moves me around and I can tell by the way I'm nearly landing on my ass five times in a row that we're on bumpy cobblestones. A door opens.

"Step up," Mable says. She sounds so happy, so excited. Not tired. Not sick.

Mable slides the scarf off my head and tells me to open my eyes. We're in a small open space—a long slab of white and green slurred marble rests on a countertop. One wall is just windows with distant views of the harbor.

"What a beautiful room!" I say and walk around. "It's so cozy." The afternoon sunlight seeps in, coating the walls until it feels like the whole place is glowing.

"I know, right?" Mable leans on the marble counter.

"And the purpose of this blindfolded visit would be . . ."

"This!" Mable walks to a small room behind the counter and comes back trying to heft a rectangular package wrapped in brown paper.

"Mable, let me help," I rush over to her before she drops it.

"Heavier than it looks, I guess," Mable says. Could it be that five months ago she could lift trays with piles of dirty mugs, plates, and water glasses?

"What is this?"

Mable begins to tear at the paper. "I haven't even seen the finished product yet. Here, you do some." We tug at the wrapping, stripping it off until the whole sign is visible.

"Slave to Grind II." I read it out loud while Mable points, like she's just teaching me the words. "I don't get it."

Mable raises her eyebrows. "It's pretty self-explanatory, isn't it?"

"Not really," I say. I look around with a different view this time. There's a huge European-style coffeemaker in the back room, stacks of orange chairs, an enormous see-through bag of cushions waiting to be unwrapped. "You're not really opening another coffee shop, are you?"

"No," Mable says. I sigh, relieved, anxiety gone. "Not today." Anxiety back.

"But, Mable, you don't even . . . What do you . . ."

"Oh, will you relax!" She pats the counter so I'll jump up there. "Listen, it might not make any sense to you, or your father, for that matter, but I need to do this. I started thinking about this years ago. And I put a deposit away before I found out I was sick. I always wanted to expand, and financially it's fine. And, well, I need . . ." She pauses. I get it.

"You need something to look forward to?"

"Exactly." Mable adjusts the sun hat on her head and looks around the room. "I mean, it's obviously much smaller than the one at home. It can be a seasonal thing. And, if you're lucky, it might lead to gainful summer employment."

She has a point. More than one, actually. "Well, I guess I'm excited for you," I say.

"You guess? You guess? You can do better than that."

"Fine!" I smile. "I'm thrilled for you."

"We are, too," bellows a voice. Attached to the hefty lungs is a familiar face. "Hi, I'm Malcolm Randall—Trip." Does he mean it's hyphenated or what?

"Hi, Mr. Randall-Trip," I say. Mable blushes. The man clears his throat.

"Not quite," he corrects. Then speaks like I'm an infant. "My name is Malcolm"—pause—"Randall"—pause—"the Third"—pause—"but people call me"— pause—(let me guess, Dickhead?)—Trip."

"Oh," I say. And when I'm about to feel swallowed up by the floor, I get pissed. Prepster Man has killed my nice moment with my aunt, but she, for some reason, is taking it like a champ.

"Love," Mable says in a peppy tone, "Trip is the landlord of the building." She gives me a look. "He's been kind enough to reserve the space for me, even though we won't open for a month or so."

I turn to her and in a hushed voice say, "I thought you were waiting until next season."

Trip interrupts. "We feel it's in the best interest of the business to do a trial run this fall—you now, gather local interest prior to the tourist brigade next spring."

What about in the best interest of my aunt? And what's with the *we we we?* I want to ask, but don't, especially when Henry, the guy I met on the ferry, shows up, and I figure out why Trip Dickhead the Ninth looks familiar—it's his dad. Whoopee! Let's hear it for the small prepster world (and "Let's Hear it for the Boy"—a ridiculous and awesomely bad yet great song on the *Footloose* soundtrack. Kevin Bacon before he was Kevin Bacon—cute like newly hatched chick, but I digress).

"Hi, Love," Henry says.

"Hi," I nod. Mable shoos me away, signing papers with Dickhead—

sorry, that's Dickhead the Third—and I go outside and sit on the stoop with Henry.

"Sorry my dad's such a colossal asshole," he says.

"That's okay," I laugh. "At least you're aware."

"More than you know," Henry says. "Or should I say more"—pause—"than"—pause—"you"—pause—"know"—pause.

"You were there for that?" I ask.

"Sadly, yes."

"Hey." I shrug it off. "Nobody puts baby in a corner." This is the first normal interaction I've had with a guy since the Euro-trash bravado at Brown made me want to swear off boy banter for the rest of summer. (I admit that this is hardly a huge threat seeing as summer is over as of this weekend, but anyway). Seeing Henry near his father makes him seem even more the rich prepster, but it's a good lesson for me with my too-snap judgments—he's not stuck up. At least not yet. I sneak a glance at Henry as we sit in the sunlight and decide he's okay. Maybe better than okay.

That night, with Dad and Viola off for a fancy feast at L'Etoile and Mable tucked into bed with a magnetic board and cutouts of counters, tables, chairs, and condiment booths (she's playing rearrange the coffee bar), I brush my teeth and slip into my Brown T-shirt and yoga pants. (Note to self: Get rid of college/prep school gear. It seems to be breeding in my wardrobe like some preppy virus.) I love my yoga pants—not that I do yoga, but I sure like the outfits. Mable nods off to sleep and I turn out the lights. I don't mind having had to give up my bedroom to my father and Viola, but I can hardly imagine her snuggling up to my dad. She's so cold she'll probably insist on a bundling board. (Bundling board = arcane way of imposing celibacy a long time ago. It's like a piece of wood that separates the two bodies so no parts stray where they shouldn't.)

I, however, could use a little contact. And by this I mean I want both the boy to adore and adore me and the girlfriend to whom I can confide said adorage.

So when I go to the bathroom and a little spotlight shines in the window, I peer out to see what it is. Sure enough, it's Prep Charming coming to rescue me (yes, I'll rescue him right back à la *Pretty Woman*) from a night of the doldrums.

I leave a note for Mable in case she wakes up and meet Henry outside under the streetlamp. The smell of the clam shack wafts over to us and we head over to where a group of his friends are munching fries and hanging out by the Chappy ferry. (Chappaquiddick is a boat ride from the Vineyard—even though it's part of it. It's like an island off of an island. How profound.)

"Tyler Scott, Jason Landry, Lissa Bond, Jay Daventree." Henry rattles off the names and they wash over me. Except for Jay.

"Jay," I say. He turns to me. He's very tall, with kid-blond hair and stubble that sort of glows in the moonlight.

"Yes?" he asks. Do I make an impression on no one? "Oh," he says, "I know you. You're that friend of Lila Lawrence's. Newport, right?"

Dear God, I have become one of those people who knows people. How odd. "The one and only Lila," I say. It feels good in a lame way to fit in via connections—like I'm finally part of that prep school people map.

"How is dear Lila doing these days?" Jay asks.

"Good," I say, my voice a little higher than it is when I'm not on the verge of lying.

Henry—possibly jealous of my minute past with Jay (basically, we hung out at Lila's palatial place in Newport for precisely one night, and no, nothing happened. And upon second glance, Jay Daventree has the appeal of a golden retriever—read: pretty, friendly, and up for a game of catch, but not a lot of heavy conversation)—comes over and says, "Is she at Brown, too?"

Ah, the moment of truth. "Actually, Lila's there, but I'm . . ." I look at the faded words on my chest. Soon the shirt that used to read Brown University will read own niversity. (Note to self: possibly good name for a band? Maybe not.) This is the perfect time to explain to Henry his mistaken assumption (aren't most assumptions mistakes?) that I'm in college.

"Well, you're *here*, obviously." Henry nudges me. Then, to Jay, he adds, "She's only a freshman—leave her alone." They share some weird guy signal. I almost correct him by saying "No, I'm a junior," but for once I keep my mouth shut.

So much for owning up to my high school status.

Later, Jay Daventree gives me a fake ID (new name = Kendra Nicoletta Bianci) and we head to Boiling Point. And yes, of course I'm aware of "getting into hot water," but I go anyway. Isn't that what you're supposed to do as a last hurrah to the end of summer?

Inside the club, Henry (who is now calling me Kenny due to my ID) gets me a cranberry vodka something and I sip at it while craning to see the band. The crowd is raucous. I'm sure we're way over the legal limit for how many people can be in this place. (All my time at Slave to the Grind has brought my attention to these little matters of real estate permits.) I'm pretty much lifted off the ground by the sheer number of bodies, and not in a good way. Henry's nearby, his buddies have dispersed, and then suddenly:

"Asshole!" This from some unidentified guy in a Polo shirt.

Then a bunch of male grunts and some shoving and suddenly I'm in the midst of a brawl.

"Watch out!" a cocktail waitress shouts and spills her held-high tray of beer. Bottles clank to the floor, my shoulder gets sprayed with foam, and some girl with massive boob-job offerings comes flying into my back.

While it's semiexciting to be witness (witness = part of?) a God-honest, Western saloon fight (minus the whores on the upstairs balcony and the pistols), it kind of freaks me out when the Polo shirt guy's cheek is bleeding. One guy swings and hits another one, a girl screams, Henry holds one of his friends back from charging at one of the band members and motions for me to go outside. When I just stand there, mesmerized, Henry shouts at me, "Go! Love, get the hell out of here!"

Maybe that's a little forceful of him, maybe he's just fiercely protecting me, but either way, I make a move.

Prying my way through the crowds and the spilled drinks, I can hear the sirens outside. I slink toward the bathrooms and out onto the balcony when there's a tap on my shoulder. A man and a woman in police gear. Shitfuckshit.

"Can we see some ID?" they ask.

I rummage in my pocket and—panic—cannot remember in which pocket I have put my real license (which I carry like the do-gooder I am in case I am the designated driver) and in which one I've stashed the fake ID. Please be the Kenny one, please let me remain Kendra Nicoletta Bianci, I think as I try to smile and charm my way out of the search. Despite the rumbling still going on inside, the police officers wait for me. I take a deep breath. If I go for the one in my left pocket, and it's the fake ID, I will go home minus Henry—I swear. I won't find Henry. I will go home like a good girl, and I will throw away the ID forever; this is what I promise to the Vineyard Gods.

I slide the thing out of my left pocket and hand it to the officers. "Thanks, Kendra," they say and hand the ID back to me.

"Actually, I go by Nicoletta," I say as they walk off. I don't know why I said it. Really. The officers pause for a minute, and I think I've doomed myself. But then they nod and keep going. With all my fake schools and imposter names, I'll be ready for a *60 Minutes* special soon. The only trouble I can foresee now is that I'm stuck on the balcony, and if I go back into Boiling Point I run the risk of bumping into the police again.

So I stay put until I see a half ladder that leads from the railing down to the beach below. I check it out. If I can manage to swing my yoga-pants–covered ass over without killing myself, I'll be free!

As I lift myself over the side, I can't help but smile. It's a fun, if slightly scary, evening, and the moon on the water looks amazing. Hard to believe in forty-eight hours I'll be back in my room at home. I snag my pants on a nail and swear at myself.

"Don't be so critical, you're doing great," Charlie says from his perch on a rock below. He's drinking a beer from a paper bag like someone playing a drunk in a school play and stands up only when I've dropped to the sand.

"Thanks for the help," I say and dust off my butt. I pull my shirt down from where it's been stuck under my bra.

"Oh, Brown this time," Charlie says, looking at the shirt (who knew wearing these clothes would prove to be such a big deal?) and sounding smug.

"And?"

"I guess community college is out of the question?" he says and offers me a sip of beer. I pass.

"What's your point?" I ask. Charlie stands up and wipes his hands through his hair so it's sort of slicked back from his face. Undoing my fleece from around my waist and slipping it on, I pull my cuffs over my hands. In between the bar and the beach, I got cold.

"Nothing." He coughs. "I'm just admiring your Ivy League wear."

"Nice attitude," I say. "I appreciate your bitterness. It's very becoming."

I walk off, leaving Charlie standing there and my footprints in the wet sand. Since I promised myself I wouldn't find Henry if the ID thing worked out, I take a back route away from the noise of the bar and go toward the cottage via the clam shack. If I had money I'd buy onion rings. But since I don't, I go and sit on the top level of the Chappy ferry terminal. (It's really just an open two-story deck.) From here, I can see the distant lights of the few Chappy houses, and the nightlife in town seems peaceful rather than policed.

I hear footsteps and look up from where I'm dangling my feet to see Charlie with a hand extended. "For your troubles," he says, his voice softer. He offers me a box of fries.

"I like onion rings better," I say, smiling slightly.

"Then onion rings it shall be." He vanishes and reappears with a collection of white-and-red plaid cardboard boxes. "What we have here," he explains as he arranges them between us, "is a veritable smorgasbord of artery-clogging digestibles."

"Consider yourself partially redeemed," I say and point my finger at him like it's a magic wand. Then I reach for an oversized onion ring.

Fries, clams, mozzarella sticks, and onion rings later, after we've traded weird food likes (he is a fan of all things orange: sweet potatoes, Cheetos, carrot soup) and dislikes (he understood my need to avoid anything resembling tapioca—seriously just thinking about it makes me heave), Charlie says, "Sorry about before. On the beach. I'm a jerk sometimes. Really."

"You should be a salesman!" I say. "With techniques like that, you'd win employee of the month in no time."

"Yeah," he laughs. "Actually, I'm kind of fun-employed right now."

"What does that mean, exactly?"

"Just that—you know—I'm sort of taking it easy for the summer."

"It's not really summer anymore." I can't help but stare at him. He's got that hard-to-find mix of prettiness and presence without any visible effort. "See, you should have accepted my father's money," I say. Charlie flinches and turns to stare at me.

"No, I really shouldn't have." He gathers all the boxes of food and stacks them up, a tower of grease-spotted cartons. "I don't need anyone's money."

I don't understand the full meaning of this, but before I can ask, I switch tacks (oh, sailing terminology—how Vineyard!). "Want to see something cool?"

I take him over to Mable's new place and, though the lights are off and the door's locked, we peer in the windows and sit right on the stoop where I sat with Henry this afternoon. The stone steps are cold, but our legs are touching. Mable always told me that she didn't believe in love at first sight, but that she'd experienced that electrical charge right off the bat (go sports imagery!) several times. This is what I have with Charlie.

From the minute I saw him on the street and again in the ocean, he's got that magnetic presence that causes me to have that weird blend of fidgets and calm. I pick at my cuticles and breathe in the salty air, trying to stay focused on what Charlie's saying—something about Boston, or school—but I'm distracted by his leg. By his voice. I look up at him.

"What?" he asks, grinning from the side of his mouth. He smells beachy. Not kegs and kelp, but bonfire and smores. Charlie would be that guy who could fend for himself if marooned, or slide into a coat and tie and whisk me away to the opera (or some other, less cliched date place that I can't think of right now because said boy is talking about learning to fish with his dad and I'm sucked in).

"Out by Lanson's Cove we'd drop these lines in—using whatever leftovers we had from our picnic. You know, hot dog remnants or whatever . . ." Charlie's voice trails off. "Anyway, it was a long time ago, I guess." He has a cloudy expression, his eyes cast downward, and I realize that part of Charlie's pull is the way he lets me half in on what he's thinking and then abruptly closes himself off again. Maybe he's that enigma that's always alluring and will leave me wanting more.

I want so much for him to kiss me. Or to have the guts to grab him myself. Then I'm suddenly reminded of Jacob and I tune back into the conversation right when Charlie's saying, "Anyway, the island's great in the fall. You think you'll come back?"

"I don't know," I falter. Did I miss crucial information when I was zoning? "With my aunt's place . . ." I thumb to the door. "Probably."

"Think about it," Charlie says and stands up. He sticks out a hand and pulls me up. "Maybe Columbus Day?"

"Will you be here?" I ask.

He thinks about it and then nods. "I guess I will."

"What—you aren't sure?"

He licks his amazing lips and turns back to me. "You know what? I am sure. I'll be here."

I assume (again, assumptions are usually wrong—get it through your head, woman!) we'll exchange email addresses or numbers, but since Charlie doesn't ask for mine, I don't offer it. Apparently, if we ever meet up again, it will be providence. This then makes me think of Lila and the crappy night, and how I have to face Hadley Hall without her. Not that I'd be thrilled to have her back at Hadley after the Brown debacle. But even a lame version of Lila would be better than a friendless fall. But Lila's a college freshman now and I am not, even though I keep pretending I am. I'm a junior. College, SATs—oh my God. I'm on the verge of a sudden panic attack.

"What's wrong?" Charlie asks, half laughing, half concerned.

"Just had a case of serious mind racing," I say, begging my palpitations to go away.

"Count the waves," he says. Without waiting for me to ask what he means, he leads me over to the water's edge where the tide laps the sand. "Just watch and count ten waves." I do. He takes my wrist in his hand and for a second I'm sure he's going to kiss me. This makes me need to count ten more waves. I do.

"Your pulse is much slower," he says.

"Thanks," I say. I take a deep breath.

"What year are you in school?" I ask. It never occurs to me that he's not a student.

"I'm nineteen, if that's what you're asking."

"I guess it's what I'm asking." We start to walk back toward town. Out in the bay, a foghorn sounds a low moan like even the ocean knows summer's over. Charlie's flip-flops flap against the cobblestones. "I'm almost seventeen," I say in case he cares.

"I thought you were a freshman in college—what're you, like one of those genius kids who took the SATs at age twelve?"

"Yes, that's me, girl wonder. No, but why would you think I'm in college? Oh, you mean my stunning array of—what did you call it? Ivy League gear?"

He's embarrassed enough to seem humbled. "Sorry—again. Yeah, I guess I just figured wrong . . ."

"No. I go to Hadley Hall—near Boston," I say.

"I know where it is," Charlie says. "It's right near . . ." His voice trails off.

"And I'm about to be a junior."

Charlie doesn't say anything. He just raises his eyebrows and does his sideways grin—a nonverbal okay—and then looks out at the water.

He walks me home and we give a brief (brief as in short, not as in annoying word for undergarments—oh, undergarments is annoying, too) hug. It's a hard call as to whether the brevity of the embrace is my doing (I got a little nervous that I was seeming clingy and so I backed off) or Charlie's mystery man emerging (he pulled me back for a double dip after I first broke the hug, but then he abruptly ended that second hug). I should be able to hug without analyzing it, but I can't. Did he pull me back in just so he could end it and establish the power dynamics of our relationship? (Do we have a relationship?) Or was he trying to kiss me? Or—and maybe this is it—it could be that since I broke the first hug out of nervousness, he tried to put me at ease (sailor!) with a second squeeze (and a bad rhyme). Before I can figure out what to think, Charlie says, "Hope I'll see you around," and he heads off into the moonlit street. Now, call me crazy, but I think he added a question mark at the end of his sentence, which would mean that he's either hoping to see me around or, if you say it like a question, that he's implying that I hope that I'll see him around.

Oh my God, I need sleep and a large dose of perspective.

I have the good fortune of being awakened by my father and Mable singing the next morning, and when I stumble out to the kitchen, Viola is head down in the Sunday papers and my dad is twirling Mable around.

"I'm heading back today," Dad says to me as he dips Mable. She stops to catch her breath, laughing. "Lots to do at Hadley."

"Blah," I say. I have the Sunday blues, even though Monday is a holiday. I want to stay on the Vineyard and never have to memorize any facts or take tests or deal with the social inanities of high school. "I dread going back."

My dad looks as though I have personally wounded him. "You're going to have a great year," my dad says like he really needs to believe—even more than I do.

The year ahead—no, the next couple of months. First term. That's what I'm plagued with as I hold out stale bread for the seagulls as my own ferry departs from Oak Bluffs. I never did ride the old carousel, never did share a kiss under the stars (despite, at least in my opinion, having come close with both Henry and Charlie—but two nearlys don't constitute a romance). But I did sing a duet with Mable this morning, testing the microphone out at Slave to the Grind II (which I think she should rename, but we're still debating). We belted out an off-tune (her) and groggy (me) version of "You Don't Bring Me Flowers," which is possibly one of the best, saddest songs ever. She sang the Streisand parts and I did the Neil Diamond, and we wound up cracking up during the heavy dramatics of it. Picturing the scene now, I could bawl though. It's one of those memories of summer that seems so funny at the time, but when you look back on it—even an hour or two later—it just reminds you that June, July, and August are finished, Labor Day has come and gone, and the rest of life drags you back from the beach and into the corridors of school.

CHAPTER SIX

♡

The Beginning of the school year

I can't breathe. Wheezing after what is probably my first attempt at exercise in months, I kick my running shoes off and allow myself to collapse on the sun-warmed mesh of the trusty pole-vaulting mat behind the gym at Hadley Hall. A quick summary of past events on said cushion: meeting my big crush Robinson Hall here, kissing him, dumping him after he slept with the vapid and vicious Lindsay Parrish (his friend-fuck from back in NYC). Ah, good times.

But it's a whole new year. A whole new me! Wow, I sound like a maxi-pad commercial (which reminds me that I should make an appointment to do another round of voice-overs at WAJS, if they'll still have me). In any case, the fall air feels good. Coolish days laced with traces of sunlight.

Actual classes start tomorrow. I can't believe how new everything seemed last year when I just started. Now I'm one of the regular faces around here. Part of me feels a certain amount of excitement to be back, to see people and to see how three months have changed them (or not) and find out what classes I have, love, or despise. I requested another English class with Mr. Chaucer, but his classes are oversubscribed so there's more than a slight chance I won't get in. Last year, Jacob and I sat across from each other and I loved jotting notes in my books and peering up through the copper curtain of my hair at Jacob, who hardly ever wrote anything down but managed to get incredible grades. (I know this because during our two seconds of being romantically linked we did a three-second swap of final transcripts—hey, our academic snoopage outclocked our dating! Let's hear it for geeks in love. But wait—we weren't really in love, were we?) I simultaneously long to see him and dread the inevitable confrontation.

I walk back to my house via the dorms, where parents and (not kidding) chauffeurs are dropping boarders off with luggage. Unlike in films, boarding students don't have trunks—except maybe in the 1950s. Here, there's just mounds of overstuffed backpacks, L.L. Bean gear, the odd Louis Vuitton case. Near Fruckner House, fellow fac brat Cordelia's acting like the cruise director, shuttling parents to the side door for easy access (something she would know about), and trying desperately to claim status as junior in the know.

The truth is, I wish Cordelia'd turned out differently. I wanted her to be a close friend, but the reality is that she's a climber, and I never felt totally relaxed around her. She's that girl with whom there's always the possibility she'll slap the proverbial *kick me* note on your back when you least expect it.

"Check it out!" Cordelia screams and rushes over to me. I can't help but smile—it feels good to at least be recognized. "It's none other than *the* Love Bukowski!" The freshmen standing around get momentarily excited as if I'm the girl who guest appeared on *The OC* who is rumored to be joining the ranks of Hadley.

"Hey, Cordelia," I say and hug her. Hadley Hall is all about the hugs. You hug your friends, your dorm mates even if you dislike them, you hug the campus dogs, even faculty members, even (wait for it— crunchy moment coming) yourself and a tree on Eco Day. "How was your summer?"

"*C'etait magnifique,*" she says without the slightest bit of irony.

Cordelia's stint in Paris is clearly taking its toll on her lingual skills. "I'm glad to be *ici, mais j'espère que . . .*" She rambles on in Franglish, trying to impress the underclass students and—sadly, I might add—succeeding.

"Oh my God, are you like, French or something?" one girl asks, making sure her collar's upright position withstands her salivating.

Cordelia just smiles and links her arm through mine and pulls me inside the dorm. Parents stand checking out the place, kids lug their crap up the stairs to their shared rooms, and I—yet again—feel like my own breed of Hadley student.

"Which room are you in, dear?" inquires a mother-father team who I saw eye me as suitable roommate material for their freshman daughter.

"Oh, I'm not," I say. From the doorway, I can hear a voice that registers as familiar, one that makes me shiver. I can feel my palms start to sweat. "I'm not a boarder." The parents look confused. "I'm not a DSG, either."

Cordelia butts in. "What she means is, she's not a day student girl. She's a faculty brat." The parents immediately lose interest and half turn away until the mother politely inquires, "What subject do your parents teach?"

"They don't," I clarify and tug at the stray bits of hair around my face. Time for a trim. "My dad's the principal—the headmaster. David Bukowski."

My voice comes out louder than normal, or maybe it's just one of those lame moments like in a movie bar scene where everyone somehow goes quiet right when the lead says the word *penis* or something. Anyway, the point is that my last name echoes like I've shouted it for effect. Cordelia rolls her eyes and mumbles *mon dieu* or *sacré bleu* or whatever French phrase she's deemed fitting for the moment.

And then, the voice from the vestibule. "Bukowski? As in Love Bukowski? Where? Point me to that bitch!"

I wish I could say I'm exaggerating or that I misheard the big B word in reference to myself, but I didn't. No subtitles needed. The parents I've been speaking with make themselves scarce, as do the few students still heaving the bags over their shoulders. I know the person attached to the Bitch comment before she pokes her enormous head through the doorway.

"Hello, Lindsay," I say as I face Lindsay Parrish—the infamous Ms. Manhattan who jumped into bed with Robinson Hall last year. Not that I would have gone that route, anyway, but she'd started a turf war before I'd even gotten my bearings. Objectively (and if you can be objective about the girl who screwed your boyfriend, don't you deserve a pat on the back? Or a medal? Something?), Lindsay Parrish is gorgeous. She's got that tall, but not super willowy physique, with toned thighs and big enough boobs to matter, and a very pretty (if not particularly unique) face crowned by thick, dark rich girl hair. I say rich girl hair because it has the sheen and grooming of a show horse—not that I'm a stable frequenter, but still.

"Love, Love, Love," Lindsay says, her mouth in a semi smile. "So lovely to see you." Then she puts her hand to her mouth. "Oops—redundant." She sticks out her huge hand to shake mine as if I hadn't just heard her prior comment.

For some reason, I take her hand and—no big surprise—judge her grip to be just a wee bit too tight. Should we arm wrestle? Behind her is a similarly tall, equine woman in tweed and expensive light wool trousers. (I say *trousers,* because a woman with Chanel earrings and perfect little heels like she's got would not stand for *pants*.) Lindsay looks at her mother and gives her some weird nod.

"Mother," she says, "this is Love Bukowski, daughter of the headmaster." I feel I should curtsy, but I don't.

"Hello, dear," Mrs. Parrish says. "Where do we put Lindsay's personal effects?"

"I'm not sure," I say. Then, because I am well trained to be polite and helpful (like a good retriever? I question suddenly) I add, "We can find the dorm parents and see which room you're in."

But we don't have to. Having stood off to the side for this little scene, Cordelia now steps in and clasps her clipboard to her chest like a prize. "I can help you," she says to Mrs. Parrish. She simultaneously points to Lindsay's bag (Birkin), announces it stunning (in French, *bien sûr*), and dramatically checks Lindsay's name off her list. "I'm Cordelia," she says, and then, looking at me, "and I think *I* have all the information you're looking for."

Suffice to say that I walk home admiring the incredible fall campus and cringing about the *Mean Girls* incident. I refuse to fall into the cruelty of female friendships. I will rise above it. I will somehow be the better woman. Not that I harbor total fantasies of making Lindsay be my long-lost best friend (and, no, I don't want her to pass along her bag to me—it's not my style), but I wouldn't mind a truce. Truce? Has a war already begun? I shake my head and sigh.

Back at fac-brat central (read: my room), I check my email twice, in case I missed something the first time. The second time, there's actually a new message.

> *Love—sorry I didn't see you more before you left. I looked for you on the ferry back but to no avail. Any chance you're up for sharing another sticky bun at some point?*
>
> *-Henry*

I write back and say maybe and ask how he got my email, though I suspect with his real-estate-mogul father, Henry can get just about anything he wants. Only time will tell if that includes me, too.

I feel funny when I compare and contrast (ode to English class there)

Charlie and Henry and their various pros and cons. It's as though they not only have their own appealing qualities, but that they represent two divergent paths for me. Charlie's natural, a bit rebellious, clearly not into material things, mysterious. Henry's totally part of the moneyed set, but so endearing and earnest. Maybe when you have to choose between liking one person or another, it says as much about you as it does about them.

"Pass the sauce, please," Dad says and takes the caper and plum tomato mixture from me. "I have a favor."

"Shoot," I say and twist a forkful of spaghetti into a tight coil.

"After classes tomorrow, do you think you can swing by Logan and collect the exchange student?" He says it like a) Logan Airport is right down the street—which it's not and b) *the exchange student* is a bag of folded laundry.

"What about extracurriculars?" The college office displays their wares, and the various societies and clubs line the hallways in the evening, plugging for membership. It's overwhelming how many groups there are to join, but the college office insists each student pick three, even if they drop out after the first meeting.

"Oh." Dad mops up his sauce with a baguette slice. "You can deal with that later."

"Why can't you get the exchange student?" I am sounding whiny. Note to self: stop.

"Because I have other things I need to do," he says, and before I can suggest it, "and no, we're not having her take a cab."

"Are you going on a date with Viola?"

"No," Dad says. He has a ring of sauce around his mouth like a pasta clown. "Mable needs to go to Mass General for testing."

I swallow hard, appetite gone. "I'll take her."

Dad stands up. "No, I will. Just remember Virgin Atlantic flight twelve."

"Okay," I say, thinking how that would be the appropriate airline for me to fly. "A name would be useful."

"Oh. Right." Dad disappears to his office for a minute and comes back with a little sign. "Arabella Piece," he says. "That's the one you're looking for."

I take the sign and am flooded with phlegmories (the icky memories you want to clear from your head, but can't quite cough up). Though I've never met her, I've considered Arabella Piece as somewhat a known entity. Her brother, Clive, the freckled and fickle, was the instigator of a fire alarm that got me busted last year for sneaking into the boys' dorm. Not only did I get suspended, but now, knowing that it was all for a possible make-out mission with Robinson Hall, I feel doubly annoyed at Clive (read: also annoyed at myself but way easier to pawn it off on Clive).

Upstairs, I check email again. My addiction is painful. Then the phone rings, no doubt paranoid parents or faculty calling to harass my father.

"Love! Phone!" he says.

I pick up in my room and clasp the phone between shoulder and ear while flinging through the clothes in my closet. I'm not in search of the latest trends, I'm just in favor of comfort and style—and the perfect vintage jeans. Mable has bequeathed some of her early eighties gear, and I dump out the contents of one shelf looking for the parachute-material bag with a giant 1985 slicked to the side: my soon-to-be book bag.

Lila's voice comes through the line. "Hey."

"Hi," I say.

"Sorry," she's quick to blurt out. "I'm a total . . ." She waits for me to interrupt with an *it's okay,* but I let her find the words to complete her apology. "Okay, okay, I get it. I suck and you'll probably never come to visit me at Brown again. But I didn't mean for it to happen that way."

"The sucky way, you mean?"

She laughs. "Yes. And by the way, lest it come as a total shock, Hans Hecklefranz and I are not, in fact, a couple."

"Really?" Faux surprise from me as I shove the rest of my clothes back into the closet, hoping the *Trading Spaces* people come to my room while I'm asleep and fix my storage crisis.

"He's maybe the lamest kisser ever and I was drunk and—to his credit—he left me to sleep off my stupor. He's cute and everything, but that's no excuse for treating you like upholstery."

"Upholstery?"

"You know, just there, in the background. Something comfortable to sit on."

"Your analogy needs work," I say.

"Okay, Mr. Chaucer," Lila says. "Speaking of which, how is he?"

"Classes don't start until tomorrow. And then I have to go pick up"— I look at the airport sign again—"Arabella Piece."

Pause from Lila. "You'll like her. She's nothing like Clive. Seriously."

"I'll believe it when I see it," I say, and then I tell her about Mable, and cry a little, and then listen to her college woes: work, work, and her inebriated mother's impending visit to campus. Then she asks about the Vineyard, to where she rightly assumed I escaped after fleeing Brown.

"Anyway," I wind down my Charlie/Henry tale, "Henry thinks I'm a freshman at Brown. But he just emailed and didn't mention anything, so maybe he forgot."

"If he shows up, what should I say?"

"You're kidding, right?"

"Sort of," Lila says. "I mean, it is possible that the guy would come looking for you."

"Just tell him the truth," I say.

"No," Lila laughs. "I'm gonna say your room is under construction and you've gone to Boston for some time off."

"Speaking of which, I'm not clear what Charlie's deal is," I say and try to remember his face. "Do you think he's like this local boy trying to get out or a college student taking time off to rough it, or what?"

"He's probably a simple fisherman," Lila jokes.

"Oh, and I'm the good catch?"

"Yeah," Lila says and then her cell battery bleeps. "I forgot my charger. Probably a good thing since the Euros always call with nothing to say and I'm left driving like a maniac without a headset. Gotta go!"

"Bye—and come visit," I say and hope she hears. I want to add, don't forget about me here at Hadley, but I keep quiet. Before Lila cuts out she adds something about *watch out* and *Lindsay,* but there's probably nothing Lila can warn me about that I don't already know.

CHAPTER SEVEN

♡

I'm not about to let a close encounter of the cruel kind kill my first-day-of-school buzz, you know, that fun (if misdirected) thrill of newness that lasts for all of two hours before you remember that despite your freshly purchased shoes and the gleaming floors, school is still school. Hadley's classrooms are sun filled and shiny, the tables glossy, the wood trim around the door and windows offset by the cream-colored walls. The only negative in my line of vision is Lindsay Parrish, and I've decided that Lila Lawrence was probably exaggerating how bad Lindsay is. I'm letting the incident in Fruckner slide—addressing it would just be too trite.

This is my plan, which holds for the first five minutes of Chaucer's English class, when the students are filing in, giving out those infamous hugs and *hey, how are yous, summer this, exotic locales that.* It's a new and bizarre experience to be asked what I did and mention *Music* magazine without having the time to explain that while it's true I interned there, it was hardly a glamorous experience what with fetching the coffee and being nameless.

Harriet Walters, our resident feminist, sees me and we exchange smiles.

"Going for the vintage librarian look, I see," I say and she's careful not to jostle her cat-eye glasses as we hug.

"Thanks for noticing," she says and sits next to me. From her bag she pulls out all the books we were required to read this summer (Eric Hobsbawm, *The Age of Empire;* William Barrett, *Irrational Man;* J. M. Coetzee, *Waiting for the Barbarians;* Fyodor Dostoevsky, *Crime and Punishment,* to name just a fraction) and all the books that were on the suggested reading list (i.e., if you are a fast reader or lame enough never to set foot outdoors, you can pile these pages onto your bedside table).

"I see you got to the beach," I joke and point to the books.

"Actually, I did so much flying this summer, I had ample time to finish," Harriet explains. Even the unassuming among Hadley's elite are, well, elite. Harriet went from Tuscany to Tunisia, where Daddy has a vineyard (who knew there even were vineyards there), to San Francisco, where she made the eyewear purchase while visiting her two moms.

Then, interrupting our burgeoning conversation, is the voice from hell. "I flew too many times to count." Lindsay leans in conspiratorially from across the table. "But when you fly private, you don't read." She says *read* like it's interchangeable with *crap*.

And just when I think Lindsay's baditude is smothering what was a fine and dandy English table, Harriet chimes back with, "Oh, I flew private. I'm just literate, that's all." Scoreboard: reaction from Lindsay, mouth open in shock; advantage, the nonbitchy team.

And so the civility I've planned on disappears. Mr. Chaucer comes in, all corduroy jacketed and smiles, blathering on about texts and what a great class we have, and how there's one student missing who will be with us shortly, and so on. While he gathers his papers and adjusts his chair so he's not blinded by the fall morning sunlight, I find a tiny smile creeping across my mouth—Jacob will be with us shortly. Cool. We met in this class last year, so maybe we can reconnect in it this term.

"Welcome," Mr. Chaucer says. "We'll be exploring various narratives this year, stories of place and culture, history of the self, and tales of survival. Man—or woman—versus nature, versus political climates . . ." He goes on. "And when our missing student arrives, I'm sure we'll have a fresh viewpoint."

Right, I think, because Jacob probably did some summer research project while abroad. I'm settling into my Jacob's return fantasy (You look beautiful, I missed you, etc.), but before I can even get to the part when I'm shouting *Inman! Inman!* like Nicole Kidman chasing Jude Law down after two hours of boring screen time in *Cold Mountain* (which Mable dragged me to see and I had to act as the tissue dispenser as she bawled throughout the whole thing), Mr. Chaucer says, "When Arabella Piece joins us from the UK, I'm sure she'll give an interesting spin to some of the class issues we'll read about in *A Passage to India* and, of course, Dickens."

"And Joan Didion," Harriet adds without raising a hand.

Mr. Chaucer nods. I can feel the words bubbling inside and they're out before my verbal gag reflux can kick in. "Is Jacob not in this class?" I ask.

Mr. Chaucer shakes his head casually. "No—he's not even at Hadley this term."

Harriet notices my (very visible) crestfallen face and writes in the margin of her notebook, *"J's at Aiglon."*

I write, *"Is that a prison or something?"*

"Sort of—it's a very posh boarding school in Switzerland."

I write, *"????"*

She writes, *"Exactly—it's a finishing school pretty much for burgeoning Euros and those destined for the throne."*

Did I miss a memo? Why does everyone on the planet (and by planet I mean my planet, which is my sad little prep school world) seem to know where Jacob is except for me? I'm always semi out of the loop when it comes to gossip (one reason I never contribute to Seen and Scene, the loosely-disguised gossip column in the school newspaper), but now that I know for sure Jacob (my Jacob!) isn't coming back to Hadley this term, I feel more out of it than ever.

Class proceeds as usual, but I'm distracted by thoughts of Jacob's absence. My plans for trying to smooth over our summer apart, picking up where we left off (minus the Crescent Beach incident) are aborted and Lindsay Parrish keeps glancing at me. Suffice to say if she had fangs (and she might—time will tell) she'd have them on display for me. Every time I make a comment (such as: "Isn't narrative one of the oldest forms of communication? Maybe we tell stories to explain our situations both from the past and into the future.") she's immediately overlapping me with her own verbage. ("I'm not sure *narrative* is the correct word. Perhaps Love means *biography,* which, when literally translated means life chart, a map. This would be a more apt choice of word.")

Um, fuck off?

I wish I had more eloquent words (or—wait, do I really mean eloquent? Perhaps I mean fluent or persuasive. They might be more *apt*) for the situation, but I don't. Right before the bell rings, we're assigned a mere tome of reading, plus an introductory essay about themes of class structure in society and literature. Due tomorrow. And I'll have all of no time to work on it after picking up Arabella at the Virgin Atlantic terminal.

I have a hectic day of running from chemistry to ethics, to literally running my five miles (if you can commit to running every day, you get out of required PE—and I want to do this not only to avoid the winter flabs, but also because if you do anything vaguely artistic after school, like the school play, you can use the PE time to practice). Then, winded and wishing for summer again, I manage to crash (also literally) into Chris the MLUT, whom I've not seen since our nonencounter at Crescent Beach (flashback: Chris leading me away to the deserted dunes just to talk—seriously—and Jacob, who wasn't supposed to be at the party, throwing a total fit in misconstrued misconduct).

"I guess this means you're happy to see me," Chris says as I peel myself off of his chest and stand up.

"Sorry," I mutter and shove my fallen books back into my bag.

"I see summer's been kind to you." He eyes me up and down.

"Oh, gross, Chris—will you ever change?" I ask and grin. He's so obvious it's funny.

"Oh, I've changed, believe me," he says, but his tone is too game-show host to be serious. "Can't a guy say a girl looks good after a three-month hiatus from Hadley without it being a come-on?"

"You tell me," I say. Chris looks like he belongs on the cover of some upscale yet trendy catalog. We walk to the student center and sit nursing coffees while the freshmen look lost, the seniors strut, and I take a deep breath for the first time all day.

"What's the big burden?" Chris asks. For some reason, I unload all of my crap on him. He nods and comments in all the right places.

"Oh my God, you must be so terrified," he says when I tell him about Mable. I nod. And when I ramble on about stupid Lindsay Parrish, he says, "Pathetic poseur—and yet, good taste in shoes."

I nod again. "She does have those Clergerie ones. I do like those." He gets me a refill on his tab and we laugh about Cordelia's Frenglish.

"It's like, oh, I stopped in Charles De Gaulle Airport and now I'm like, officially French—*comprennez-vous?*" He says, doing a perfect impression. "Meanwhile, whatever became of Jacob the Great and Moody?"

I blush. "Yeah, well, nothing. Not really." I remember sitting talking with Chris on the dunes and then I suddenly recall something. "Hey, what'd you want to tell me at Crescent Beach?"

Chris falters for the first time in our conversation. He shakes his head. "Nothing."

"Come on . . ." I poke him in the ribs, but he's totally stone-faced.

"Nothing!" he says too loudly, so I drop it.

We walk with Chris's mystery hanging in the air between us. I won't ask again. I'm way too familiar with this routine from my dad. So, instead of Chris revealing himself, I blather on about my adventures in guyville (nod to Liz Phair there) on the Vineyard.

"So," Chris says, gallantly holding the dining hall door open for me, "if you had to choose between them, would it be Posh Henry or Poor Charlie?" He grins and gives a coy, English wink.

"I couldn't choose," I say. "Besides, it's not like they've been throwing themselves at me, demanding I declare my emotions. And I don't really know them. Not yet, anyway."

"Go on," Chris nudges. "Get naked . . ." He waits.

"Chris . . ." I laugh, but I remember Chris's love for the quick kiss, the, um, ins and outs of his sluthood.

"I meant emotionally naked," he says and guides me over to the addictive burrito bar. I scoop black beans and cheese into a salsified (read: artificially red) wrap and wait my turn for nukage at the microwave.

"Why do you assume it's a case of *Pretty in Pink* richer or poorer?" I ask.

"Listen," Chris says, "all I was wondering is if money matters to you—and it matters to everyone, right? And—more important—which one of these Vineyard boys would be the lucky winner of your amorous advances."

We stand there, amid the bustle of the eating frenzy, and I ask myself Chris's question again in my head to see if I come up with another answer. And again, I'm annoyed at myself because I realize that my answer isn't dependent on what I feel, but rather I take the passive way out. Shouldn't I be able to tell what I feel without someone else telling me what my options are first? With goopy cheddar sliding out of my burrito and a tall glass of milk (I could, in fact, get a job promoting the American Dairy Association—please don't let me ever develop lactose intolerance), I decide that neither Charlie nor Henry has made enough of an emotional impact to (get ready for a driving analogy) overtake Jacob's place in my brain. (I say brain because heart seems just too vulnerable—plus *place in my heart* is just too Mariah Carey former hit single you can't free from your mind or stop from humming.)

On the way back from lunch, I have another body impact, this time with Mr. Chaucer. (Note to self: Don't pick cuticles while walking across street. Bad for digit hygiene and dork factor). He asks about my summer (required teacher-student banter) and then about Jacob (certainly extracurricular banter).

"Are you two still in touch?" he asks, obviously familiar with the flare-up, fade-out nature of student love.

"Not really," I say and semi hope that Mr. Chaucer has a message for me.

"Me neither," Chaucer says. Yeah, but you didn't trip in love with him (and I say trip because I kind of stopped short of falling). "Anyway, I hope you'll be on board this year."

He means on the board of the literary review, which, though award-winning in the prep school circuit, is a gathering of dysfunctional-family literature and thinly veiled crush poems. Next.

"I doubt it," I say.

And yet, after my first college counseling meeting, it's highly likely I will beg to be on the lit review staff—I'll even beg to be an editor. Or at least submit some writing. All this because I am informed that my "ECs" (that's extracurriculars for five hundred, Alec) are sadly lacking.

At Hadley Hall, the college process starts without much fanfare but with all the pressure of a life-making or -breaking decision. TCP (the college process—not kidding about that abbreviation—the faculty send notes like "Time to start thinking about TCP," which the stoners find hilarious) starts early at Hadley.

On an assigned day in the early fall, each junior is excused from a class to meet with their counselor to discuss their options. Like a less-cool Emma Peele (I've been doing some late-night viewing on BBC America and am semi obsessed with *The Avengers,* and definitely way too into *The Prisoner*—Patrick McGoohan is so hot in that retro spy way), I spy walk out of class and down the halls, past the student center and outside into the amazing fall day (orange and red leaves, air so crisp and clean I wonder if it's perhaps paid for by a wealthy trustee) and listen to the clip-clop of my clunky heels on the pavement that leads to Garrison, the stone building complete with its own rotunda where the college counselors hand out their (usually dismal) news.

I squeak onto the leather couch in the waiting area and gaze at the built-in bookshelves. Floor-to-ceiling college catalogs. Thumbing through, it's hard to tell them apart—each one is more multicultural than the next, with images of smiling student scientists (Oh, I love nuclear physics!), dramatic stage presentations (I'm a drama major but not at all messed up!), and the inevitable dorm shots that make the freshmen accommodations look like suites designed by Philip Starke. Where will I wind up? Wyoming? Santa Cruz? New York? Nowhere?

"Hello, Love." Mrs. Dandy-Patinko's gentle voice wafts over me. When she walks into the room, she fills me with an immediate sense of calm and paisley. Known for her head-to-toe plaids and full-length corduroy skirt and cardigan combos, Mrs. Dandy-Patinko is like a sitcom mom, all full-busted and vanilla smelling. For some reason, when she shakes my hand, I start grinning and can't stop.

Me: Um, hi.
Mrs. Dandy-Patinko (Not joking! Direct quote from her = "I used to be a young dandy; then I traded it in for Patinko. Could be worse—pa-stinko!"): So, what thought have you given to the college process? (Leans in, overly eager.)

Me: Just that, well, it seems—daunting.

Dandy-P: That's why I'm here—to help you . . .

Me (feeling suspiciously like I'm on a douche commercial and she's about to tell me how I can feel *fresher*): I just want to go somewhere—somewhere that is really the best fit for me, that feels right. (Um, am I describing a college or a bra?)

Dandy-P: I certainly understand that. Why don't you make a list of all the schools you've been interested in so far, and I'll add some suggestions of my own, based on your choices and interests, and then we'll run them in the SIBOF (statistical information based on facts = computer program from hell that plugs in all your info and spits out how likely it is that you'll get accepted into all these places—or not) and see what comes out. We should have the results instantly, but—of course—I'm not at liberty to divulge them until our next meeting.

Me (with stupid smile that switches on when speaking to adult I don't know whom I know is judging me): Sure!

And so my first college counseling session begins with the two of us going into her cozy little office and me coming up with a bunch of schools based not on anything that has to do with my life, but more to do with people I've met (Lila = Brown, random person in New York = NYU, *Music* magazine editor = Stanford, dad = Harvard, Mable=Sarah Lawrence). Mrs. Dandy-Patinko and I swap lists and see that there are a couple of overlaps (Brown, SLC) and a couple that inspire her to pause.

"Would you be happy to spend another four years in Boston?" she asks. She is able, somehow, to sound completely nonjudgmental. Maybe this is code for what chance in hell do you have of attending Harvard University, never mind the fact that I don't really want to go there anyway, even if Hadley is basically a feeder school.

I shrug. "I don't know."

"Is it important to you that a school has its own, well-defined campus?"

"I'm not sure."

"Ideally, would you have small classes or lecture-type academics?"

I open my mouth, but nothing comes out. The truth is, I have no fucking clue about college. I know I'm supposed to have a goal—like I've always dreamed of going to Harvard like my dad or something, but I don't. Not that I'm unmotivated or need to be on the depressive-tendency watch list. (Yes, the list exists and it's in my father's home office. Certain students need "more support" at stressful times likes winter exams or during TCP so they don't drink themselves into a coma and get Hadley Hall sued.) I just want to be happy and figure out what I want to do as it comes to me.

At the same time, I'm a functional person and well aware of the fact that applications need to be in and SATs need to be taken and college visits planned.

"So," I say to Dandy, "what's your advice?"

She turns to her computer screen where the SIBOF program lives. "Let's see what SIBOF says." Ah, the magic eight ball of the college process. She's quiet for a minute and then, "Love, you need to sign up for some ECs. Have you ever thought about the chess club?"

On the way to Logan Airport, I make a mental list of clubs and societies to join. *Me Gusta Spanish* club—some of the students in it are fluent, others just stoners looking for ECs and free food on the multicultural meals nights. Possibly the literary review. And possibly—maybe—the school play. I'm not one for the drama of drama, but I do like to sing, and since the fall play is *Guys and Dolls* (arguably one of the best musicals ever, not that I think arguing about musicals is the best use of time) I just might audition. Besides, Chris is insisting I try out since he's in charge of set design.

Airports are just filled to the brim with emotional good-byes and greetings, and it's a weird feeling to be picking up someone I've never met when all around me are couples making out, grandmas welcoming new babies, and parents returning home from business trips. All I know of Arabella Piece, the English exchange student who will grace our hallowed halls this term, is the random cell phone message she left for me on Labor Day. I vaguely remember her sounding haughty, but maybe that's just the British accent. For a minute, standing there at the international arrivals (*Bonjour, Jaques! Guten tag, Lindstrom*), I watch the anonymous people parade out and wonder if my mother has ever come through the swinging doors, passport in hand, scanning the crowd for familiar faces. She could be anyone here, but the truth is, the older I get without her, the more she becomes a haunting nonpresence in my life.

And then, jolting me out of maternal-influenced funk (and other new music categories), comes a voice. "Hadley? Hadley Hall?"

In picturing Arabella, I have been mentally aided by the fact that her brother, Clive, also did the program last year. However, I suppose I've been picturing Arabella as a female Clive (read: blotchy, snivling, and lame—and if it sounds like I have leftover resentment from Clive having gotten me in trouble last year when he pulled the fire alarm, it's because I do harbor resentment. I can own up to my stupidity at being in the boys' dorm after hours, but I refuse to take the blame for Clive's pot-induced paranoia). So basically, I kind of hold a grudge about the Clive incident and, by way of sibling connections, I displace it onto Arabella. Arabella, whom I assume to be the female version of her rodent brother.

My point being that when a tumble of chestnut hair (the thick kind with just the tiniest bit of blond fringe at the front—no doubt from ponytailed summers in Sardinia or somewhere) attached to a broad smile attached to a stunningly figured woman appears in front of me, I have no idea who she is, though the entire package is attached to a lovely English lilt.

"It's me," the woman says. She points to the sign I'm holding like a chauffeur. "I'm Arabella Piece."

"Love. Love Bukowski," I say, and we lock eyes. Arabella looks at me like I'm from another universe.

An hour later, we're back on Hadley Hall grounds and yet have said practically nothing. I'm partly to blame; the rain was so heavy when we exited the international terminal that we were both nearly soaked, and (being still kind of new to driving and very new to the loops and lanes of Logan) I missed the Ted Williams Tunnel exit and wound up driving fifteen minutes in the wrong direction.

"Did you see a sign?" I asked and pointed out the window.

"Do you mean a sign like an omen or a road sign?" she asked.

"What?" I had to actually look at her face to check if she was kidding— did she not get how stressed I was on the road?

"I'm not positive. What exactly are you looking for?" Arabella's accent was cool and upper crust, but her directional abilities left much to be desired.

"Never mind," I said and circled back through the airport.

"I don't drive," she explained and shrugged, like I was only her chauffeur and she couldn't possibly be expected to be helpful. Fine.

I kept saying a combination of "Wait, where the hell are we?" and "what did that sign say?" as the rain pounded the car's roof and I grew progressively more tense, while Arabella checked her hair in the visor mirror and had the nerve to complain that she couldn't see her whole head while I struggled to find change for the tolls in the glove compartment.

Now, I am driving Arabella to Deals, the girls' dorm next to Frucker. If the dorms have stereotypes in terms of their occupants, then Fruckner has the glossy, the bitchy, and the beautiful, and Deals has the willowy, the wistful, and the blue-blooded. Arabella is, potentially, all three.

"Well, thanks for the ride," she says. "Sorry to keep you from your big night of . . . what did you call it?"

"Extracurriculars," I say, and it sounds lame even to me. "It's fine. Glad you arrived safely." Oh my God, we can compete in the Inane Conversation Olympics.

"Okay, then, bye!" She chirpily finishes unloading the last of her luggage (tasteful, nonostentatious brown canvas with leather straps, no crest, no initials—an anomaly among the well heeled at Hadley). Her old-style trunk is "arriving by steamer" she told me before, like we're in some black-and-white grainy film.

Back at home, my dad hands me a mug of cranberry tea and tells me to sit down. Good news does not come with tea and sympathetic tones, so I know his afternoon can't have gone well.

"The thing is, Love, that Mable's cancer is spreading," Dad says. His shoulders are slightly slumped, his shirt crinkled. I start to cry looking at him—not so much because I know he's about to tell me more about Mable and her sickness, but because my father doesn't seem paternal, he seems like a brother with a sick sister.

I decide to shove the tears away and be stoic. It's actually kind of easy. I take a huge breath and count to ten on the inhales and exhales, like I did while counting the waves on the beach with Charlie, then pretend I'm about to have a job interview or something requiring composure.

"So what's the plan?" I ask. I sound so efficient I should have a clipboard or prop of some kind to demonstrate this.

"She needs a round of radiation on top of the chemo," he says. He picks up but doesn't sip his own tea while I spoon sugar into mine and gulp it like it's water (which, okay, fine it is, but I mean I chug like it's ice water and I'm Sahara parched).

"I'm sure the doctors know what they're doing, right?" I say less like a question, more definitively. "Because she'll be fine and we can just rally and totally support her and be there and . . ."

Dad licks lips and sighs. "Sure. Good plan." His voice is quiet. My guess is that if I poked or prodded right now, he would lose it—just break down, and since I can't cope with that, I just give him a hug and he pats my back. I go upstairs to my lair, which is free of cancer textbooks (Dad has accumulated four in recent weeks), free of words like *oncology* and *radiology,* free of English exchange students and college counselors.

One of the bizarrities that makes high school its own peculiar bubble is the day-in day-out ant colony feeling. We tread along the same worn paths to classes, sit in circles, talk, eat together, and then march along.

I say this to Chris as we nonchalantly walk toward the drama board to see if my tryout for *Guys and Dolls* has led to anything other than humiliation and a used-up afternoon.

"Oh my God, you are so quoting Dave Matthews," he says.

"I am not," defensive Love says, rearing her ugly head.

" 'Ants Marching'—give me a break. That is so college boy with a Mean People Suck bumper sticker on his Jeep circa late nineties."

"Like you would even know that crap, Mr. English guy too busy kissing everything in a skirt," I say and slip my arm around his waist. In the past couple of weeks Chris and I have merged our banter into something like a very good friendship—only we just don't reference the fact that we kissed (once, briefly) last year.

"Hey, don't just limit my exploits to skirts." He smiles and we head into the Dramatics Arena (are we Spartans? Romans? Dueling on stage?).

I pause and wait for clarification. "Not just skirts? You mean pants?"

Chris swallows and waits a minute. Then he laughs. "Miniskirts, too," he says.

I turn and tug on his shirt so he'll stop moving. "Seriously, Chris, you're a changed man," I say.

He blushes and does the guy nod: chin out, lips pursed. "Yes, my MLUT days are gone."

"So you're aware of your former huge MLUT status?" I ask. For some reason I always thought he was in the dark (obviously the right place to be for his line of duty) about how bad his reputation was, but I guess not.

"Let's just say I'm pretty well aware of a lot of things," he says.

"Ohhh, man of mystery!" I say and exaggerate my tone. Then I think for a split second about Charlie, who really is a man of mystery, his enigmatic presence still right on the tip of my brain (or, um, tongue).

I'm broken from my Vineyard reverie by Chris. Excited, he says, "Check it out!"

I look to where his finger is pointing to the cast list. Rather than chorus person #3, which is what I thought I'd get (since prime roles usually go to drama-heavy seniors who get choked up during final bows), I find I am to play Sarah Brown, the Save-a-Soul mission woman who gets semicorrupted by lust and love and winds up getting a dreamy kiss from Sky Masterson in Havana.

I sit on the massive, empty stage and kick my heels against the theater's edge while Chris goes and stands in the two-dimensional stage set forest and pretends to be one of the trees.

"You're going to be great," he says. "I'll put in a good word for you with Harriet Walters."

"Why?"

"She's in charge of costumes. Gotta have a sexy salvation thing happening—you know, innocence corrupted and all that."

I stand up and join him as we play with the log cabin (more remnants from the summer school's production of a creepy Hansel and Gretel). "I'm not that innocent," I say and sound decidedly un-Britney.

"Now you're just stealing from *The Breakfast Club*," Chris says as he chops with a fake ax.

"Fine," I say. "You caught me. But the point is, I'm not some little faculty brat who's, like, never been anywhere or done anything."

"Yeah, right," Chris says.

"What's that supposed to mean?"

"You take a lot of almost risks, that's for sure."

Before I can comment (and before I get pissed off, which I will when I think about what Chris said, and not just because he's probably right), our little scene is interrupted by a round of applause.

Chris and I turn toward the audience (and by this point I have basically forgotten that we're on a stage—I just like to mime woodworking all the time) and see Arabella Piece in the front row. She's got a hat on—one of those 1940s men's hats—and is gorgeous enough to pull it off without looking like she, too, raided the prop room.

She notices me staring at the hat. "Oh," she explains, "I raided the prop room."

Chris holds my hands as I jump down from the stage. "I'm Arabella Piece," she says and holds out a hand to Chris.

"This is Chris," I say, and before I can add a qualifying adjective, Chris butts in.

"So you're Arabella Piece," he says. "Your reputation precedes you."

"Really?" Arabella is too cool, too British, too tall. I'm too petty. "How so?"

I jump into the conversation. "No doubt you've been ranked in the boys' dorms."

Chris fiddles with his hair. Is he nervous? Does he have a thing for her already? "Suffice to say that guys are gross."

"I can only imagine," Arabella says. She takes off her hat and says to me, like I'm her lady-in-waiting (I've seen enough Jane Austen remakes to know about this role), "Hold this?"

I take the hat, try it on, and then, right when I'm about to give it back, a piercing *bleep bleep* echoes in the auditorium.

Immediately, Arabella grabs her back pocket, slides out her cell phone, and skitters off like a too-tall fawn (an elk?) without so much as a good-bye. Cell phone usage is frowned upon by the administration and you can actually get in trouble if you buzz or ring in class (one kid downloaded a Ferris Bueller-type coughing ring to disguise it), but Arabella doesn't seem to care—we can hear her gabbing in the highs and lows of her English accent.

"So much for Catherine Zeta-Jones gone Hadley," Chris says, his own accent muted by the loudness of Arabella's shouting into her international phone.

"Catherine Zeta-Jones is Welsh, anyway," I say, like that sums it all up.

"No shit," Chris says.

CHAPTER EIGHT

♡

Let me state for the record that I think of myself as a nice person. And in this vein, I have pulled out my biggest smiles, my best relaxation techniques, and my most fervent go-with-the-flow-ness (note to self: need to study for verbal section of the SATs) when dealing with Lindsay Parrish and her new sidekicks Cordelia and Sue Smith. You'd think that Sue Smith, with her unfussy name and her pleated kilts and brushed hair would be kind and affable—but you'd be wrong. I am no longer capable of giving all three of them the benefit of the doubt. After countless (okay, four) times of being challenged in class, on the track (when is it necessary to side check someone while jogging?), and in the student center (yes, it's true they pinned a pair of polyester granny underwear on the Questions and Comments board and tactlessly wrote my name on the tag for all to see), I am done.

I'm fed up with being a disciple of my father, the patient headmaster, the man so principled he became one. So—and Chris is with me on this one—I have begun to think of Lindsay, Sue, and Cordelia as the Triad from Hell. Especially evil potent is Cordelia, whom I still counted among my friends until her recent venture to the dark side. Plus, there might be a fourth—Arabella Piece. The tall and potentially treacherous Brit I picked up from the airport strikes me as their silent partner. She's that not-quite-sidekick girl whose intentions are unclear. On the one hand, she wasn't the one who wrote my name on the grannypants, but on the other hand (or ass), she cackled when she saw the less-than-charming undergarments.

But then, just when I was about to write her off, Arabella appeared in front of me in the crowded snack bar and presented me with a hot cocoa and a smile.

"To what do I owe this honor?" I asked her.

"Just thought you could use a pick-me-up," she said.

I reached into my pocket to hand her a couple of dollars, but she shooed my hand away. "Do you want to sit down?" I moved my book bag to clear a seat for her, but just as she started to join me, the obnoxious *bleeeepppp* of her cell phone called her away with only a shrug as an explanation.

Between the Triad, Arabella's hit-or-miss attitude, Mable's radiation treatments (I'm heading to Mass General after practice today to meet her for a soft serve she won't touch), and the slur of words and wisdom being spewed at me from my Other Nations teacher Mrs. Daniels, my head is clogged. I need liquid brain-o.

"Why was the treaty so important?" Mrs. Daniels asks. It's weird that she's even a missus. Mrs. Daniels is only six or so years older than we are. She's petite and semihot, as far as teachers go, and she just got married to one of the fugliest but nicest physicists ever, who teaches interdisciplinary something something for science-obsessed seniors who need individual challenges.

Harriet Walters raises her hand. "Because it demonstrated solidarity among struggling nations." She and I have a record four classes together this term.

"Go on," Mrs. Daniels says and nods in that teacher way, like it's the first time any student has ever answered the question correctly.

"Well, certain nations were without means, like they didn't have a national export product or were somehow barred from having sister nations, connecting with others . . ." Harriet explains her theory and people take notes, while I find myself drawn into her words. I'm a struggling nation! I'm without a sister nation. Poor me.

I find Chris in the library, when I'm not so much looking for him as I am looking for Harriet Walters, who, while not my best friend, certainly makes for some fun conversation. Instead, I find Chris looking dapper among the stacks.

"The good news is that you're a hot saddie," Chris says when I tell him my female troubles (no, not that kind).

"Huh?" I ask. I shove forty pounds of text into my 1985 bag and then heft the thing onto my shoulders and calculate how much homework I need to do. Three papers (ten, twelve, and five pages), six chapters, and one test, plus I have to think of an ethics question. The pathetic thing is that the ethics question assignment will probably take the longest out of everything. The papers I've done most of the research for, and the reading is heavy but interesting (mainly about the Massachusetts mills and women in factories—go team!), whereas the ethics question is petty but time-consuming. And even though all the questions wind up being put into a box (the Box of Wonder—yes, this does illicit one or two snickers from the puerile) for *anonymity,* my cheeks light up at the sound of my own queries, so I have to try to slide under the radar or prepare to at least pose a question I wouldn't mind the whole class knowing I wrote and then answering myself.

"Hello?" Chris taps on my head like he expects an echo.

"What were you saying?"

"I was saying, o distracted one, that you have the advantage of looking really pretty when you're sad."

"And this is a good thing?" I ask and get out the *Guys and Dolls* script.

"Can I walk you to practice?" he asks.

"Sure," I say, gladly accepting his offer.

Chris winks when we're outside. "In some cases, looking hot when sad might come in handy."

"I could see that," I say and imagine Jacob coming back or visiting Charlie on the Vineyard and my looking so hot and sad that he comes back to Hadley with me.

Chris goes backstage to join the other set designers and crew but adds, "By the way, I'm more than happy to come with you to the hospital— you know, if you want the company or your aunt wouldn't mind."

I smile. A huge sense of relief. "That'd be great," I say, surprised at how glad I am to have someone to talk to about Mable—someone who will wince with me when Mable coughs and laugh with me when Mable does her imitation of the wacko nurse who told her she liked to dress her cats in doll clothes and talk to them.

At Mass General, Chris and I take turns talking about school, about work, trying to smooth over the fact that we're here (here = subterranean café with—strangely—the best fro-yo around) with my sick aunt. My aunt who could die. Seeing the rings under her eyes, the pallid cheeks, isn't the worst—it's that Mable seems deflated. She always has this brashness, a veritable carnival of fun around her, which now seems gone. Or just on hold.

But Chris, with his accents and quick comments, manages to make us forget. He stands up and does his Jude Law impersonation for Mable.

"Where'd you find this one?" Mable asks me while gesturing to Chris.

"The lost and found," I say.

"Heh," Chris says and kneels down by Mable, who is rapt. Chris is very good-looking in that English shaggy-haired way, and Mable clearly likes the attention. "Now, I know we're years apart, Mable, but will you be my prom date?"

Mable giggles. "Why, of course."

"Fantastic. Now hold that thought. Nature calls."

When he goes to the bathroom, I expect Mable will ask me the inevitable, "Are you two a couple?" But she doesn't say anything.

I hug Mable good-bye.

"I'm off for my next appointment," she says. "I swear it's never ending, this whole process." She sighs. "I've got to go see Mighty Mouse."

"She has a lilliputian but really well respected oncologist," I explain to Chris. "Bye." I watch my aunt disappear down the hall.

Chris and I sit in my car, the one in which I've had so many fun times with Mable, and look out at the Boston skyline.

"We should go," I say. "I don't want to deal with Storrow Drive in the dark."

Chris pats my hand, quiet for once, but still a steadying force. It doesn't occur to me until later that Mable didn't even wonder if Chris and I were going out—and, come to think of it, he hasn't brought up the subject either. But then again, neither have I.

One night, after we do the Havana scene three times and I still can't hit the highest note, I go home, do the routine check of email (twice—once upon arriving home, once while brushing teeth, once before bed—oh, wait, that's three times. Note to self: deal with computer addiction and clearly flailing math skills) and rather than find nothing, I see Jacob's name glaring at me, unread.

> Yup, this is the email you've probably dreaded getting. Or maybe you deleted it without opening it, like it's viral. If you are taking the time to read this little ditty, please accept my humble apologies for what was quite possibly the biggest overreaction ever. Suffice to

say, summer has given me the perspective I was
lacking and now (from the safe distance of the
Alps) I am ready to talk. Are you?

Luckily, he hasn't signed his name, so I can write back without the
aforementioned crisis of how to sign my email. So I write back and say

J—
I'm writing okay, even though I'm wary. Does
that make sense? In some ways it's been a
long time and a lot has happened, but in
other ways it's like nothing's changed. What
I guess I'm trying to say (albeit not in
the most eloquent way) is that yeah, I want
to be in touch, if you're really up for it.
                                            —Love

This is what I email, even though I miss him (which I don't say in
the note), even though I don't want to get roped into a long-distance
courtship scenario where I'm drifting off in class picturing him in leder-
hosen (do they wear those in the Alps?) yodeling to me.

And, just like that, we are back in touch. Not totally comfortable, but
decent enough to email daily (or nearly every day) about Hadley, about
the glamorous students at Aiglon, the princes and contessas he's com-
muning with while learning German, French, Italian, and the international language of partying. Of course, I neglect to tell him I've been
spending the bulk of my free time with Chris the MLUT. Some things
are better left unsaid.

In fact, Chris and I spend so much time together that we're assumed to
be a campus couple. Sometimes we even play it up for the underclass-

men, with Chris saying things like "you were so hot last night" in an überloud voice just for shock value. Then I call him Tiger or Gypsy Stud or something and watch the newbies blush.

Today, it's my turn to blush as we continue round twenty of ethics questions that are more about truth or dares than real ethical scenarios.

"I guess if I had to, I would," Lindsay Parrish says in reference to the bogus "If you had the power to kill someone just by blinking at them and would never be held accountable, would you?"

"Isn't the point that we are all accountable for everything?" I ask. I've been trying to be a solid presence in class both because it's semiinteresting and to get out of answering the questions, plus there are no grades, just acceptable (read: spoke and showed up) and unacceptable (did neither of those). I've found that four times out of five I can get by without telling my "innermost thoughts" by talking just prior to the question and just after. The teacher then skips over me. Today, Lindsay makes sure my trick doesn't work.

"I think Love should answer," she says. "Would you off someone just by blinking?" She wants me to say *maybe,* but I won't.

"Oh, it's a pretty simple case of no I wouldn't," I say. A couple of nods and me-neither's. This is the only class where Lindsay and I are without our friends for side-impact protection.

"Because you're just so nice, right?" She glares at me.

"Not killing someone isn't just *nice,* Lindsay."

"You know what, you're right," she says, but then, before I can even think she's serious, I notice her blinking at me repeatedly. Instead of looking wounded, I put my arms to my chest in a fake dramatic death scene.

It's no surprise, then, when two days later, at the first of what I am sure will be many off-campus parties, Lindsay instigates "blink, blink, death," a new and twisted version of duck, duck, goose that seems to involve sitting in a circle and drinking whatever absentee parent liquor is on hand.

"This is lame," Chris says.

"I know, but what else are we going to do?" I whine and drink a soda. After last year's puking incident, I am the designated driver.

"We could leave," Arabella Piece says. She and Chris have also become quite chummy, and I can't say it doesn't piss me off. I'm not jealous, I just haven't figured her out. On one hand, she's obviously interesting and more than a step up from her brother. On the other hand, she's snooty. Plus, she and Chris get all English when they're together, and since I've never been to London, there's not much for me to do except smile, nod, and say "Oh that sounds like fun" when really I'm not sure.

We end up driving to Slave to the Grind, where Mable is noticeably absent and where Arabella insists on finding organic milk for her coffee. We take the java to go, but since I can't guarantee the Grind's milk is untreated and that the cows were hand fed grass stalks or whatever, she asks me to stop at three different places before being satisfied with Whole Foods. While she's inside, Chris fiddles with the radio station in my car and says, "I have to tell you something, Love."

"You sound so serious, Gypsy Stud," I say.

"I am serious," he says. "You remember Crescent Beach, right?"

Chris, me, the dunes, Jacob's shoutfest. "Yup," I say. My heart speeds up just a tiny bit. Could I really picture dating Chris rather than our act? Not really. He's just—

He sighs. "Okay, the thing is, when I asked you to take that walk— you know, in the dunes? I wanted to talk to you and just see if . . ."

Arabella opens Chris's door and gracefully swooshes into the car with her now-lactosed coffee, her cashmere wrap, and her piles of hair. "I'm so in love with that market!"

"What were you saying?" I ask Chris.

He turns to Arabella and asks for a sip of her drink. "Nothing," he says. "Let's go."

We're back and the campus is buzzing with students trying to soak up the last minutes of freedom before curfew. The sophomores mill around near the now-empty movie theater. Clumps of seniors lounge on the day student cars, causing the faculty to hover just in case they decide to go for a drive without permission. Like good little kiddies, we took the necessary precautions, and when I drop Arabella back at her dorm where she kisses me on both cheeks, Chris, too, and then gallops away. She's like a fine steed—or mare. Is steed only male? Note to self: Learn horse terminology.

Chris walks back, past the cemetery, where the Hadley Goths and Les Miserables (not drama geeks, not Francophiles, just the truly depressed and downtrodden) go to smoke or cry or ink Smiths' lyrics onto each other's legs, without telling me what he'd wanted to earlier.

I, on the other hand, manage to get a flat tire by main campus. Conveniently, my auto mishap happens near a parking space, so I go into Neutral (not a state in which I find myself all that frequently) and then into Park, figuring I'll deal with it tomorrow. I lock the door and then grab my jacket—the wind is cold at night now and fall is at its peak, with clear night skies and temperatures that turn my cheeks and nose red like they're in competition with my hair.

Just as I'm crunching on the fallen leaves by the library, I hear a moan. I look around for a cat in heat, or a couple of day students tempting the campus security by pawing each other after hours, but see no one. Until, that is, I nearly stumble and step on the one and only Lindsay Parrish.

"I don't have any clue," I say to my dad later.

"You mean to tell me you just found her there?" He gestures to Lindsay, who is slumped on our couch.

"She was spread-eagle, passed out—or whatever the stage is before passed out. I mean, she was moaning, so she wasn't totally gone, but . . ."

"Okay, I get your point." Dad has his principal voice on. "I'll drive her back to the dorm." He pauses, thinking of something.

"What?" I wait for him to explain.

"You know what?" His voice is overly friendly. Something's up. "Let's just have Lindsay stay here."

I shake my head, way overemphatic. "No. Dad, seriously? No. The girl fake killed me in ethics. The last thing I want is for her to be in my house unguarded."

Dad smirks. "It doesn't look like she's going to cause you too much trouble." Lindsay finally gives in to gravity and liquor and falls face-first on the sofa. "I'll just ring the dorm and explain and then we can bring her back tomorrow."

"Fine," I say. "But don't make it seem like I invited her."

He agrees, but when I'm upstairs (yes, checking my email) I can hear him say into the phone, "I know it's last minute, but Love has invited Lindsay for a sleepover."

Gag.

Today is the day not only when I am supposed to have all my cues and lines learned (which I sort of do), but also the day I find out what the college stat cruncher has to say about my future. In other words, my SIBOF results are in, as evidenced by the note I get in my campus mailbox (thrillingly, it reads "The college counseling office is pleased to inform __ that her/his SIBOF scores have been tabulated." The blank is where someone—probably Mrs. Dandy-Patinko, judging from the purple marker—has scrawled my name. Thoughtfully, they've also made an X over the *her* so it reads *blah blah blah* pleased to inform Love that *his* scores are in. Even though I support the transgendered students here at Hadley and worldwide, I don't count myself among them, but I smile at

the thought of them mixing up my boy/girl status when they're supposed to help me decide about the next four years of my life post-
Hadley Hall.

On my way to Dandy-P's office, Arabella trots over to me (I swear I
can't help the horse talk) and says, "Did you hear about Lindsay Parrish?"

"What about her?"

After his cross-quad wave, Chris sidles up to us and slips right into
the conversation. "Rumor has it she was drugged at that party."

"I'm guessing Roofies," Arabella says.

"You guys—"

"We're just speculating," Chris says. "Becca Feldman said she saw her
about to pass out."

Arabella adds, "Rob Garcia told me he got off with her."

I pause. "I need a station identification." Arabella looks confused.

Chris clarifies. "Love doesn't know what that means."

Arabella sighs, remembering I'm not one of the UK's spawn.
"Hooked up with. Garcia said he hooked up with Lindsay."

"Doubtful," I say. We're almost to the college counseling office.
Through the stained-glass window that displays the Hadley crest, I can
see a tinted Patinko head nodding into the phone. I get a little nervous
thinking she has the information that could point me toward my whole
college existence.

"It's possible," Chris says.

"It's likely, I think," Arabella says. "Lindsay's a slag-in-waiting."
Luckily, Chris has already taught me (and no, not from personal experience) that slag is like slut, only I think it's better because it's like slut
meets hag.

"Actually, I picked her up from the middle of the quad after I
dropped you guys off," I say. "And she was drunk. Not drugged. Simple,
plain, barfy drunk. And my dad made her spend the night."

"Oh my God, you poor little duck," Arabella says.

"Pity party," Chris says and gives me a hug—any excuse for touching. "Don't tell me you had to clean up her hurl?"

I pull back and look at them, rolling my eyes. "I refused. You've gotta draw the line somewhere."

"Well," Chris reasons, "at least she'll get DC'd and then have to go home for a while."

After getting Discipline Committeed, students had (like any reality show castoff) to immediately go to their dorms, pack their bags, and go home for either two-, four-, or seven-day suspensions. I figured Lindsay would get four days—but only because she was new and this was her first offense. Otherwise, she'd face seven days or be kicked out. This last slim possibility was just too much to hope for. I'd had only the briefest of encounters with her at my house. Hungover at our kitchen table the morning after I found her, she nursed some seltzer water and gave me the fakest smile ever. When my dad went into his office I couldn't help but smile at her, knowing she was on her way to getting DC'd. But Lindsay just held her head and sneered, saying softly, "You gloat now, but don't think I'm not getting out of this."

I'm still trying to figure out what Lindsay meant, but am also aware that she shouldn't be of concern to me. Not, for example, as much of a concern as where I'll spend the four years after Hadley.

"Love?" Mrs. Dandy-P's voice pulls me back into the reality of the college counseling office. Sometimes I don't know where to draw the line between my rich inner thoughts and the real world in front of me.

Two minutes later, Mrs. Dandy-P is also drawing lines—three of them, in fact.

"See, all the schools above this line are your safeties—the ones you're quite likely to get into; the ones in the middle section are your swing schools, which could go either way; and the ones below here"—she takes a deep breath like she's submerging into Arctic water—"these are your reaches. They're . . ."

"Something to reach for?" I say and sound like a crappy Hallmark card and stating the obvious. Mrs. Dandy-Patinko looks at me with what I assume is kindness but might be pathos. It's not that the list is bad (note to self: copy said list into my journal), just that it's so defined. As though there's no point in even researching any other colleges because it's all about likelihoods and percentages.

I wish I could say that the list in front of me inspired dreams of semi-adulthood, stating a major, bonding with people from all over the country or world, taking classes with names like Intro to Women's Studies and Linear Readings of Noncohesive Texts. The reality that hits me when I look at the list of my reaches, safeties, and swings is that college sounds a hell of a lot like Hadley, only without parietals and my father's watchful eye—which, to be honest, hasn't been particularly watchful as of late.

"Is there a problem, Love?" Dandy-Patinko asks. "Are you disappointed with the SIBOF?"

"No," I say, "It's fine. It's all fine."

I write and tell Jacob about my SIBOF snafu and putter around packing for the Vineyard for the Columbus Day weekend while I wait for a response. When I get a reply, Jacob skims over my precollege malaise with the following:

> What was that trite but probably true saying about sweating the small stuff? And before you point-counterpoint me with a "college isn't the small stuff," just take a breath and remember Harvard or UCLA or Cape Cod Community is still two years (I know, I know, more like twenty-two months) away. How are you otherwise? I think I miss you.
>   —J.

Of course, I need to read this a thousand times to interpret and reinterpret the last line, which is dumb because it's a pretty simple statement. And yet, on the phone, I tell Mable three different times what the email said.

"I'm sure he does miss you," she says.

"I'm not questioning that," I say. "I'm wondering if it's like miss you or *miss* you, or it could be just a quick kind of miss you, like he's signing off."

And when we hang up and I call Chris, he hands the phone to Arabella.

"I hope you got parietals," I say.

"Nope," Arabella says, semiproud of herself. She tends to think she can bend the rules.

"I'm just reminding you that you should. I mean, trust me, I got busted last year and it wasn't worth it."

"So, do tell," Arabella says. I can hear her chewing on her nails.

"Tell what? Where'd Chris go?" I didn't sign up for Arabella and her Brit-speak, I just wanted Chris's guy view of my email.

"Chris is otherwise engaged." Arabella giggles. I can't fathom what he'd be doing with—or, um, to—her that would make her laugh so much, so I let it drop. "But I'm just as good at interpreting stuff, so tell me. What did the boy say?"

I gather from her tone that Chris has filled her in on some of the background of my past, present, and potential future with Jacob, so I tell her what the email said. Arabella's quiet after I read it, and I keep waiting for her cell phone to interrupt us, but it doesn't. "So, Professor, what do you think Jacob means?"

"You're overlooking one key thing," Arabella says. "*I think I miss you* doesn't exactly set things in stone now, does it?"

CHAPTER NINE

♡

Columbus Day

"Can I be brutally honest with you?" This from Arabella, who is driving me nuts on the ferry. My father's brilliant plan to "show the exchange student some island hospitality,"—as if, personally, I am Jamaica—has turned into Arabella questioning all things American (i.e., "Why wouldn't they just build a bridge rather than these boats?" "Is there an actual Vineyard on the Vineyard? And, if not, why is it so called?" "My boyfriend has [insert name of luxury good here] or [insert name of wonderfully sensitive yet manly quality here]). "I'm not a fan of the ocean." Um, then why come to an island, which by definition is surrounded by water?

"You talk a lot about this boyfriend. Where is he, exactly?" I ask and zip up my sweatshirt.

"It looks better like this." Arabella unzips my prior zippage. I rezip. She undoes it.

"Oh my God, will you stop?"

"I'm just trying to help," she says.

"Well, you're not," I say. Mable comes over to us with a Styrofoam cup of tea, which she holds but doesn't drink.

"Girls girls girls." Mable shakes her head. "Enough with the bickering. What are you guys, long-lost sisters?"

"Hardly," I quip before I can stop myself.

"Yeah," Arabella adds. "It's bad enough we're trapped on a boat as friends—don't go making us related."

Then we start cracking up. Being annoyed takes too much energy. Plus, when I go to the bathroom, I look at my sweatshirt all zipped up and see it creates a massive uniboob effect, whereas unzipped as she suggested looks good. One point for Arabella.

As if she can read my mind, Arabella pulls me over to one of the porthole windows and says, without looking at me, "I do have your interests in mind. Even if I show it rather oddly. And I know I have a tendency for driveling about my boyfriend, it's just I miss him and I'm lonely and I'm . . ." She turns to me. "I'm not some horsey snotty brat, okay?"

She whinnies to prove a point and makes me laugh. She can't be all bad. "Okay. Let's start over."

"Okay. So tell me again why they wouldn't just build a bridge to this place?"

"Don't test me." I smile and we look out at the lighthouse ahead.

"Fine." Arabella puts her arm over my shoulder and our heads knock together as we vie for a better view. "Let's go onto the deck. I want the dramatic entrance. Plus, Chris told me to ask you about a certain guy here. No, wait—two guys. Explain, *s'il vous plaît.*"

"Now you sound like Cordelia with her faux French."

"Actually, it's real French, it's just totally affected and ridiculous. Um, hi, I spent two weeks in the Dordogne and now I can't help but think in French."

"Hey, that's the first time I haven't heard you take their side."

"*Their*?" Arabella asks.

"You know," I explain. "The Triad from Hell."

I don't have to say more. Arabella sighs and looks me right in the eye. "Look, I'm really sorry if you thought—and probably rightly so—that I was one of them. I just . . . I don't know. I was lonely, I think, and not really sure of all the American social scenes, and well . . ."

"It's okay," I say and really mean it.

"Chris does nothing but sing your praises—and my brother, Clive, did, too, believe it or not, even though I'm fully aware he led to your dorm demise last year."

"Well, I'm glad to get that all cleared up."

We pause and look at the water, listen to the squawking seagulls.

"All right," I say to my newish friend. "Brave the bow with me and I'll let you in on the nonromance of Labor Day and my Tale of Two Hotties—Charlie the penniless boat boy and posh Henry."

I tug on Mable's hand as Arabella and I walk past her and onto the windy deck, but Mable gestures to the cold outside like she's a cartoon character, all rubbing arms and shakes. "I'm staying here," she says. "You girls go."

She looks silly and vulnerable at the same time, but waves us to go on without her. It's not a sentiment I want to think about.

The cottage is just as appealing as I remember it; the windows are decked with fall flower boxes, courtesy of my dad's weird fondness for marigolds and mums. (I can't help but exaggerate the word *mum* each fall when he gets into foliage, just to see if he'll finally break and spill the beans about the woman who brought me into this world—so far, *nada*—or, as Cordelia would say, *rien*).

"You girls can have the big room," Mable says. "I won't be here all that much—the café is in dire need of my supervision." Even though Mable has hired a new head barista, Rhiannon (ode to Stevie Nicks), she's been coming down here each week. The combination of that plus her radiation has made her thinner, more drawn, so tired my father actually yelled at her (yes, I overheard him on the phone) that she would collapse if she didn't slow down. But so far, she's fairly upbeat and smiley. "In fact . . ." She checks her watch and drops her bags by the kitchen counter. "I have to go. Enjoy. Help yourself to moldy cheese or whatever you find in the fridge."

Arabella opens the refrigerator after Mable leaves. "I assume she doesn't mean the microbrews?" She holds up a six-pack of beer.

"That'd be a no," I say. "Besides, it's almost dinner and there's a box of fried clams with my name on it."

As we lick the oil and bread crumbs from our fingers, I tell Arabella every detail of my interactions with Charlie.

"We sat right here," I say and pat the exact plank where our legs had touched while eating the same food just a month and a half before. "It just feels like so long ago."

"Just think, you didn't even know me then," Arabella says. She stops eating and wipes her mouth with a papery napkin. "It's so odd how far away summer seems after school starts. Everything—all the people, that summery feeling of anything being possible—it evaporates."

"I know." I look at our box of fries. "The other thing that's evaporated is our fries. Chowhound."

"You ate them all," she says. "I was busy with the clams."

"That sounds like an album from some English new-wave group—Busy with the Clams," I say and stand up. A shower of crumbs falls from my shirt. There is a lovely oil spot near my belly button as if I have an oozing wound. "I'll go get more."

On my way down the steps, my cell phone makes my ass buzz (let's hear it for vibrate mode) and I talk into it only to hear, "Love—it's . . . I'm . . . need . . . you."

"Chris?" I ask. The line at the clam shack is growing, so despite my aversion to public displays of cellfection, I join the crowd while still talking.

"It's . . . need to tell you about . . ." For all its beauty and charm, this particular vantage point over Edgartown Harbor does not have good cell phone coverage, so I hear about every fifth word and can piece together only that Chris needs to tell me something. Of course, this piques my interest, so I try to decipher the scratchy sounds and holes in his sentences.

Finally, I'm reduced to going totally yellular, whereby I am screaming into my phone as if this will magically make the reception better. "Chris? Wait—say that again? What? What?" Insert massively dirty looks from patrons of the fried food hut. "I can't hear you. Call me later?" Click. Phone back in pocket, shameful eyes cast downward, trying to make amends with the annoyed customers.

"Can I have a large fries?" I ask at the counter.

The girl smirks and says back, "Don't you want to yell for it?" Laughs from the people waiting for their food.

"No, thanks." I step aside. "I'll just wait here."

"Well, your fries might take a while." This is clearly an affront—not a measure of their deep fryer. I am being punished for my lack of phone etiquette.

So, like Julia Roberts in that scene with the bitchy salesgirls, I slowly walk away. Cue the heartfelt ballad! Big mistake! Huge!

Being right back where I was over Labor Day makes me think of course about when I met Charlie. Charlie and his closed-mouth grin, Charlie and his ruddy cheeks, Charlie with some sort of chip on his shoulder, Charlie who had a kind of drawl even though he's not Southern. Just when I think I've forgotten him, I'll get a memory of what it felt like to spar with him, to sit with our legs touching, loving the chemistry between us.

I climb the rickety stairs back to Arabella, ready to explain my lack of snacks to her, when a large container of hot fries is thrust toward me by none other than the chemistry man himself, Charlie. He's every bit as hot as he is in my memories, but taller, suspicious of me.

"Here, take these," he says but not in an entirely friendly way.

"That's okay," I say and push the fries back. "We don't really need more. But thanks."

"We?" He looks up to the balcony but can't see Arabella. "I saw your screechfest back there."

"Yeah—it's . . ." I'm about to apologize, but then I get that burst of adrenaline that makes me haughty, so I say, "You know what, though? It's just not that big a deal—so I was a little loud on my phone."

"Even the whales could hear you," he says and gestures far out into the Atlantic.

"Well, they have really good hearing, right?"

"The point is, you were kind of rude. But I guess it's to be expected."

"Excuse me?" I hand him back his stupid fries. "All I did was try to hear my friend Chris . . ." I muzzle myself before leaking further explanation—which Charlie doesn't deserve. And yet I want to explain that Chris is not my boyfriend, just in case it matters (to me, or to Charlie? Not sure on this one).

He takes a deep breath, eats a fry, and licks his (incredibly beautiful, soft-looking) lips and then scratches his (slightly stubbly, still-tanned, gorgeous) face. "The crowd you run in is pretty loud, that's what I mean. You're all always yelling and celling and generally driving the locals crazy."

"The locals, meaning you?"

He doesn't answer. "Look, take these." He hands me the fries again.

"Don't placate me with fast food," I say and smile, trying to make this a flirty fight rather than a town-gown locales vs. weekenders rumble.

"See you around," he says and turns to go.

"That's it?" I say. "You're just gonna go?"

He pauses and starts back toward me. Cardiac issues abound (read: racing and fluttering on my part). And then just as he's about to say something (*Say Anything*?) our "In Your Eyes" Cusack moment is interrupted by Arabella's throaty laugh and her Rapunzel-style hair draping over the balcony above us.

"Bukowski! Get up here, stat!" Arabella likes to use American hospital lingo she's learned from imported television shows like *ER*. Before she can request a CBC and Chem panel, I shout up, "One sec!"

Then I look at Charlie, who is all but shaking his head at my shouting. Before I can justify the laughs, or introduce them, Arabella trots halfway down the stairs and says, "Guess who's here?"

"Love Bukowski! The girl who never emailed me back!" Henry bellows from above us. I tilt my head skyward to see him. He and his group of well-heeled friends have apparently adopted Arabella.

"As I said before—see you around. Have fun with your *friends*." Charlie walks away, not in a huff, but quiet and—or am I just interpreting to my benefit here—disappointed. Maybe he wanted to continue our sparring. Maybe he wanted to do the boy-challenges-girl, boy-finds-girl-alluring, boy-kisses-girl-in-rainstorm thing. Or maybe he just thinks I'm part of the rich crowd and has no interest in them or me.

"If you won't come up, we're coming down," Henry says, and suddenly I am surrounded by soon-to-be friends. I'm part of the group.

"I think you'd be well served to go for it," Arabella says, still slightly subdued from one too many rum and cokes. Henry had tried to insist on sneaking us into Boiling Point, but I told him there was no way in hell (or anywhere else) that I'd risk going back there. Instead, we've wound up lounging in someone's cozy beach house (and by cozy I mean six thousand square feet of ocean views, imported fabrics, stainless-steel appliances, and too many bedrooms to count. Not that I've seen them from any other view than from the doorway (which is more than I can say for a couple of the, um, couples who seem magnetized toward the king-sized beds and high-thread-count sheets).

What I find really interesting is how comfortable all the prepsters are in houses like this. They chill by the wet bar or just seem to know where the gourmet chips are stashed. The girls raised half in seaside spreads and half on the Upper West Side or Beacon Hill are able to lie back on a chaise longue without looking like a lame-ass heroine from a romance novel. And it's not like I'm an unsophisticated, uncultured person. My breadth of knowledge of music, books, even other countries isn't paltry (it isn't Paltrow, though), but somehow, I feel like I'm being studied for my non-blue-blooded background. But I am proud to say that even I know what a bidet is used for and that when Henry asks someone to open the champagne bottle while he turns on the hot tub, I not only volunteer, but get the damn bottle open without knocking out my eye or someone else's.

"I'll take some of that," Arabella says and slides her fluted glass my way. We've established a subgroup (the non-bedroom-goers) including Arabella, me, Henry, Lissa Bond, and Jay Daventree. Not because I'm an idiot, but because I seem to be a big bag of distraction lately, I'm surprised when Henry asks Arabella what her major is. Only then does it dawn on me that a) Henry still thinks I'm a first year at Brown and that b) I have not explained this to Arabella. I try to kick her under the table but knock my foot against Lissa's instead.

"Stop it, Jay," Lissa says, and I'm grateful my clunky boot feels like Jay's. As Henry waits for Arabella's reply, I make a plea for more chips even though the bowl is still half empty. (Oh my God, I really am a pessimist, even when it comes to corn products.)

"Major?" Arabella crinkles her brow. I've noticed she does this while also turning the sides of her mouth down, which gives the illusion that she's very seriously considering something even though I know from her poking me in the thigh that she's clicked into the fact that (at least in this case) I'm a big liar. I poke her back. "Possibly European studies. I mean, I am, after all, European and, um, studying, so . . ."

We make a clichéd bathroom trek, and while Arabella glosses her lips,

I look around for a counter on which to hoist myself up, but there isn't one. It's one of those bathrooms that's as big as a den and yet amazingly uncomfortable: freestanding sinks, a toilet that's tucked behind a frosted glass half wall, various medicine cabinets shaped like trapezoids (see, I really did pay attention in geometry!).

"Check it out," Arabella says and demonstrates the various functions of the retractable mirror. "You can look for blackheads, check and see how your ass looks, and use the bidet at the same time."

"Yum," I say. Arabella starts to rummage through one of the cabinets but I swat her hand away. "I don't think that's a good idea."

"Oh, come on. I'm sure it's just the usual prescription fest." Sure enough, she digs up the social-anxiety semi-OCD just-need-to-relax potions made out to Henry's father.

"Trip Randall the third," Arabella reads.

"No, it's more like . . ." I imitate the guy's voice, doing an over-the-top half-British half-Trump "Hel-loooo, I'm Trip. Randall. The. Third." Arabella laughs. I look in the mirror and continue. "But, anyway, Trip owns the Slave to the Grind space, so I can't really be too hard on him lest he overcharge Mable or something."

"Listen, why don't you just tell Henry the truth?" Then, in her British mummy (the maternal kind, not the wrapped in gauze, deteriorating kind) voice she says, "Are you worried he won't like you if he finds out you're still in high school?"

Maybe. No. Yes. "I don't know, actually. It's more like it's really awkward now because he assumed one thing and I just kept my little charade going."

"So now you'll look like an ass if you come clean."

"Pretty much."

"Fine. But I'm not going to major in European studies! I'm going to drop out and go to hair school."

Back outside, Arabella announces her beauty school dropout intentions (complete with a nod to that scene in *Grease,* which only Lissa and I catch). But instead of finding her comments funny or surprising, Henry and Jay Daventree exchange glances.

Then Jay offers up, "I wouldn't be so quick to drop out of college. Brown's a good school. And, well, let's just say we have friends who've *taken some time off . . .*" Henry finishes the thought. "And they're still not back. It's like, once you let yourself get off track, it's impossible to pick up where you left off."

But maybe their friend didn't want to get back on track. "Maybe the point of dropping out of college isn't to get back on track. Maybe it's to totally change your point of view, and if you do rejoin the ranks of academics you make a conscious decision to be different."

But my thoughts and speech are wasted on The Wasted. The house party continues, and I'm half there, playing the prep-school name game, which is bound to happen, the "Do you know so and so," or "You look familiar," and then you go around and pretty much everyone is one or two steps away from either having hooked up with or summered with or whose parents are friends with and so on. Again, I'm only just getting connected to the boarding school/top colleges map, but even Arabella seems to know a bunch of the names mentioned. Including Lila Lawrence's.

On the way back to Mable's cottage I ask, "I guess I remember Lila saying she kind of knew you. Did you guys meet in London or something?"

Arabella shakes her head and pauses to steady herself on one of the benches thoughtfully placed on the cobblestone streets (as if the town planner knew the drunken masses would have to navigate through there). "No. Lila is . . ." Arabella's voice wavers.

"Are you going puke?"

"No. Not now, anyway," Arabella responds, always composed. "Lila's mum went to school with my mum's sister and . . ."

"Oh," I say. "Just more preppy geography." I wish I knew where my own mother went to school. Or if she finished. Or her name, come to think of it.

That night, when the house is silent (silent save for the hum of the ancient refrigerator that recharges itself every eight minutes) I pad out to the living room in my hospital scrubs, which Mable stole for me from one of her radiation sessions. As quiet as I can be, I reach into the apple-shaped pot on the centerboard and find the skeleton key I saw Mable put there. It easily unlocks the large drawer, which is surprisingly and disappointingly empty. All I can say is that when you have a part of your life that is unclear—and in my case it's still the ongoing issues of my parents' unraveling marriage or at least my mother's disappearance—it seems like clues could be everywhere. But the drawer is empty.

The cabinet below, however, is full. Folders with income tax receipts (boring), old electric company bills (also nonexciting), and a deed to the cottage, which I'm about to toss aside when I see that the owner is listed not as Mable, not as David Bukowski, but to one Galadriel Bukowski. And just like that I have my mother's name. I say it in my head and then out load. Galadriel. I'm cross-legged on the floor, the blue light from outside slants across the wood floor, and I am one step closer to either finding out what happened to my mother or just to finding her.

In the morning, Arabella nurses her hangover with scones and enormous blueberry muffins from the Black Dog. We eat our baked goods and coffee and I try not to feel guilty for going somewhere besides Mable's new café. Slave to the Grind II is in semioperation, a kind of trial run at the very end of the season to figure out any kinks prior to shutting the whole place down for the winter. Judging from Mable's excitement about her new venture, the place will be great—but then again, Mable's forever the optimist. The jagged cough she has now tells a different story.

She and I decide to show Arabella the wilder side of the island, where the wind rages and the houses are closed up for the season.

"This is like Cornwall," Arabella yells to me from one side of a dune.

"What?" I yell back.

"Cornwall," Mable shouts. "Like *Pirates of Penzance*."

I can't really hear what else she says, but I love the feeling of being on the windy beach, running and laughing with Arabella until we fall down, our legs splashed with freezing ocean water. Behind us are houses shut down for the winter, empty balconies a seasonal reminder.

"I love it here," Arabella tells Mable when we're back in the car.

"Me, too." I rub my cold cheeks.

"I knew you would," Mable says and backs up so we can take a last look at the crashing surf and peopleless beach.

Back at her new place, Mable wants to catch up on the girl talk—what little of it there is—with me and Arabella while we drink maple chai after closing up for the night.

"I love it here," Arabella says again, and before I can ask where she means, she says, "The island, this place. Everything." She sounds relieved.

"Ohh . . . I hear a summer job," Mable jests. But once the words are out, Arabella lights up.

"I would love to come back here next summer," she says. For some reason, I've been unable to think more than twenty-four hours in advance recently. Okay, it doesn't take a genius to realize that part of my living in the moment has to do with Mable. Basically, when I try to picture next summer or college or even opening night for *Guys and Dolls* in three weeks, I just can't guarantee that she'll be there. And so I don't like to think about it.

Arabella turns to me and grabs my shoulder. "Can't you see it? The two of us working here, spending an entire summer surrounded by beach, boys, and brews?" She does have a gift for gab.

"Maybe," I say. "It's so far away, though."

Mable and Arabella look at me like I've spilled weak coffee all over their plans, and Arabella fake pouts, which annoys me. But I'm also happy that I have a friend I like enough that her annoying features are still endearing.

"Don't fake pout," I instruct.

"Don't be a wet rag, then," Arabella says back. She stirs her chai and licks the wooden stirrer. "You need to lighten up."

"She's a brick all right," Mable says and adds, "Minnie Driver here is right, though. Just relax." Mable coughs and goes toward the kitchen, then turns back. "But think about it. It could work—you know—both of you here next summer? Good tips!"

The rest of Columbus Day is a blur of beach walks with Arabella and voice messages from Chris that say things like "Hey, just trying to catch you for a minute so we can connect." Not sure what, if anything, he has to say. Before I leave, Arabella and I fit in a last-minute coffee with Henry and his friends at Slave to the Grind II before we rush to the ferry. With our mugs stacked and ready for clearing, Henry leans in and plants an unexpected kiss on my cheek—which isn't unpleasant. In fact, I'm just a little thrilled (I mean, it has been a while since my lips or face or any part of me has seen any action and—let's face it—he's hot, if a little standard) until, out the window, I see Charlie in his faded jeans and black flannel shirt, hair blowing over his eyes. The eyes that are staring at me. Or maybe he's just checking out his reflection in the window.

"No, he totally saw," Arabella says when I ask her on the ferry back. "And now he thinks you're not only one of *them*, but even worse . . ."

"He thinks I'm Henry's girlfriend?" I ask and wonder if anyone (Jacob?) has ever called me his girlfriend and meant it.

"Would that be such a bad thing?" Arabella asks.

I shrug. "Could be worse."

★   ★   ★

Back in my room a mere day and a half later, it occurs to me that I haven't seen Lindsay Parrish for a blissful four days (she took Friday off—and actually had the tacky taste to leave campus in a limo, which, despite the moneyed members of Hadley's student body, isn't really done all that much, usually it's just Lincolns or drivered SUVs). And I won't have to see her for another three days because she should be suspended until later this week for her drunken display of dysfunction on the quad. But when I get back home and check my email, I find out from Chris that he bumped into Lindsay in the library and she is, in no uncertain terms, not suspended.

"Dad," I call downstairs. Dad's been cloistered in his study, dealing with some faculty faux pas that I'm not supposed to know about but am aware of the gist if not the specifics of. (Read: Some teacher is, um, too close to a certain student—I'm sure if I were less distracted I would find out who.) He's been so focused and frantic with the start of school that I found out he and Viola had broken up only when I heard her clipped and cold message on the answering machine asking for her scarf back. It's weird to picture my dad even having girlfriends, let alone one "forgetting" her accessories in his bedroom—it's too familiar. (And I'd be willing to bet she did the intentional leave, where it's just an excuse to reclaim the item and have face time with your ex.)

"How can I help?" Dad has his squash racket in hand, ready for court time.

"I don't need help, I'm just wondering about disciplinary actions," I say.

"Are you writing an article for the Hadley paper?"

"No," I say. "Just, if someone is caught drinking or something, they get suspended, right?"

"Listen, Love, there are issues in the administration that you aren't privy to." He puts his hands on my shoulders like he's either going to knight me or head butt me—the latter is closer. "Lindsay's not getting suspended. She had a small, private disciplinary hearing, and it's been the decision of the board that Lindsay do some community service and go to class as scheduled. She'll also receive some alcohol counseling."

"The decision of *the board?* Aren't *you* the board? And what about her record?" I look at Dad, but he looks away, fiddles with the stack of papers on his desk. "It's not even going on her record?" I don't give him a chance to answer because I know what he'll say. "Dad, that's so messed up. She should be an example—aren't you always saying that? That Hadley Hall is built on good examples?"

"Her mother happens to be one of the biggest contributors to the school's endowment," Dad says. "It's really out of my hands."

We stare at each other—not so much as father and daughter but student and administrator. "I'm disappointed in you," I say and sound just like a parent. "Don't you get that every time someone buys into her whole aura of privilege, she just gets stronger and more . . ." I can't even finish my thought because I'm so frustrated. Not to mention this whole conversation waylays my plan to drop the name Galadriel and see what kind of reaction my dad has.

"Well, I can understand that," Dad says, ever the diplomat. "But not everything is going to make sense to you at your age." I *hate* when age is brought into arguments. It's such a lame way of saying *I can't deal with talking about this anymore.* "Besides, what has Lindsay Parrish ever done to you?"

The answer, of course, is not that much. The fact that she bedded down with Robinson Hall is vaguely humiliating, but not tragic by any means. It's more the fact that she creates drama in my everyday life and I don't like it. Right now, in class, Lindsay is so smug about her nonsuspension that she keeps looking at me and smiling just to make me react. Which I'm doing only internally. On the outside, I'm just taking notes and occasionally making comments about our reading assignments. Mr. Chaucer is his usual energetic self, bedecked in teacher garb from the 1970s: blazer with sueded elbows, boat shoes. Looking around the sturdy oval table, we are all visions of youth and health. It's nearly sickening, but also kind of like getting to be in a Neutrogena ad.

But when I pause on Lindsay Parrish, I can't help but think there's more to her than soapy-clean fun. Linsday Parrish isn't pretty. She's more than that. She's like that really alluring girl who gets cast as the beautiful bitch on *The Real World* and who has the hot-tub/hot-guy kiss or barfs but still looks amazing. It's disheartening to see what a cruel person Lindsay can be—how she uses her looks for evil, in comparison to say, Lila Lawrence. So, sitting across from her and underlining key passages in *A Room with a View,* I can't help but wish that if Lindsay were cast on *The Real World,* it would be *The Real World—Duluth*! Not that there's anything wrong with Duluth—I'm sure it's an awesome town—but it's just my mind-set right now that I wouldn't want Lindsay to be cavorting with her posse of impossibly fashionable frenemies on the Champs-Elysees or L.A. That'd be too much.

At lunch Arabella and I decide that we should name our escapades the way E. M. Forster named his chapters.

"Well then, this chapter would be called something like 'In which Love is proven to be an ass,' " I say after I tell Arabella that Cordelia has invited us over to her house next weekend.

"Why dumb ass?" Arabella asks.

"First of all, not dumb ass—just ass. Second of all, because I feel like Cordelia exploits my naïve tendencies."

"Oh, you little innocent fawn," Arabella coos and shovels canned corn into her mouth. She has a fondness for the dining hall cuisine that surpasses normalcy. "How about 'In which the redhead is made to reconsider.' "

"Cool," I say, although I have no idea what it is I'd be reconsidering. "I don't totally get it, but it sounds good."

My current audio stimulation is in the form of Love and Rockets (specifically "No New Tale to Tell" —a must-have as far as I am concerned), and my current visual stim is the one photograph (aside from his mug shot in the Faces of Hadley Hall) I have of Jacob. In the picture he's sitting on my porch with his elbows resting on his knees, his head turned to the side like he's looking at something out of range of the camera. Right now I'm wishing I knew what that something was.

I'm especially curious about Jacob after I received a letter from him today. An actual paper letter airmailed from Switzerland.

L-O-V-E—

Greetings from the neutral country. I'm staring out at an alp (can it really be called an alp? Does it have to be plural? You're the grammarian—you tell me.) I'm going to cut to the chase because I have about ten minutes before some required tea (I can hear you laughing all the way from Hadley) to go to. I'd just like to set the record straight and tell you I know I completely overreacted at Crescent Beach. I know I said this before, but I'm reiterating based on some recently garnered information. Life here at least affords me that perspective—and since I'm sort of reiterating, I'd like to propose an idea. Electronic correspondence aside, how about exchanging some real letters and maybe talking about less day-to-day shit and more of what's underneath (is that an album name, what's underneath? If not, it should be—your album!). We can ask questions of each other and take our time answering.

You can ask me anything you want. Plus there's the added bonus of not having to see each other (joke—pretty much). Anyway, here goes nothing:

What are your thoughts about virginity?

Neutrally yours, Jacob

And if that seems like an abrupt end, it is, but I must admit, Jacob got my attention. So now I am plagued with remembering his kisses and dealing with this letter (not to mention the fifteen-page paper I have waiting to be completed on themes of modern courtship and confinement in later English literature—or, as I describe to Arabella and Chris 'In which Love bullshits her way and throws in words like dichotomy and duality in order to seem knowledgeable.') I want so much to be the kind of person who keeps a letter like this totally hidden and unto myself, but now that I have two decent friends, I want their opinions. In fact, after reading it, I feel that if I don't bounce some ideas off someone else's brain wall, I will go nuts.

"But why is it, do you think, that Jacob keeps saying he's so sorry about overreacting at Crescent Beach?" I ask Arabella and Chris. Arabella shrugs.

Chris offers this, "Listen, there're probably a couple of good reasons for his groveling, the first of which is that he's clearly still into you."

"I don't know," I say.

"Any guy wanting to write about sex with you is obviously expressing more than just friendship. Otherwise he wouldn't have had that be his, um, opener."

We laugh and I gnaw at the dry skin on my lower lip. "I don't know, you guys, I guess part of me thinks he's seeing someone. Why wouldn't he be?"

"You're so bizarre. Why draw that conclusion from what he said?"

Chris asks. I reread the letter and can't pinpoint anything; there's no specific phrase.

"Just a gut feeling," I say. Chris runs off to paint scenery for *Guys and Dolls,* but Arabella and I spend the next fifteen minutes speculating and deciphering what Jacob means. Arabella sticks to the premise that he still likes me—and maybe he does. Maybe he loves me, even. Or just wants to have sex with me. Or maybe he has lost his virginity in Switzerland— talk about not neutral.

CHAPTER TEN

♡

As psyched as I am about Arabella's presence in my life and at Hadley, I'm still hesitant about two things. One is that I am hyperaware that she's here only for the term and I can easily flash forward to second term, when I will be stuck in the snow with the powers that bitch (namely Lindsay and her girl gang) breathing down my pale and vulnerable neck. Of course, I'll still have Chris—as long as he doesn't defect.

The other part of Arabella that gives me pause is a feeling that there's more to her life than she's letting on. For one thing, her invisible boyfriend seems, well, like a figment of her British mind. She goes yellular talk-screaming to him on the quad every now and again, and to her credit seems devoted to him, but she so far hasn't shown me a photo. ("I have one somewhere . . . just can't locate it right now" was one excuse. Another was "He's camera shy," whatever that means.) And it's not like I care about the thing itself—either she has a boyfriend or loves her imaginary friend, but my point is that I don't like the feeling of starting such a good friendship with her only to have her either a) disappear when she goes back to the UK, or b) keep things hidden from me, or c) both.

Case in point today (Saturday), when I was treading my ass off at the Lowenthal Outdoor Gymnasium (affectionately called the LOG by

Hadley students—it's an all-season workout space with one wall that's completely glass but like some sort of massive garage door, so the entire thing can roll up, making the gym half outside with a view of the woods behind the school—say yay for alumni spending!). So I'm trying to trick myself into doing a full fifty minutes on the elliptical trainer by flipping through an ancient *People* magazine and pressing the various functions on the control pad—miles completed, calories burned, minutes of life wasted (although I counteract this last one by rationalizing that keeping fit adds time on to your life span, so I am balancing mind-numbing— and ass-numbing—moments with a healthy body). Then Marjorie Gundalsmann, our German PE teacher (our sort of workout godmother but more manly), arrives. She unlocks the entertainment system and plays music (no idea what band, but something with a beat that cancels out the blah blah blah in my head) and switches on E! I lip-read about star gossip. Then I let my mind wander, thinking about what Arabella and I will do later today, where we'll go downtown for lunch, what my topic sentence will be for my paper, whether the SIBOF scores will determine my life, and so on. Then, back on the television I swear I see Arabella. Just a quick snapshot of her, or someone very similar. I immediately focus and wait for the program to repeat the image, but they don't.

"So you have a doppelganger," I say to Arabella over hot white chocolate at Burdick's in Harvard Square. They have milk, dark, and white hot chocolate and serve the drinks in massive mugs while all the Harvard hotties read their Russian lit. (My fantasy is to find some brown-haired guy who can quote Anna Akhmatova *and* Dylan—and of course this poet-songster would arrive in faded 501s and help me fix my flat tire, all the while knowing I am perfectly capable of jacking the thing up myself—but I digress.) "Anyway, your doppelganger is quite something."

"Sorry?" Arabella raises her eyebrows and sips her drink. Then she folds the page down from her guidebook—she's been trying to make sure she sees all the Boston sites, walks the Freedom Trail, and goes on a duck tour (an amphibious boat that rides the streets of downtown and then plunges into the Charles River for a scenic ride).

"Doppelganger—a double," I explain. "I was watching TV at the LOG and you were on E!"

"I'm European and speak German. I'm quite aware of what the term means." Arabella blushes and tucks a lock of her ridiculously thick chestnut hair behind her ear. "But doubtful." She laughs.

"Are you positive? I mean, are you famous and just not telling me?" I ask and smile.

"Yeah, right," she says and goes back to her book. "Not last time I checked."

Later, we meet up with Chris, who gives us a tour of made-up historical places and then convinces us that we should go to Cordelia's house.

"What's the worst that can happen?" he asks and pauses to tie his shoe. His scarf trails on the sidewalk, and when he stands up a leaf is stuck to him. I reach over and pluck it off, and he bows in gratitude.

"I don't think you want me to answer that," I say.

"Yeah," Arabella agrees, "the worst could be fairly horrific."

"Can something actually be *fairly* horrific?" I ask.

"Will you shut her up for God's sake?" Arabella pleads with Chris. They exchange some English banter that goes over my head—every once in a while it's like they're from another planet and I'm shocked they're using words that I know, but I still don't get what the hell they're talking about. "Have you lost the plot?" "You're round the bend." "That slag snogged her?" "Those shoes are so twee/naf." "He's a real salad dodger." "I've been sacked." "Watch where you're driving—don't hit the bollard!"

"Fine," I say. "We can go, but I think we should have some signal. You know, like pulling on your right ear if you think we should leave."

"By signal I'm assuming you don't mean moonwalking or groin grabbing?" Chris says.

"That'd be a no," I say. "More like a subtle thing—you do remember the notion of subtlety, don't you, Chris?"

"More than you know," he shoots back, making some weird joke with himself. I look at Arabella to see if she has any suggestions, but her magic cell phone has made eyes at her, so she speaks into it in a hushed tone for once while Chris and I stand and wait for her to finish.

Suddenly, I remember something. "Hey—what was all that drama while I was on the Vineyard?" I ask. Chris frowns like he doesn't know what I'm talking about. "You know, your millions of messages—"

"There weren't millions," he interrupts.

"Fine—a bunch of messages, and you got cut off. What's the deal?"

He takes a deep breath and looks at a couple walking by holding hands. She's doing that head lean onto the guy's shoulder, and he pats her face, and it's hard to tell whether it's the most tender moment you've stolen a glance at or whether the guy just totally patronized her with his doglike motion. "I don't know," Chris says. Then he looks at me and for some reason seems absolutely terrified. "Maybe I just wanted to talk. It's not . . ."

"Okay." Arabella rejoins the world of the real people. "All sorted. I'm back."

"How's your boyfriend?" I ask. Every time I say it, I picture Ernie or Bert or some Muppet, since I have no idea what the guy looks like.

"Fine," Arabella says softly. "He's okay. Just misses me."

"You should tell him to visit," Chris says. He seems totally fine with the idea that Arabella may have invented a long-distance lover.

"That might be tricky," she says, and we head back to my car, on which, of course, is a fifteen-dollar ticket for going literally two minutes past the meter time. Arabella takes pity on me and takes the orange ticket from my windshield. "I'll pay it—it's my fault for keeping you standing there."

"That's okay," I say and reach for it back, but she insists.

"What were you guys talking about anyway?" she asks when she's buckled into the passenger seat.

Chris leans forward from the back and says firmly, "Nothing. Nothing at all."

In the four hours between when we get back to campus and when we meet up at the dining hall prior to venturing into the unknown social world at Cordelia's, I manage to do a miraculous number of things and yet complete none of them. I write eleven of my required fifteen pages of my Communism, Socialism, Realism paper. I write two stanzas of a poem/pathetic cringe-worthy lyric set of a song I'll never perform. And then I try to go over my lines. Memorizing my part for the play has been one of the only times my dad and I have been exchanging words without driving each other crazy, so I recruit him to go over act one with me, which he does, including his own funny version of "Sit Down, You're Rocking the Boat," but then we're interrupted by whatever faculty fire he needs to douse, so I trudge back upstairs to do something else half-assed. The only task I manage to complete is one I thought I might never get to. With a deep breath and a handful of red Swedish fish on which to nibble, I respond to Jacob's letter.

J-

You asked about my thoughts on virginity . . . I guess I am more interested in the second time. The first time is so pressure filled (ignore any weird impulse to be punny here) that I kind of always figured it would suck (ditto with this). Then again, I know how important losing your virginity is—at least to me—because for the rest of my life, that's the story I'll have to tell—to my friends, college roommates—or, even if I tell no one, it's the event I'll have to relive in my head every time the word virginity comes up. So I never really wanted to focus on the first time, but I know it's meaningful enough to me to not want to rush through it or just run out and find some hot summer guy to spend the night with . . . at least I don't think so. What I do know is that whomever I get naked with is going to have to be my good friend, at least I hope he will be, so that there's a second time and a third, etc., with the same person. You know, like a relationship? People do have those still, don't they?

-L

On the way to Cordelia's, Arabella tells me and Chris about her anxiety dreams.

"It's just not fair that I keep having them," she complains. "I'm not even in the bloody play and yet I'm the one standing there, racked with panic because I don't know my lines!"

"Maybe you just love drama," Chris offers. He looks cute in his Hadley sweatshirt. The hems are frayed, the collar stretched out.

I remind him I want to borrow it later. "Sure," he says. "Just don't perfume it."

"I don't even use perfume," I say quickly, then reconsider. "Well, sometimes I do, I guess, but not as a general rule. I mean, I don't know why it is that women have to smell nice all the time. Not that I want to be all garlicky or anything either, but . . ."

"Oh my God, you have to chill out," Chris says. "It's not like Lindsay's going to be there—it's just Cordelia and some friends, right?"

*   *   *

But of course, Cordelia had failed to mention that Lindsay, who had been in New York (probably shagging the living daylights out of my old flame Robinson Hall, but that's another story—one for the STD clinics, maybe) for some charity event her mother chairs, managed to arrive back just in time to give her hale and hearty greetings when we walk in the door.

"Salutations," she trills. Chris mutters, "Okay, Veronica," under his breath and I'm at least relieved he's attuned to Lindsay's subversive ways. "Love, let me just say, I hope we can get back on track." Oh, like we had this great train friendship that just momentarily derailed?

"Um, okay," I say, noncommittal, but still nice. I am clinging—however inanely—to the notion that I don't have to sink to her scum level.

And to her credit, the evening flies by with nary a mean look in my direction. Did she renew a prescription or something? Whatever the reason for her lack of cutting remarks, paucity of pithy comments, I am glad. It's a sort of typical nonparty Hadley party. The more raucous bashes rage with full-frontal liquor, smoking, and some lame senior playing DJ. House parties like this one come under the guise of "get-together" so that the faculty are thrown off scent and the tone is more mellow (i.e., if you're going to get high or drink, please be discreet). And since Cordelia's parents are both Hadley profs who regularly have groups of students over, it seems normal. Not that her faculty folks are there. But it's all hush-hush, so there are some trips to the bathroom with someone's engraved silver flask and the lush flush on Cordelia's face from the wine she consumed earlier out of a Snapple bottle, but nothing terribly overt.

"Salsa?" Cordelia walks around with a little dip bowl, ever the thoughtful hostess when she isn't following in her evil stepsister's shoes. "The chips are organic."

"Oh, organic!" Chris eats a mouthful and settles into the oversized chair like a king. He always seems comfortable wherever he is, which makes his afternoon falter even more bizarre in my mind. I really, really, really, really hope that he's not fighting some crush on me (could I be more conceited? God, now I really do sound like an extra from *The Breakfast Club,* which reminds me of my crappy trip to NYC last year when I first met Lindsay and we reenacted that scene), or Chris could have some familial issue, or he could be madly in love with Arabella, which would be complicated. Just as I'm thinking this, I see Lindsay perch (like a vulture, not a blue jay) on the arm of Chris's chair. She leans in and whispers something in his ear, and he laughs. Upon closer eavespection, I hear, "And those pants really do suit you." Which is Chris's English way of saying "You look hot."

Chris puts a hand on Lindsay's thigh. (The pants in question are the same ones Mable and I ogled a couple of weeks ago in a boutique on Charles Street. Suffice to say they were of the Marc Jacobs/six-hundred-dollar variety, which just goes to show what good taste and a lot of money can buy you—um, really tasteful trousers.) Then Chris pulls Lindsay onto his lap and she giggles like I've never heard her do before—who even knew her voice had the range of two octaves up?

Despite the fractured social groups all present here, the tie that binds is, well, boredom. There's a sort of unwritten rule that if you're not a complete outcast, you're always welcome at any party. Thus, frenemies and post hookups and current quests are all found in the social blender of Hadley gatherings.

"Okay, okay." Cordelia clusters everyone around her and we all listen as she details her party games. Skipping "Spin the Bottle," and since no one's drunk enough (or a twelve-year-old at day camp), we bypass the orange-under-the-neck passing circle, and head right for "Would You Rather." Which is, in Cordelia's terms, just an excuse to find out who wants to hook up with her.

"Chris, would you rather me naked on an island in the Caribbean or Lindsay, clothed?" Cordelia asks.

"Is Lindsay in the tropics, too?" he asks.

Laughter and more chips. Harriet Walters, complete with feminist brain, slices up brownies and hands them out. "Does it matter?"

"I'm geographically challenged," Chris says and avoids the question completely. The game continues until enough of the people have drifted away to suck back whatever liquor they can find. Then they make use of a communal toothbrush Jon Chesterton (Chesty, to his friends who want to get their asses kicked) has thoughtfully brought along with Listermint and Life Savers (which are, in fact, true to their name if you happen to have a run-in with the Von Tausigs or any other dorm parent after a night spent drinking).

Then, just as the party is on the verge of splintering, Lindsay leaves her position near Chris and suggests truth or dare.

"That's so clichéd," Arabella protests.

"Yeah, but it's so clichéd that it's not clichéd," Harriet Walters says and plops herself down next to Lindsay.

"Fine, whatever," Arabella acquiesces and ties her hair back with the purple rubber band she keeps on her right wrist at all times. She pats the space next to her and I go over, squashing myself onto the not-built-for-two ottoman.

As if she's prepping for her future young debutante meetings, Lindsay clasps her hands together and demurely (and when I say demurely I mean in the swaying, slightly drunken way) informs us that we each have one "NFW" card to play during the truth or dare game.

"So," Lindsay clarifies, examining for a moment her perfectly (and no doubt costly) highlighted hair, then tossing the mass of it back. "If, for some reason, I—or anyone else—asks you a question you just can't deal with, you may use your No Fucking Way card. But only once."

We (we = me, Arabella, Chris) survive round one, narrowly escaping the make out with someone in the room, what's the most immoral thing you've ever done, if you had to have sex with Hairy Leaf Man (the guy who trods along Hadley campus with no shoes, even in winter and "brushes" his teeth with leaves) or Fairy Princess (the bright but strange Potter-obsessed girl who carries a bag of "magic dust" to class), which would it be?

But then:

"Arabella Piece," Lindsay says like she's taking roll call.

Arabella rises to the occasion, "Present and accounted for."

Lindsay grins; the shadow from the brass standing lamp next to her casts an eerie glow, making her look like a witch of darkness, which I guess she sort of is. "Truth or dare?"

Arabella picks at her cuticle, tugging at it with her teeth to show how nonchalant she is. "Truth."

"Who is your *really serious boyfriend* and why are you so pathetically secretive about your relationship?" Lindsay is clearly pleased with herself. And, I have to be honest, so is everyone else. It's like Lindsay called Arabella at her bluff—or not.

"You'd love to know, wouldn't you?" Arabella says, her accent thick. "Well, too bad. I'm using my NFW card."

"Didn't you already?" Harriet Walters asks. Dissention among the troops. Some claim yes, during the *describe your first time* question (which, honestly, isn't really a question, is it?).

"No, I fucking didn't," Arabella quips. "Don't put words in my mouth."

"Believe me," Lindsay says. "I have no intention of going anywhere near your dirty mouth."

"Meowfest," Chris says.

"Shut up, Chris," Cordelia says. She's instantly protective of Lindsay, standing by her side to show some lame support of this lame game.

"I'll take the dare," Arabella says and looks at me. I give her our signal—a tug on my right ear to show her we could leave right now—but she shakes me off. Chris raises his eyebrows at me and I shrug.

"Fine." Lindsay thinks for all of one second and spits out, "Clothes off. Time for a naked run around the flagpole."

"Screw that," Arabella says, her haughty self in full force.

"Oh, you're gonna weasel out of it, little miss priss?" Lindsay all but whinnies.

"Fine. I'll do it, but in my underwear."

The nation's flag and the Hadley Hall crest flap proudly in the night air. The boys' dorms form a semicircle around a patch of grass, and it's in the center of this grassy knoll that the flagpole protrudes. Various boys lean out the Whitcomb windows, aware of the rustling below. We all stand around as Arabella defiantly strips down, covers her breasts Garden of Eden style, and sprints around the entire circle, shouting, "The British are coming! The British are coming!" as instructed by the dare-meister, Lindsay Parrish.

When she's done, and at least partially clothed, Chris is complimentary. "You should totally go out for track!"

"Bite me." Arabella smiles at him.

"Nice ass," I say and hand her shoes back to her.

"Until next time?" Lindsay stands with her hands on her hips, looking at the three of us.

We don't say anything. We just walk off, semi-proud, waiting to exhale. Then Chris looks back over his shoulder and gives Lindsay a wink. Perhaps this is his way of joking with her, but to me (and Arabella, who nudges my ribs with her elbow) it looks suspiciously like flirting.

Sunday morning. The dreaded school-the-next-day feeling has been creeping into my brain earlier and earlier. Used to be that I'd wake up and feel fine until about four o'clock in the afternoon, when the reality of having to deal with class the next day hit, but with a full rehearsal for

Guys and Dolls tonight and a page to go on that damn Communism paper, not to mention a bad taste in my mouth from Cordelia's house last night, I wake up at seven a.m. and can't fall back to sleep no matter how many times I roll over, count backwards from fifty, or—Mable's trick—pick a mellow song and replace all the lyrics with *blahblahblah* while keeping the tune. I wind up propping myself up in bed and writing in my journal. Rather than write about Mable's condition or my father's growing remoteness, I focus on subjects that don't make me spiral into an abyss of doom. Yes, my three non-boyfriends. I figure that if Arabella is allowed to have her mystery man, I can indulge my crushes. Half an hour later (the sun is only just rising over the nearly bare elm trees out my window, causing the sky to turn the color of a ripe peach), I have three columns (marked *Charlie, Jacob,* and *Henry*), along with various pros (i.e., Charlie = rugged, non-Hadley, real. Jacob = familiar, my age, knows me, sweet. Henry = exciting, daring) and cons (Charlie = distant, clearly dislikes me/what he perceives me to be. Jacob = in Switzerland, too dramatic, all talk, no rock. Henry = uses money in a gaudy way, his father could complicate things with Mable's café, thinks he owns the world) for each one.

I love that I can waste an entire hour (yes, I spent an additional thirty minutes trying to think of songs that would describe how I feel about each guy—fun and also gets me out of having to write my own lyrics) doting on boys with whom I have no actual romance. Ah, productivity at its best. I should list this on my college applications or future résumés.

I venture down to the kitchen in my boys' pajamas. (I like to go to the little boys' section in clothing stores to buy T-shirts that are way cheap—these seersucker pj's were clearly a sample gone wrong. Who wants orange seersucker? Give it to the redhead for five bucks.) My father hands me a plate of Belgian waffles and we sit down like civilized human beings with the Sunday papers and coffee.

Civilized and normal until, "Love?"

"Hmm," I respond as I dip my waffle into a puddle of syrup. Rather than get my breakfast bread products soggy, I like to keep the syrup separate (segregation of the sweets, if you will).

"Will you help me write something later?"

"Sure," I say and then wonder a) when I'll have the time and b) if I've just committed myself to drafting a chapel service about the good-natured hearts of Hadley students. (Yeah, we're all really good-natured. That's why we have to run naked laps around the flagpole.)

"Good. I'm placing a personals ad later today," he says. He points to the *Bostonian* magazine.

I choke on a Belgian waffle (note to self: Google them and find out what makes them truly Belgian) and sputter, "You're doing what?" And then, before I can chastise my dad, I find myself doling out advice. "I mean, at least do it online so you can check out their pictures. There are like a thousand sites that'll show you your match."

And this is how I find myself bagging the work I have, straying from my line memorization, not returning Chris's phone message from late last night (he whispered into his cell and told me—yep—that when he got back to the dorm he remembered what he needed to talk to me about), and hunched over my dad's shoulder in his study, building his online profile at some relationshipswhensortofoverthehill.com kind of place.

"No," I instruct him. "Don't say you like walks on the beach. That's totally lame and clichéd."

"But they have a box to check if you do. And I do."

"Look, Dad, do you want to get some remnant girlfriend from 1982 who thinks the band Journey is the height of beauty and longs to wear flowing skirts while taking walks on the beach?"

"Don't I?" He laughs. He tips his head backwards so he looks at me upside down. "It doesn't sound bad—especially after Viola's uptight behavior this summer. She wouldn't even go barefoot on the sand."

"Yeesh," I sigh. "Anyway, click there—yes, you are well read—and don't click there—even if you like cats, you can't say that you want to be with a woman who likes cats or you'll just meet aging hippies with bad hair."

"I'm glad you're here to decipher all this code." He gives my hand a squeeze without making eye contact. It's the most fun we've had together since I got in trouble last year, or since I got back from New York, or since Mable got sick. It feels good.

CHAPTER ELEVEN

♡

Midterms and Mayhem

"I will call this day 'In which the British girl and the American continue their ruse of niceness prior to having a luncheon,'" Arabella says. She's referring to the fact that we're having lunch—at my house—with Cordelia and Lindsay—at my invitation.

"Too long," I say. "Forster would have written something like "The two women go running—dogs follow.""

"True." Arabella breaths hard, keeping pace with me as we dodge the fallen branches on the cross-country trail.

"This whole thing could be a huge mistake—or it could be a very smart move," I say. "Maybe if we just fly low under the radar with them they'll move on to bigger and better bitchiness that doesn't involve us."

"Well, again, let me just say how impressed I am with your apparent ability to suck it up," Arabella says. "I'm going to stop here. Two miles is plenty for me and my British bum. I'll see you back at yours in a couple of hours."

She heads back toward the LOG and shouts over her shoulder something about studying for exams. Which of course I need to do if I'm going to do well. Of course doing well is a necessity if I'm going to apply to any of the reach schools on my SIBOF sheet. And also true, according to prep-school dogma, is that I need to go to a reach school to be a success in life, which of course I need to do to be part of the social norm and not a complete failure.

But I keep running for another two miles, my body enjoying the dichotomy of inner heat and outer cold—sweat on the forehead that freezes against my skin. Then, in the huddle of birch trees near my old pole-vaulting cushion, I see two figures. I pause, jogging in place, then stop and stretch, craning for a better view. Mr. Chaucer and Harriet Walters? I can tell only by Harriet's hair (which has been amber hued these days) and Chaucer's fluorescent-orange scarf, which he wears all fall and winter. And the two colors (amber and orange) are way visible—even from here.

Not that I know what seeing them together means, if it even means anything. There are always the faculty-student slightly-too-close-for-comfort connections, but you never know when one might cross the line (or where on the person that line actually runs).

I walk home with every intention of talking to my dad about faculty gossip without mentioning names, but when I get there, sitting on my front stoop is none other than my long-lost blond buddy Lila Lawrence.

"Will wonders never cease?" I ask, and she stands up to hug me.

"Surprise!"

"To what do we—and by we I mean all of Hadley—owe this honor?" I ask, and we sit on a bunch of fallen red and yellow leaves that crunch under our butts.

"Just on my way back to Brown for exams," she says. "I was up in Vermont at my parents' cabin."

"I always forget you have property in every state." I poke her. She grins.

"Not every state," she corrects. "Only six. Not counting Europe."

"Hard life," I say. "It's so good to see you. Tell me what's new."

"Not much, really. Just the usual hookups and heartaches and heaving into the bushes behind the chancellor of the college's office and then nearly failing one class but getting an A in biology."

"You always were good at the birds and the bees," I say, intentionally cheesy. She goes on to describe life at Brown and then I take my turn and tell her about the play, about Arabella and Chris.

"And what ever happened with Lindsay Parrish?" Lila asks.

"Oh . . . she's just your standard everyday top-of-the-line sleeze with good hair," I say. Then I remember I'm still trying for a truce. "But she's okay—sort of. I mean, I'm hoping her queen bitch act is fading now that it's nearly Thanksgiving."

"Listen," Lila says and tucks a piece of my hair behind my ear. "Don't ever let yourself be fooled by her. She will always come back and bite you on the ass."

"I thought she didn't eat meat," I say, and Lila shakes her head, then checks her watch. "Do you have to go already?"

"Cartier is telling me that I do, yes." She stands up. "How's Mable, by the way? I'm so sorry I haven't even asked about her yet."

I sigh loudly. "We're all sort of waiting to find out. She had a course of radiation that we hope will be successful, but if it's not she's going in for a lumpectomy."

"My cousin had one," Lila says. "Then she was okay."

I perk up. I like hearing breast cancer success stories. "Hey," I say. "Want to do the Avon Breast Cancer Walk next spring?" I've been thinking about it but haven't wanted to commit to doing it because it's so far off.

"Totally." Lila's psyched. "We can raise so much money—especially if I hit my mother up for cash when she's loaded." We look at each other. "Which, of course, she nearly always is."

Lila laughs and I join in. At least she's aware of her monetary situation and how odd it is.

"And I can maybe try to get Slave to the Grind to put a donation sheet by the counter—and Hadley administration."

"See?" Lila does her college counselor voice. "You *can* make a difference."

"That's me," I say. "Proactive Bukowski."

We do the arms around the shoulder crappy public service announcement pose with twisted fake smiles and faux-concerned brows.

"I *can* make a difference!" I say.

"That's right," Lila says, voice dripping with gooey sarcasm. "As long as you don't get pregnant."

"Or do drugs."

"Or binge drink."

"Or sniff bleach."

"Or only get into your safety school," Lila says.

"Seriously." I nod and seamlessly segue into Hadley's preferred topic of choice for juniors. "The college process sucks."

Lila smiles. "Oh, it gets better. Just think of all of those weekend visits." She waves her hands over my eyes like she's casting a spell and dreamily describes the freedom of colleges you'll see only once.

"I just want to get through this term," I say. How many times can I repeat that phrase? Many. I walk Lila to her antique BMW. It's purple and perfect for her. She looks like she's in a movie poster when she leans out from the driver's side window. "By the way, I wanted to catch Arabella Piece—it's too late now, but say hi for me, okay?"

"Oh, yeah, I forgot you guys kind of know each other," I say. It's weird when two sectors of your life overlap, like a summer friend invades a school, or a vacation fling (like the myriad ones I have on my sex roster) surfaces in your hometown.

"Um, more than *kind of*." Lila wrinkles her forehead. "Our mothers were like sisters or something in college . . . university, as they say in England. Hasn't Arabella filled you in on her—ah—family situation?"

"No." I shake my head. "Tell me. What's the deal?"

Lila thinks about it for a minute, then slides back into the driver's seat. "You'll have to ask Arabella," she says and starts the engine. It's so bizarre. I mean, just when I think Lila's a normal person, she gets all upper crusty and closed off. Not in a mean way, just in a *what's proper etiquette for the moneyed* way—like there's a whole set of codes and expectations among the connected elite.

Arabella and I have chosen to serve a simple lunch of several different kinds of tarts.

"Of course, they won't know this is my subversive way of suggesting you are what you eat," I say as I take the chevre-and-tomato tart from the oven and place it on the table near the salad and sliced peasant bread.

"Clever girl," Arabella says and goes to open the door to let in Lindsay Parrish and her caped (literally—she's taken the poncho thing to another level) crusader Cordelia.

In all honesty, I figured lunch would degenerate into a slurfest or at least verge on the snippy and snide, but the reality of the meal was that it was . . . fine.

"I'm not saying I'd want the girl on my island tribe or anything," I whisper to Arabella in the kitchen with the tap running as noise cover. "But she's not atrocious."

This time, Arabella agrees. "I think she's upped her meds—but you're right. She's been decent today."

Over sticky toffee pudding (which Arabella made—it's perhaps the most calorific and completely awe-inspiring dessert ever) served in white ramekins, Cordelia turns the topic of conversation toward me.

"How's the play going?"

I sigh. "Good. We're getting there."

Arabella turns to me. "Can you reserve a seat for me?"

Lindsay semi-good-naturedly rolls her eyes. "Looks as though you have at least one groupie." Then she sees my eyes narrow and corrects herself. "I mean, of course we'll be there, too."

Cordelia scoops the last of her pudding. "Love's got a great voice.

I'm sure the play will rock. Hey, what ever happened to your voice-over gig?"

"It's kind of on hold right now," I explain. Then Lindsay asks what gig and I go over a couple of the ads I did last year for the mattress store and—when pushed—go upstairs and get my demo reels.

"Play them. Oh my God, classic!" Cordelia laughs. Arabella raises her eyebrows when she hears the maxi-pad ad and then gives me a thumbs-up.

"Something to play for my grandchildren someday." I smirk.

Then Arabella and I clear the dishes, wash a couple, and encourage (in a pleasant, gentle way that suggests we are all on okay terms now) our guests to leave.

"Work beckons," I say.

"Thanks for having us," Cordelia overlaps with Lindsay.

"Oh, thanks for coming," Arabella says. When the door is closed she turns to me. "I don't trust those girls for one second."

I shake my head and pick lint from Arabella's shoulder. "You are way too paranoid. The war is over." And it wasn't really a full-on war anyway—more like a skirmish.

"So will you do it?" Mable asks.

"Of course," I say and sign up for the Avon Breast Cancer Walk in the spring. Aside from a vague notion of college visits, it's the first long-term thing I've committed to since her diagnosis.

"It'll be great. We'll get some sort of double iPod thing going so we can listen to synchronized eighties music and nudge each other when the bad lyrics come on." Looking at Mable, I'm in awe of her strength.

"You're incredible," I say.

"Don't eulogize me," she says. I've been in the habit of telling her how much I love her and how cool she is, and my free-flowing lovefest is driving her crazy. "Just tell me what's new."

I put down the coverless *Newsweek* magazine that seems to grace every doctor's office in the country. Other patients read quietly and smile at us—they probably think we're mother and daughter.

"It's your typical not-typical high school deal," I say. "Love life is a whopping zero. The kiss I get from Dan Dearborn—aka Sky Masterson—is the highlight of my fall. Unless you count my ever-growing relationship with Mrs. Dandy-Patinko, who puts the counselor back in college counseling—I'm in serious need of rehab. I abuse the fact that she's all ears and tell her everything."

"Okay, a stage kiss is better than nothing. And, if memory serves, Dan Dearborn is one of the better looking and not flagrantly gay drama guys. And if Mrs. Dandy-Patinko is the depository of deep thoughts or angst, then so be it."

"Ah, the blessings of an inordinately expensive education."

Mable gets called in for her appointment and I sit on the squeaky Leatherette chairs and cross, then uncross, my legs. Every once in a while it dawns on me that I am only going to Hadley because of my dad—and maybe other people are aware of this fact. Not that it's a subject of concern for me, but I'm not one of the privileged by birth (i.e. my ancestors weren't on the Mayflower, as many of the Hadley student roster reveals) and I'm not fundamentally brilliant like the financial aid–worthy lot. I'm just there. Which is fine, but it makes me feel slightly on the outskirts of the semi-invisible financial lines drawn through the student body. (Okay, I know there's no such thing as semi-invisible, but it's like a line we all know exists but don't ever talk about.)

While Mable gets poked and prodded, her margins assessed, I pace around the office and read the poster verbage about self-checking for lumps and how genetics are a big factor and then get depressed and sit down, thinking again about the wealth and status issues around me.

I mean, I don't want to become one of the JABs (the Jaded and Bitters). They're the girls who went to St. Bart's in fifth grade and now think it's totally out and Nevis is in, but next year or two years from now, somewhere else will be the must-mellow-at spot. First of all, I don't have the money that seems to go along with the JAB attitude, but I can see how it happens. You go to parties with quasi-celebs at home in L.A., vacation all over the world, have sex with a handful of hot if unmemorable guys, and pretty soon there's not much out there to pique your interest. The JABs aren't bad people—they just seem tired. Tired and kind of disappointed.

On the other hand, the other extreme sucks, too. The wide-eyed innocents, the day students who think life is all about two-parent families and dinners at home and parents who live for their kids' lacrosse games and mothers who obsess over SAT scores and college acceptance letters make me feel itchy and sick. There are a lot of groups in between these two, but I don't seem to gel with any particular one. I roam somewhere in the middle—in the middle of wealth and scholarship (I certainly wouldn't have the tuition funds without dad working here), neither the class brain, nor the class hookah (like the caterpillar in *Alice in Wonderland,* who smokes hash or whatever crap is in that pipe, not a sex worker), not a raging party girl, but I've obviously indulged occasionally. This makes me comfortable, but it doesn't exactly bond me to a group, doesn't make me inseparable from a cohesive set of friends.

"Which is why I am so lucky to have you," I say to Arabella after I tell her all my thoughts and about Mable's visit.

"Me, too," she says. "If only I could bring you home with me."

"Don't," I say. We've made a pact not to talk about the fact that she's leaving for London at the end of the term.

"I know—it's just . . ." She rifles through her desk drawer and hands me a bound book. "It's the course catalog for LADAM." The cover spells out The London Academy of Drama and Music. "I thought you might help me pick out some courses for the spring term."

Spring? It's not even Thanksgiving yet and already Arabella is telling me about the afternoons spent lolling in Hyde Park and night in the campus bar—the catalog contains pictures of stages set with glittering winter scenes and packed houses. She points out friends with nicknames like Fizzy and real names like Goliath. With offerings like vocal range I, set design, pop, jazz, and classical song arrangements, I am overwhelmed with jealousy, but agree to the task. "I can't believe you get actual credit for this stuff," I say.

She's defensive. "Well, it's not as if you do only this—there are, in fact, proper academics, too."

"I wasn't trying to say that you don't do work, only that I wish Hadley were more . . . I don't know. Like there wasn't such a set track of what you have to do."

Arabella looks down, thinking of something but not telling me. We've gotten to that point in our friendship where we can decipher gestures. "There's a track at home, too. It's just a different set of rules."

"Meaning?"

"Meaning . . ." She starts but then stops. "Just, my family is very set in their ways, and there's still all the class issues in England and, well, it's just complicated."

"Try me. I can understand complex ideas," I say and wait. She shakes her head and walks to her closet to change out of her gym clothes. I look around her room; it's spare and neat. A burgundy duvet cover in a style that suggests Calvin Klein journeyed to Bangladesh and bought fabric there, several black and white prints on the wall—in actual frames—and a photo of a group of her friends from LADAM whose names I can never keep straight. Noticeably missing are any family photos. When I've asked, she's just shrugged and said her parents aren't much for the camera. Her brother, Clive, however, graces the cover of one of those fake magazines you can order from the Internet. This one's on Arabella's desk and has pimply annoying Clive as the lead story called "England's Eligible Elite."

Despite the fact that Arabella is doing no drama here at Hadley, the roles she's played according to her head shot are numerous and impressive. She showed me the gorgeous photo only after Chris told me she showed it to him and I got pissed off. Of course, she's stunning and natural and the photo is very professional. Arabella's way more into acting than I am. For me, it's just about the singing. "Anyway," she says as if we've been talking the whole time, "I can't wait to see you tonight—break a leg."

Luckily, it's only the rehearsal and not the real thing, because I nearly do break my leg. In typical "Love as lamely coordinated loser," I manage to trip over—no, not a wire or a stage prop—but my own foot and come toppling down. Chris laughs from stage left, where he's about to roll a prop lamppost onto the set.

I recover and pick up where I left off. After the show, I hear applause—not just from Arabella and my father, who are seated off to the side, but from Cordelia and Lindsay Parrish, who are visible in the front row. I smile at Arabella and Dad and remind myself to say "I told you so" to Arabella regarding the bitch turnaround from Lindsay. It's semi-restorative in terms of the Queen Bee Syndrome and its predictable fallout. I'm glad when Lindsay pats me on the shoulder and says, "Well done." It's not as freakish as if she had hugged me and not as cold and threatening as she used to be.

"You were really great!" Dad is filled with praise and parental pleasure back at home. We're doing our biweekly browsing of the responses he's got in his in-box from the personals ad. So far, he hasn't even met up with anyone, and he's only written back to two people. "I don't care how casual email is, I still think grammar is important."

"So you'll only date people who use caps and lowercase? What's your policy on abbreviations?" I ask and scratch at my stage makeup. The base is like tar and takes many washes before revealing my untanned self underneath its cakey mess.

Dad ignores me and keeps scrolling through other profiles. "I have the faculty meetings tomorrow night, so you're on your own for dinner."

"Fine," I say. "I'm doing a big fall cleanup anyway." I have lofty notions of making my room as neat and as organized as Arabella's, even though part of me is aware that it's easier to be organized with only a suitcase of things with you.

"I'm glad—the party's in two days." Dad has mentioned this to me morning, noon (if I see him in the dining hall), and night. (A favorite dinner debate is the merits of melted brie versus fondue.) "I think everyone's coming." In honor of faculty morale and the frantic fall pace, Dad is hosting the first annual faculty soiree (read: I watch my teachers get drunk and try to avoid the trappage of uncomfortable social situations with Mr. Kenglebud (the art guy who wears cowboy boots and favors an Art Garfunkel white man's afro) and Mr. Washburn (the kind of old guy who makes you sad so you have to listen to him talk about his model trains just because you feel too guilty to walk away) or Madame Le Lune (called Looney by everyone, including my father on one occasion—'nuff said).

"Don't worry," I say as Dad logs off. "I'm sure the party'll be wonderful— with a lame social life like most of the teachers have, it'll be a big deal."

"Gee, thanks, Love," he says, and then, out of nowhere, like he's just imagined me as a little kid, "I love you very much."

"Me, too, Dad." It worries me when he gets like this recently, because it makes me wonder if he knows something about Mable and isn't telling me—or if he's just gotten to the sentimental parent stage, where they're convinced you're changing way too fast.

An eighty minute cd, four trash bags, and a pile of crap later, I've piled some books onto shelves, moved my bed to the other side of the room (in effect creating more space for more crap), and reread my pile of letters from Jacob. The word's still out on his answer to my last question (panicked by the thought of another round of sex-themed letters, I went with the staple *Where do you see yourself in five years?* Hopefully, his response won't be a one-word answer—i.e., not *Abroad*). And I've made a pile of things to donate (bye-bye platform shoes from Mable's brief glam period) to the drama department. One thing I can't find is my Vineyard sweatshirt—that said, I can't locate a variety of items: one of Arabella's green British welly boots, cd four in the seventies collection Mable sent me last year, my voice-over reels, random notebooks, and my coffee mug, which has a poor-quality photo of Engelbert Humperdink on it that I picked up in some junk store in the village over the summer. It's priceless if you ask me. I make a nonmental (nonmental = visual so I have some hope in hell of actually seeing/remembering to do it) note to continue the search-and-rescue mission—mainly I want my MV sweatshirt back (possibly it is now residing with Arabella) and my voice reels (which are micro sized and therefore very tricky to locate).

"I so know what you mean." Mr. Chaucer takes a mini Charleston Chew from the orange plastic pumpkin and nods. He's cool enough and funny enough to get away with teenspeak. Looking at his rumpled French blue button-down, his skinny cords, and Stan Smiths, it's easy to imagine Chaucer a decade and a half younger (my age for instance).

"Well, I don't know," I say and rummage in the squash skull for something good, but the loot is fairly picked through, so I'm left with those gross plasticky chocolate-covered marshmallows that crack when you bite them. My sugar jones is bigger than my candy snobbery, however, so I graciously accept the choco dandruff and I munch away. "I bet it was all easy for you," I say.

"It's never easy, is it?" Chaucer sips his red wine. He's had enough that his limbs seem looser, but not enough that his teeth are maroon. "High schools are all the same, and very different."

"You can take the teacher out of the classroom, but . . ."

"Sorry. What I mean is, whether you're here at Hadley—or in a Bulgarian Catholic school somewhere—"

"Presumably in Bulgaria . . ." I add.

"Right. You are still you. That's the kicker—and, I'm afraid to tell you, it doesn't get any better. It doesn't get any worse, really, but your perception of life will always be filtered through the lens of where you come from. That's why childhood—and I know you're not a child—is the subject of so much discussion, so many texts."

I'm about to ask him to tell me about his own childhood or talk to him about my mother issues, when I remember he's my teacher. Not that I think he'd ever use anything against me, but I don't really want to overshare. What did Lila call it? Mitin. More information than I needed.

"Yeah," I say, trying to change the subject. "I guess it's all just part of the learning process." This is a phrase I learned from my dad and it's very useful as a way of making closure on a topic while not really saying anything—it's universal management code and it works in most scenarios. Even now.

"Oh, speaking of learning process . . ." Chaucer reaches into his back pocket and pulls out a slightly worse for wear photo and hands it to me. Staring back (albeit from a distance) is Jacob circa last winter; ruddy cheeks, tousled hair, semi smile. "I found this in my desk—it's leftover from those classroom candids." Chaucer's faculty head of the yearbook staff.

"Um, thanks?" I don't mean for it to come out so sarcastically, but it does.

"So you're not still dating?"

"Well, we weren't so much dating as, you know, about to date? But then—"

Chaucer interrupts. "But then, long-distance relationships are hard. His loss, anyway." Weird comment from a teacher, but then, Hadley is so incestuous that it takes a minute to realize this is half flirting and half mentor speak. Arabella is convinced that Chaucer is "mutton dressed as lamb" —the old guy in a hottie's clothing with dubious intentions.

"Love! There you are," Dad bounds over to us and brushes the fallen chocolate flakes from my shoulder. "You're missing all the excitement in the other room." He says this with his headmaster-of-school tone, but his eyes tell me he's aware (and by aware I mean suspicious) of the way Chaucer and I are cloistered away in the half-light of the kitchen.

"Oh yeah?" I shrug at Chaucer as a good-bye, grab a Coke, and follow my dad to where Lana Gabovitch, movement teacher and scarf-loving hippy, is doing interpretive dance—in the middle of a cocktail party. Either she's high (rumors abound) or just an oddball (proven—though I think she's sweet). Either way, she gave her students two classes off when Phish disbanded, ditto for when Garcia died or for any political issue she deems *too dire,* and asks students to reflect or form bonding circles, leg over leg.

In the middle of the late buzz, the sounds of clinking ice and faculty chatter, my dad misses the phone when it rings (I have hearing like a canine when it comes to phones), so I go to pick it up. And when it's Mass General calling to say Mable's been admitted, it takes me completely by surprise.

CHAPTER TWELVE

♡

Pre-Thanksgiving—"In which I try to feel grateful but in reality feel annoyed, stressed, and hormonally challenged"

This is the time of year when, all across the Hadley campus, shampoo and soap consumption drops way low. Exams are an excuse to sleep fifteen minutes longer before the later morning assembly, therefore negating shower time, therefore increasing the wafting scents of the collective student body. Suffice to say that though we're all padding around in sweats (everything from Juicy to Old Navy to Hadley track pants and last night's pajamas) no one's getting any bedtime action. The library is jammed with people cramming for midterms and I, sadly, am not one of them, due to the fact that during the insanity of academics I still have to be a Salvation Army-type good girl in the play. I have to do "I'll Know When My Love Comes Along" for the fifth time, and sit backstage with Chris as Sky Masterson/Dan Dearborn struggles with his own songs.

Chris and I are writing the program notes together (he volunteered us) so we include tidbits for the Dramatics (the group of Hadley students who are, like, totally sure they're gonna make it to Broadway and walk around singing "Seasons of Love" from *Rent* like it's the national anthem and consider Sondheim their personal hero).

"We should say that the show is based on "The Idyll of Miss Sarah Brown," Chris offers while lighting fucks up their cue again.

"Do you think people care about Damon Runyon's short story?" I ask. I've become disenchanted with the production lately—possibly preshow jitters but, more likely, this is my realization that I am not a drama wannabe. I'm just a singer trapped in a musical.

By the time lighting has their mark, we've jotted down:

Guys and Dolls revolves around Nathan Detroit, the organizer of "the oldest established permanent floating crap game in New York," who makes a bet with fellow gambler Sky Masterson that he can't make the next girl he sees fall in love with him. The girl he spots happens to be Miss Sarah Brown, a pure-at-heart love-a-soul sort of reformer, and the stage is set for a variety of complications and misunderstandings—all tied up with a bow at the end.

"It doesn't suck," Chris says.

"Unlike my life," I say.

"Oh my God, you are so ridiculous." Chris talks me through the better points of my life right now. "For starters, you have the best hair of any female on campus."

"Let me guess, you have the best in the male category?"

"Don't interrupt. So—good hair. Good friends—that'd be me and Arabella. Good grades . . ."

I nod. "They're not bad, I guess."

"And a kick-ass voice." He pauses. "And if that's not enough, Lindsay Parrish didn't eat you alive this fall."

"That's true," I say. "But the downside . . ."

"I know, when people are sick it shakes everything up . . ." He stops talking and hugs me tightly.

"Did I already tell you she has a secondary infection?" I say into Chris's chest. I emailed Jacob about it in my last short and semi-coherent letter. "Mable's back in the hospital."

"Will she be in long? Should we maybe bake something and bring it to her?"

"Not a bad idea, but she's not eating all that much—maybe just a visit. Would you be up for that? I'd ask Arabella, but she went with me once and for some reason it really got to her, and I don't think she wants to go back. Plus, Mable thought you were a riot."

"No problem," Chris says. "Name the time."

"You're so great," I say. "Thanks for being my emotional cushion. And I'm sorry I haven't been the most available to you the past couple of weeks." Has it been weeks? Or a month? I can't even remember.

"Just do the same for me sometime," he says and then stands up, opens his mouth to talk, and then just waves good-bye on his way to format the programs.

After the rehearsal ends, instead of flipping through flashcards or highlighting more passages in my *isms* text, I decide to go and find Chris and ask him—once and for all—what he keeps wanting to tell me. There's something—or there was—and enough's enough.

"Hey," I say when Chris comes downstairs to the common room in the boys' dorm. The fire's emitting heat, and the room is empty except for us. He gives me a hug and sits on one end of the leather couch. I take the opposite side and stretch my feet out onto his lap. It's after nine p.m., too late for parietals, the dorm room visitation rule (but not quite curfew), so we have to meet here rather than his room (like being away from an actual bed would prevent anything). But it feels cozy here anyway.

"So." He says the word like it's a full sentence and takes a huge breath. "I'm glad you found me. You obviously know me really well by now—and you also know that I've been trying to find a time to talk . . ."

"Yeah, and that's why—I'm sorry it's been such a long time coming. I just want you to tell me whatever it is and I promise I won't step on your toes with my own bullshit."

"And no cell phones," he adds.

"Right."

Chris leans in, slips my feet off of his lap, and touches his face with his hands. He's got exam-time stubble, which suits him. "So, all this has been building, okay? And it's like, I wanted to talk about it with you, and after hanging out at Crescent Beach—and I know you now have seriously shitty associations with that night, but . . ."

"Whatever, it's in the past—Jacob's not the subject here."

"Right. Well, after that night and then hanging so much this fall . . ." He stands up, then sits down right next to me. Mr. Von Tausig, the dorm parent walks in, fake checking the fire (read: making sure we aren't pawing each other in our easy-access sweats) and coughs—Chris moves away slightly.

"It's been fun," I say, and Chris looks confused for a second. "I mean, I love being with you." I hope that didn't sound too clingy. The ambiguousness of this moment is killing me. And just when I thought it couldn't get any more tense . . .

"I thought I'd find you here!" a big shout out from Lindsay Parrish, looking rather like she's just come back from riding a stallion (which, um, maybe she was?) complete with camel-colored britches, knee-high leather boots, and a fitted velvet jacket. Annoyingly, she looks lovely, albeit like she's auditioning as an extra for *The Black Stallion*.

"So much for the fireside chat." Chris quickly makes a big gap between us and says hi to Lindsay.

Completely aware (and yet completely unapologetic) that she's interrupted us, Lindsay sits between us and turns to Chris. "I'm guessing you'd be game for coming with me to the upcoming formal." Just like that. Like asking someone to a dance without asking them is normal or that Chris would actually—

"We'll see," Chris says and then puts his hand to his mouth like the acceptance was a mere burp and he wants to take it back. I look at him like he's nuts, but before I can comment on his early signs of dementia,

Lindsay's notorious cell phone rings (a Japanese version of Right Said Fred's "I'm too Sexy").

"I'm taking that as a maybe—with the likelihood that it becomes a yes," Lindsay says to Chris and then grabs for her phone. "Hi, lover." Lindsay draws out the r so it sounds like she's revving a car (knowing her, it'd be a Hummer or whatever vehicle of destruction she can get her long legs into). "Oh, of course! And—why don't you say hi to my little friend here." Lindsay's huge smile tells me she's a Stepford bitch hiding in the guise of a student, but she hands me her lilliputian cell phone and orders, "Speak."

"Hello?" I ask.

"Love? Hey, it's Robinson." Robinson Hall—last year's crush, last spring's boyfriend, this moment's awkwardness.

"Oh, hi. How's it going?" I want to hand the phone back to Lindsay, but she's in the middle of coercing Chris into some color scheme for the formal.

"Glad to know you and Lindsay have kissed and made up. She's the best, right?" Oh my God—he's at college and still pining for Ms. Manhattan and semi-dissing me into the phone. Robinson would make the perfect cardboard-cutout boyfriend. Good-looking, good listener, two-dimensional.

"I gotta go—take care," I say. I never use the *take care* clause, which really translates into *don't really give a shit what happens, just trying to wrap up the conversation.*

"Maybe I'll see you around?" His voice still gets at a tiny, tiny part of me (not sure if it's the tiny part that will always think of him as my first successful campus crush or if it's the part of me I cringe at that fell for his BS), so I flick the phone onto Lindsay's lap and stand up.

"Wait—" Chris catches me at the door. "Meet me?"

Ironically, Chris and I wind up meeting on the blue mesh of the pole-vaulting mat, the inanimate witness to my prior passions (if that's what you'd call them, and at this point I have my doubts) with Robinson Hall. It's early in the morning, the sky still eggplant dark with just traces of rose over the back buildings.

Chris bounces on the mat, his sneakers squeaking.

"It's freezing out here," I say.

"It's good," he says. "It's private." He looks at me, holds my gaze, and then looks away. "The place of many a Hadley hookup." He looks at the mat as if there are ghosts of his prior trysts splayed on the cushion.

"What?" I say it softly so he knows I'm ready for whatever he has to say.

"I've been feeling—I've wanted to tell you for a while, as I was trying—have been attempting, seriously pathetically trying to spit it out." I nod, afraid if I speak, I'll derail his thoughts. The wind whips my hair into my eyes, causing that stingy feeling in my eyes. "The thing is, Love—I'm gay."

He's not in love with me. Not sleeping with Lindsay Parrish. Not dying, not leaving Hadley Hall, not going into to rehab.

"I'm so relieved," I say and then think that might be anticlimactic for him, so I add, "Not that I'm, like, worried or anything, but I just had no idea—but then . . ." I do a quick inventory of Chris—the former MLUT—the guy who tongued half of Hadley's most eligible girls (the thwarted attempt with myself included) but never really dated anyone, never really had a girlfriend. "It makes total sense."

Chris smiles and rubs his hands together for warmth. "I know, right? I mean, looking back, isn't it just so totally obvious?"

"And yet . . ."

"Don't say it—"

"And yet you're seriously considering going to the formal with Miss Lindsay Parrish." I make a big frown. "And here I thought I was your hag."

Chris hugs me. "You are. I'm just messing with Lindsay's head to get her back for the way she treated Arabella at that stupid games night." We dismount (heh) from the mat.

"Do you feel better?" I ask. We walk toward the dining hall. During midterms, students can eat either in their dorms for breakfast or go up to the main hall, which opens at six in the morning so students can carbo load before cramming.

"Having told you? Yeah. But the weird thing is, it's more normal than it was before. Does that make sense? For so long—forever, really—there was this part of me that was never comfortable. Of course, I'm a brilliant master of disguise and I can appear however I want, but—and don't be freaked out—when I tried to kiss you last year . . ."

"Ah, the infamous field hockey hickey incident—you were such a slut. But actually, you didn't try all that hard, come to think of it."

"Exactly. It was like I just gave up. Here you were, this innocent, beautiful girl and I wanted to be . . . well, like we are now, but I had to try to jump you instead, and when you refused, I was so fucking relieved I thought—I don't know—screw it. The jig's up. I have to deal with all of it. So that's what I did."

"How I spent my summer vacation, by Chris Avalon . . ." I say in my best speech team voice (read: way too overpronounced).

"Coming out . . . right. Puts that paper I did freshman year into perspective."

"I wasn't here freshman year, remember?"

"Oh, I hardly remember a time without you—heh. Yeah. So I did a paper called *Gay Viking—themes of homosexuality in Norse Literature.*"

I laugh. "And this wasn't a bat signal to everyone?"

"I know." We crack up and then he hugs me really hard and whispers, "Thanks. Thank you so much, Love."

At Slave to the Grind, which is being run in a semi-shoddy fashion by an interim barista, Dad and I read the printed-out responses from his new online personal ad.

"Mable was right," Dad says and swigs his latte. "I needed bigger age brackets."

"As long as you don't date someone of my generation," I say.

"The idea of that is absolutely revolting," Dad says.

"You think Reese Witherspoon is—what did you say?—appealing," I counter.

"Appealing is not sign me up. I'd like to have an adult relationship with this person," Dad corrects. "What about this one?" He pushes a grainy photo toward me.

"Hey, she's not bad—and check it out—no cats, likes the outdoors, lives within twenty miles . . ."

"And she eats smushed fruit on her bagels like I do, not jam. Isn't that an odd coincidence?"

"God, you sound like a fifteen-year-old girl," I say and shake my head. "Are you going to meet her?"

"I think so," Dad says. "I'll email her tonight after the show—how's that sound?"

"If I can actually make it through opening night," I say, nursing my sore throat with honey and lemon and hot water, "I'll help you ask her out."

"I just might be able to do that part on my own—"

I frown. "If you're sure . . ."

"Well, maybe you can proofread for lameness," Dad suggests, and we head out the door so I can change into my A-line skirt, red blazer, and tuck my hair into its bun for the show.

Before I'm about to go on, I get a tap on the shoulder from one of the freshman stagehands—they all dress in black to blend in with the background so I can't tell them apart.

"Here," the stagehand says. "You got these. Are you like, famous or something?" She hands me a bouquet—rosy hydrangea in the middle, purple peonies on the side, all set into a celadon green enameled box that is sort of antiqued with the word *Sugar* in red on the front. The card reads *Wishing you a sweet opening night—you know I want to be there. xMable.*

I try not to cry (which would not only disrupt my preshow game face but seriously streak the pancaked base I have on) and put the flowers in the dressing room. Of course I wish Mable were here, and I know it's incredibly hard for her to be stuck at home in quasi-quarantine after her discharge from the hospital this evening, but there's just too much sickness here, all the campus germs and her lowered immune system. Which I understand, but part of me feels empty when I scan the seats and don't see her face. My father, however, is one of the first to arrive, proudly taking a spot right in the front row. He spies Arabella and motions for her to sit near him. They confer about something and I decide to ask about it later, but right now, I'm on.

"You were so good!" Dad says. "Broadway bound?"

"No way," I say. "But thanks." I have that public performance high, and I give my dad Mable's flowers to take home. Six more shows and we're done. It's weird to work on something for so long and then have it over it a week of shows. But I feel good—the songs went well—and Arabella pushes past the crowded hall to me.

"Fantastic. Well done, you!" she gloats. "This is my girl!" She twirls me around. "And guess what I got?"

"What?" I smile at her and start to scratch at my makeup. She swats away my hand.

"An invitation . . ."

"What, are you going to the fall formal with Chris, too?" I joke. Arabella laughs.

"No. But I am spending Thanksgiving with you! Your dad offered, and since I couldn't really go home just now—"

"Why not? I thought your boyfriend was *desperate* to see you."

Blushing from the English girl. "He is. Obviously. But he had to go out of town suddenly. And it's not as though the British celebrate it anyway. So here I am, on my own for—what is it? Turkey day?"

I hug her. "Cool—you can try all the Americana: yams with marshmallows, corn pudding—"

Chris interrupts me. "Hey, it's not break yet. You still have one more week to get through before overindulging."

And I get through the week, but by the time the closing night of *Guys and Dolls* rolls around, I am tired, tired, tired. Five exams, one twenty-page research paper, and a massive cold (the kind with a runny nose that leaves you with a red trail of chaffed skin and blotchy cheeks and requires major Sudafed action in order to sing) later, I'm onstage, looking out at the packed audience. Mrs. Dandy-Patinko gives me a thumbs-up, Harriet Walters leads a standing ovation, even Lindsay Parrish and Cordelia shout their best.

Then it's time for each of our main character bows. Sky Masterson, Nathan Detroit, Adelaide. Then my turn. I do a courtly bow and then, when there's a pause in the applause, a crackling starts on the school broadcasting system. We are all so Pavlovian trained that everyone listens in case the building's on fire or there's some campus emergency.

But it's not. It's my voice coming out of the speakers at full blast. And, to my complete horror, lines from my voice reels are slung together so everything's out of context—all the pizza, maxi-pad, and mattress ads are clipped so it sounds like "Oh . . . how I love myself. I am so . . . comfortable and hot. Everyone is cheesy, but not me . . . I'm the best—and you know it. Sit there and . . . watch me shine . . . even when I have my period." All of this and the spotlight is on me, too.

I have a total out-of-body experience where I can look down (or up, from the hell I'm in) at myself and the erupting laughter from the crowd as I back away.

Chris is there behind the set and he says, "What the hell was that?"

"I have no idea," I say and unpin my hair. My whole head hurts. "Clearly someone thinks they're very funny."

Arabella's backstage in an instant and says, "Well you can bloody bet I have a good idea as to who—I've just seen a certain Miss Parrish and her sidekick by the sound system."

"I just saw them in the audience!" I say.

"Well they're not there any more." Arabella raises her eyebrows and sighs.

Which, sadly, is our only ammunition the next day. It's the half day before Thanksgiving break, so there's only a couple of hours in which to try to convince people that I'm not a conceited idiot (and, I might add, if I were going to announce myself as so wonderful, would I have done it in a polyester-blend outfit?) and it was obviously a joke gone wrong. But most people (or this could be my interpretation) avoid me like I'm walking mono. A couple just mutter words like *poseur* under their breath or roll their eyes.

"Never mind," Chris says when I walk him to his taxi. He's flying to Chicago to visit some cousins for the break. "We'll get them back. Or at least I will."

"My gay action hero." I sigh.

"That's me," he says. "Complete with great accessories. Anyway, have a good break. Don't let Arabella talk you into doing anything stupid."

"We'll see," I say and kiss his cheek.

CHAPTER THIRTEEN

♡

"**H**ow about orange?" Arabella holds up a tester strip of paint to my bedroom wall.

"I'm not sure I could sleep in that—I'm just not that into pumpkin living," I say and consider the others. We've decided to star in our own vacation version of Extreme Fakeover, where we redo my room before my dad comes home from his faculty meetings, which doesn't give us all that much time. Part of me is slightly concerned because I'm not sure if changing the decor is considered illegal (not by some style council—which is a favorite band of Mable's from the eighties; note to self: copy her cd—but illegal in terms of my room technically being Hadley property, which is semidisturbing in its own right).

"What about this? It's mossy, and it would look really good with your hair." Arabella shows me.

"You mean for all those times I drape my hair on the wall?"

She shoots me a look. "I think it's perfect. The question now is what technique? Sponging? Rag rolling?"

"I've never done any of them—well, except for the unintentional splatter painting toddler years."

"Oh, mini-Jackson Pollocks weren't we all. I think we should just go with a glaze."

I page through the book we've taken out from the library, ignoring the fact that checking out decorating books for vacation is venturing into geek territory uncharted for me. But it's fun. "Let's do it."

Songs of the moment include: "Dance Hall Days" by Wang Chung, The Kinks singing "Come Dancing," and Blondie "The Tide Is High," which Arabella has currently set on repeat.

"I can't take much more of this," I say and wipe my hair from my face after it escapes the prison of my bra-strap headband. Already streaks of the mossy paint (officially named *retreat,* which is pretty much what I hope my room feels like when we're done) grace my forelocks and Arabella's managed to dip the end of her ponytail into the can near her, and now it's dried into a crunchy greenish point.

"The painting?"

"No—the song. How many times can you possibly listen to Debby Harry talk about being his number one?" I sing this last part along with the song so she'll get my point.

"Fine. It's just . . . it reminds me of something and I like that—you know, time traveling through music."

"I'm as big a fan of songs cuing an emotional flashback as anyone, but you'll have to give me specifics if you want me to have enough empathy to allow you this continuous play."

Arabella puts her paintbrush down, carefully setting it into the rolling tray. I'm impressed that her brush is only painty at the tip—mine is covered all the way to the handle, which translates into my left hand being kind of Hulk-like. Arabella takes a piece of the *Boston Globe* from our recycled stack and sits her butt on the arts and leisure section so she doesn't get the room any more splattered than it already is.

"By far the best holiday of my life was in Cornwall," she says. "Which is lame—it's like Cape Cod, but not. Well, anyway, my mum and dad dragged me there, and I was just dreading it. Some friends had rented a chalet in France and invited me, but for one reason or another I couldn't go."

"I love that you just throw that in there, like you could have gone to France, no big deal . . ."

"It's not that big a deal—it's like flying to New York from here."

"Okay, go on." I listen to her talk as I finish the last corner of the room. The roller won't fit into the corners, so I have to paint by hand there, and I go slowly, not so much for neatness but so that Arabella doesn't suddenly stop her story; it's one of the first times she's rambled on without checking herself.

"So, did you ever have those times where you just forget who you are? So often I find that I'm completely fixated on everyone watching me—of course this is partly due to my acting and all that, but on this trip I guess I was just annoyed that I had to be there while Clive got to go rafting in South America. So I just slept in my disgusting old tracky bums, barely washed my hair, took two-hour walks every morning—and you know how much I loathe exercising."

By the time I've finished the walls, crumpled up the papers, and found a perch (on the business section) next to her, Arabella has, if not spilled, then tipped over slightly, the proverbial beans. "So it was on one of those walks that I met him."

"Him as in God?" I'm only partly kidding.

"No, idiot. My boyfriend." She pauses. "Toby."

"Oh my God—a name? You're revealing a name? Has the earth stopped on its axis? Hath hell gone arctic?"

Arabella examines the green on her ponytail and laughs. "Okay, I'll admit I'm fairly secretive, but I've got my reasons. Toby—Tobias, really—he's just very . . . He's very sweet. And private."

"You make him sound like an elite club," I say. Arabella shrugs like it's true. She goes on to tell me how they met on some rugged cliff and sat and talked about the ocean and *Wuthering Heights* and quoted *Withnail and I,* some film she insists I *have* to see. And then they met the next day and so on, for the whole month that Arabella was "stuck in the seven dwarfs' cottage" with her parents.

"Didn't they mind you disappearing every day?" I ask. "I think if my dad and I went on vacation together and I just abandoned him completely, he'd be pissed."

Arabella waves her hand in front of her face. "These fumes are getting to me. Let's let the room dry and raid the basement for hat boxes and shit that can double as cool new furniture." We stand up and head downstairs. "But to answer your question, no—my parents are really kind of different." She pauses. "I'm not sure how to explain them, so I won't try. Let's just say that they're on the eccentric side and don't care that much about what I do."

"And yet you don't want them to know about your boyfriend?" I ask, referencing the conversation we had once where she pretty much admitted her boyfriend—Tobias to those of us now in the know—was off-limits, and so far she's been successful at keeping their romance hidden from her parents.

"I said they don't care what I do, but they care very much about whom I do it with."

Case closed. For now. While my room is drying out and I'm planning my justification of said decor change to my dad, we roam around the massive basement looking for treasures, but find mainly items from the Eras of Crap: shag rugs that have lost their shag, castoffs from other faculty apartments, chairs without seats that my dad bought at some flea market but never had recaned. Then Arabella finds a trunk, an old-world steamer type. "This is your new footboard," she announces. "Like I use mine."

"Cool," I say. "This is my new ugly coatrack. Check it out—the thing actually has antlers. This is just wrong in so many ways."

Arabella comes closer for inspection and groans. Then she notices a pile of huge boxes in the corner. "What's all that?"

I turn to look and open one of the flaps. "Just more junk—my dad never throws anything out, so we've hauled all this around with us forever. Probably my third-grade book reports are in there yellowing and decaying."

"Can I have a snoop?" Arabella Englishly queries and goes over before I can object.

"You'll be seriously unimpressed—unless you like crocheted potholders."

Arabella ignores me and rifles through one box, holds up an old school photograph of me with my front teeth missing. "The pirate look suits you."

"Funny, funny. I was just dentally challenged." There's so much stuff in here (mental note: have a yard sale this spring. I suddenly imagine a productive next term where I'm donating our unused goods to charity, doing the Avon Breast Cancer Walk with Mable miraculously in remission, my room on the cover of a nonexistent teen makeover mag, and so on).

"Now this is the best." Arabella snaps me out of my fog and holds up a dress so that it covers her body. "Am I not a vision of retro funk?"

"Actually," I agree, "you are. Where'd that come from?" I go over and look at the thing—it's a shade of green lighter than an avocado, but darker than lime, with geometric patterns in various shades of purples and pink. I check the tag—it reads Pappagallo, which means nothing to me. Arabella points out the box from whence the dress came and I look through it.

"This is awesome," I say and display the contents: pencil leg jeans, a tight-bodied sweater with a cowl neck, and then a pair of blue suede boots. The basement is a repository for the entire faculty house, with years of dumpage, boxes no one's claimed or crates former faculty members have left behind.

"Oh, Elvis," Arabella says in a decent Southern drawl and mock faints.

"And they fit! I'm so keeping these."

Arabella grabs the cowl-neck sweater and we go upstairs to change before venturing to rent movies and deal with my dad's probable paint-induced wrath.

But when he sees the room, he's totally fine with it. I can tell from his face that he's trapped in a mire of faculty issues, which isn't unusual after a hard fall, but what is weird is hearing him swear under his breath (well within range of Arabella, whom he still treats as a sort of dignitary or ambassador) about how much goddamn bureaucratic bullshit exists.

"Bad day?" I ask.

Dad shakes his head. "Bad choices." Then he reconsiders and no doubt mentally reminds himself not to share faculty secrets. "Never mind. Wow—quite a change. It's very calm." He touches the walls for dryness. "Not a bad job, either—maybe I'll hire you girls for the dining room."

I'm so glad he didn't mind the paint job, so relieved to have him just be mellow dad, that I'm totally caught off guard by his sudden Sybil switch of personalities. One minute he's saying, "Isn't a green room supposed to be the most soothing color? It's very . . ." and then interrupts himself with, "Jesus Christ, Love. What the fuck are those doing on your feet?"

Not only is this a) the *first* time in my life I've heard my dad say fuck (okay, second, but the first time was when he shut his finger in a pickup truck door and he had no idea I was in the back, and I was eight so I didn't even really get it), but also b) it takes me a minute to register he means my boots (which, fine, aren't really technically mine, but which are on my feet—and, I might add, looking damn good).

He demands an answer. "Where did you get them?"

Arabella steps in, trying to be my buddy shield. "We were in the basement—all my idea I'm afraid, and there was this box . . ."

"There are *lots* of boxes in the basement," Dad says, still way louder than normal. "But in my recollection, none of them are specifically yours." He turns to me.

"Well, actually, a couple of them are . . ." I say and then stop. It's moments like this that I wish I could remember not to be on the defensive and just to say yes, you're right, and so on, but I can't. "I mean, Dad, some of that stuff is mine."

"And a good deal of it isn't." He takes a deep breath. "Take them off." He points to the boots like they're made of 100 percent dung. "Now."

I start to unlace them, and when they're off, I'm a barefoot, confused Cinderella, busted for some criminal shoe offense.

Of course, my dad storms out to answer his study phone and leaves me here with Arabella in accessory fallout.

"Um, that was fucked up," I say.

"Tell me about it," Arabella says. "Not to flake out on you, but do you mind if I skip out on our coffee? I'm knackered."

Knackered = tired, so I forgive my friend for her lack of caffeine compulsion and head to Slave to the Grind myself. I'm in one of those moods (courtesy of my dad's shitfit) where every song drives me bonkers, so I flip through stations, driving with one hand on the wheel, the other with my pointer fixed on the scan button. By the time I reach the café, I realize I haven't heard any song all the way through.

Slave to the Grind is holding up well despite Mable's absence. She's been back in the hospital, cooped up, first with the infection, now scheduled to have a lumpectomy, which is pretty much what it sounds like—with the surgeon trying to cut out the lump of cancer. I check my watch—one hour and then I can go to the hospital to see her. My stomach flips and turns when I imagine Mable in the thin robe, tucked into the white sheets there. Part of it is that I'm totally guilt ridden, that I'm living my teenage existence without her—which of course I have to do while she's gone, but it feels bad. Also until our fight today (or rather, my dad's irrational boot behavior), with Mable less present, I've been with my dad more—and I have to say I kind of like it. But if it's a trade-off of sick Mable/closer Dad, it feels wrong.

I wash down my sorrows with a caramel misto (which I refuse to accept on the house, even though I'm well aware my bank account is dwindling rapidly. Note to self: must earn money soon) and write to Jacob on the back of the free postcards on display by the sugar cart. In fits and starts I try to explain my current state of brain mush and respond to the serious hints from an earlier letter, where he mentioned a certain Beatrice who was reading over his shoulder as he wrote (Beatrice whom I'm assuming is more than just a Shakespeareanly named friend).

> Hey J—
> I'm at Slave to the Grind, caught in that weird Thanks-
> giving mode of not fall/not winter. The pumpkins are out,
> so are the turkeys and the Christmas lights, and shitty
> Musak abounds (thankfully not here—Mable has way
> too much class for that). And speaking of Mable, she's
> not great—and I wish you were here to talk to or to visit
> her with me.

I pause. Maybe the *I wish you were* part is too much. Especially if we're supposed to be neutral. But I leave it in anyway—what's the worst that can happen? He could assume I still like him, which is partly true (though I don't want him to think that), or just chalk it up to sadness regarding Mable. Whatever. I'm not going to line edit a damn card.

> On to #2—
> How goes life in the Alps? I'm sure you're a regular ski
> bunny now, or whatever they call guys—ski elk? Moose?
> Chris said to say hi to you—he's gone off to Chicago in

search of cute Midwestern boys (yes, boys—a story for another time, though I'm guessing you figured this out before I did. Is that why you were so repentant about the Crescent Beach fiasco?). Arabella and I are here, trying not to dwell on the fact that she leaves for the UK in less than a month and then I'll go back to being alone.

That last part sounds so pathetic that I hate myself for writing it, dislike myself even more for feeling like it's true. It's not that I have no other friends, it's just that Arabella is such an integral part of my life now. But I don't need to have Jacob with his arm around some gorgeous Euro-girl pitying me, so I cross that part out and go on to the next postcard, which, when I look at the picture on the front, has the tour dates for Jamie Cullem, whose upcoming show is at Boiling Point on the Vineyard. I use this as my segue into describing the cottage, my tame exploits there, and then—since we're so neutral and he mentioned Beatrice, I throw in:

And I'm psyched to go back there. My dad mentioned going back to pack up Grind II and winterize the cottage (not sure exactly what this entails—giving it a hat and mittens?). I met some new people there (Charlie and Henry to name a couple) and I'm curious how all of that will pan out.

Of course I feel a little catty writing this, knowing full well that he'll interpret it how I have interpreted Beatrice (read: I am in no way, shape, or form pining over you. I am dating other people or at least I want you to think I am). And it's the truth. If I could export myself to the island right now, I would. Picturing Charlie's eyes, the way his voice dipped down when he chided me for talking too loudly on my phone. I can't help but want to explain myself to him, and it's way easy to imagine being pressed against his flannel-clad rugged sailing exterior. Yum. Not exactly what I'd say to Jacob, but fun to think about. And Henry—who knows about him? He's probably forgotten me by now (being, it seems, the kind of guy who frequently finds friends and flings and discards them just as easily), but he's the kind of guy that sucks the breath from your lungs immediately.

> Anyway, I hope you have a good holiday season in the land of snow—and I'm looking forward to catching up with you next term. Chaucer passed along a photo of you from last year and it seems like a long time ago, even though it wasn't.
>
> X on both cheeks,
> Love

He's gone into detail about the Euro two kisses (or three or four, depending on the locale) so I figure I'm safe signing off that way. I don't reread my words for fear of overediting, I just shove the cards into an envelope (note to self: get stamps) and chuck my cup into the garbage on my way to go see Mable.

"You know the thing that annoys me most?" I ask.

Mable shakes her head. She has the softest baby chick fuzz growing in on her head and I keep touching it until she grabs my hand to make me stop. "What?"

"I just hate thinking one thing and then having something else happen."

"You'll have to be more specific, Love." Mable adjusts her pillow and raises the automatic hospital bed up more. She actually looks remarkably well, better rested than before.

"It's like, I just thought he'd be so mad about the painting and changing my room around without asking, since it's Hadley property and everything. But instead, he's like 'Oh, that looks nice,' charming and whatnot—"

"I hate the word *whatnot.*"

"Oh, right. Sorry. And then he goes and throws a total tantrum about a pair of goddamn shoes." Mable looks at my feet. "No, not these. He made me take the other ones off."

"Did you look like a hooker or something? I know he doesn't go in for the stiletto style."

I shake my head and rub my cheeks where the wind chapped them. "Not even. They're these cool electric-blue boots with a—"

Mable overlaps with me. ". . . a fold-down cuff at the top?"

I jerk my head like a pigeon. "Yeah."

Sighing, Mable swings her legs from the bed and slowly, carefully stands up. "I've got to be careful—I get dizzy from the meds." I wait for her to explain. She holds herself up on the drop-leaf table. "But those shoes—they were your mom's signature thing. She must've gone through four pairs of them."

"These were almost brand-new."

"Then they must have been the last ones she had before . . ." Mable stares out at the Boston cityscape. The gray sky, the faint twinkling of holiday lights.

"Before what?" I stand up and stand next to her but look out the window, too.

"Before she left," Mable says, point-blank and then looks to check my reaction.

Chills. The kind that start at the top of the neck, then spread downward, racing from shoulders to arms. "Oh."

"So, I'm guessing that your dad's outburst today was a mixture of surprise and—I don't know—horror, probably, because he hasn't seen those things—you know how a song or clothing can just totally bring back the essence of someone—he hasn't seen them in a long time. Where'd you find them, anyway?"

"A box in the basement. Arabella did, actually."

I wait for Mable to tell me to leave the stuff alone, to pack up the shoes and not ask more or defend my dad like she usually does, but instead she offers this: "I think you should wear them." I raise my eyebrows. "The boots. They fit, right? And they're totally in now—actually, they're timeless—and if David—your dad—has such colossal issues with them, then he should practice what he preaches and express himself."

"Oh, I think he expressed himself pretty clearly," I say, doubtful of Mable's advice, particularly when I envision the wrath he could impose on me—not to mention the house arrest he could demand during the rest of break.

"It's just time," Mable says, and part of her sounds like she's giving up on something, which makes me panic. "This is all . . ." She waves her hands. "It's all just his shit to deal with. It doesn't really have to do with you."

But it does, I think but don't say. I'm the product of whatever he had with my mother. My mother, who as I've just found out, left.

"So, she's still alive, then?" I ask. I almost pause on that word, since it more than hints at death, which I more than don't want to suggest around Mable.

"Ah . . ."

"You can't just drop the abandonment bomb on me and then nothing," I say. "Come on—is she alive? In Prison? What?"

"As far as I know, she's not behind bars," Mable says as the nurse comes in to give her medicine. From a white cup—the kind you squirt ketchup into at a snack bar—she picks up two red pills and swallows them at the same time. "But more than that . . . Listen, Love, I don't want to do this without some sort of consent."

"You mean my dad controls what you say?"

Mable is vastly annoyed with my comment. "Love, usually I think you're very perceptive and far wiser than your age suggests. But you know what? Every time this subject comes up, you wind up pushing it too far . . ."

Now it's my turn to feel slapped. Annoyed. My face burns, partly with the dry revolting Mass General heat and partly with the knowledge Mable's right. Which is not to say that I think I should act otherwise. "Well, maybe if you and my dad weren't so childish about it, I wouldn't be forced to act like this."

Of course, this is all said in front of the nurse, who helps Mable back into bed. She's probably heard lots of wacky family conversations. So in a moment of levity I add, "It's not like when you shot me in the foot!" The nurse doesn't flinch, but Mable suppresses a smile.

"That was once and you only bled a little," Mable responds without missing a beat.

The nurse leaves and I hug Mable, leaning into her bony chest, wondering if I'm hurting her. She pats my hair. "You look like her, you know."

I pull back. "Really? Galadriel?"

Mable nods slowly, not questioning how I know the name. Then she deliberately considers my face, my hair. "It must be really hard for your dad. I know it's hard for you, but you never knew anything else. He lost the only great love of his life. And yes, she had the *exact* same hair as yours, copper with these summery strands of whitish gold at the front. But your eyes are greener." Mable's tone changes to a sour one. "If memory serves, hers are gray."

And that's where we leave it. Odd yet monumental moments in Mass General. That's how I'll describe the scene to Arabella.

*   *   *

In the parking garage, I sit and freeze my ass off trying to remember whether I've parked on floor A or D and, in wandering around with my breath coming out in white puffs, my hands tucked under my arms for warmth, I have a complete epiphany.

CHAPTER FOURTEEN

♡

"So," I say to Arabella when we go to Whole Foods to shop for the Thanksgiving dinner, "here's what I decided. First, I'm applying—albeit late, and we'll have to express the thing over and maybe call—to LAMAD."

"For next year? Great!"

"No," I say. "For next term. I read in the brochure you have that they accept some foreign students with special qualifications, and I'm hoping that since I have you as a personal reference, and Chaucer will obviously write a good academic rec, that might work."

"But—not to sound discouraging or anything"— Arabella holds up a garnet yam and after I approve of it, drops it into our cart, or as she calls it, trolley—"you need to audition. They're really formal about that."

"Which brings me to the second thing. I am going to come home with you for Christmas . . ." I watch her face to see if she freaks out or—unlikely—gets pissed off with me for inviting myself to her home. "And meet with them if need be. And in the meantime, I'll send my *now recovered and relocated* voice reels."

"So what's the third thing?"

"Oh, I need to go by WAJS, the radio station where I did them, and ask if they have any spot jobs for right now. Otherwise, I don't think my bank account can handle international travel."

Arabella pauses by the bulk bread crumbs and rolled oats. "I could . . . get your ticket for you?" I shake my head. "Not buy—no—just lend you the money. You know you'd do the same for me."

"True," I say. "But I don't want to get in over my head before I've even landed. Oh, and p.s.—I'm not telling my dad." Arabella makes a face and smells the leeks I hand her. "Yum—and good luck."

With my mother's blue boots on, I record two thirty-second spots for WAJS. Originally, they claimed they had nothing for me, but when I (and I wasn't acting, really) teared up, I finagled a quickie preholiday sale ad for the Men's Big and Tall Store (why they want a short, non-male advertising this is beyond me, but I graciously accepted) and a way too chipper jingly tune about sending a teddy bear as a gift for your long-distance girlfriend (let me state for the record that this gift is not on my wish list, particularly not from a boyfriend). And I leave the studio with a hefty (in my world, not in the world of most Hadley people, who'd probably use the whole thing in a matter of days) check and a recipe for collard greens, which I pass along to Arabella when we get home.

My dad says nothing further about the additions I've made to my wardrobe. (I absconded with the dress Arabella found, a boxy suede jacket, and a shirt all from that infamous box in the basement.) In the middle of stuffing and turkey, Arabella (as we've planned) invites me home to her house for Christmas, to which Dad (without tons of time to consider) says, "Potentially."

"I have my own money for the ticket," I say, and produce the check from my pocket.

He shovels a mouthful of yam onto his fork. "Well, then, I don't think I have any arguments."

Not exactly a warm, *thrilled that my daughter will experience life abroad,* but not a *forget about it* either.

"It'll be a fun time," I say.

"Yes," Dad agrees. "A good two weeks away."

I swallow and try to ignore Arabella's foot against my shin, reminding me that two weeks away might just be the beginning.

CHAPTER FIFTEEN

♡

The totally bizarre time between Thanksgiving break and Christmas recess

The two weeks in between breaks are just useless in terms of academics. Exams are handed back (A, A, B+, A-, and a crappy B-/C+, which kills my average but serves me right for not really studying for calculus, a weak spot for me anyway, not to mention that there's zero chance of bullshitting your way through any of the questions). It's a Hadley tradition that you can dispute a midterm grade—and many kids do, even if they know damn well they deserve what they were given, but I just don't feel like I have the right. I mean, maybe that's what I'm lacking, the feeling since birth that I am somehow entitled to whatever I want. I watch Healy Warner argue with Mr. Chaucer over the B he received and, even though Chaucer is notoriously firm about his grading system, he gets bumped to a B+. Then again, Healy Warner's dad is on the board of trustees and his grandfather and all his relatives (male, of course) have gone here since the school opened (by candlelight, prior to the invention of the wheel).

So I suck up my grades and report to Mrs. Dandy-Patinko, who says, "Love! You star. What a simply wonderful performance in *Guys and Dolls*. And I've seen the fall issue of the literary magazine, which I'm pleased includes a poem from you." True, I did submit one—and miraculously got it accepted. And it's not so much a poem as it is cribbed notes from my journal, songs as of yet unsung. And just when I think Dandy-P will continue to lift my spirits, being the human equivalent to one of those flotation tanks where you leave your worries behind upon immersion, she adds, "But the C+ isn't going to do you any favors, and there's a certain lack of diversity among your credentials, which, upon reflection, is going to hurt your chances of getting into those reach schools."

"It was actually a B-/C+," I say defensively.

"Call it what you like, Love, but I can tell you as a former admissions head, a C-slash is still a C."

"Oh." I look at Mrs. Dandy-Patinko's Christmas tree vest, the quilted fur and 3-D boxes of presents, the buttons in the shape of candy canes and for some reason, start to crack up. Not the kind of laughter you can brush off with an *Oh I was thinking of something humorous from earlier in the day,* the kind of laughter that got me sent out into the hallway in fourth grade. Pretty soon, I'm hiccupping with hysteria and Mrs. Dandy-P actually joins in, and I can see the remains of her lunch caught in her back teeth (spinach? broccoli?), which makes me think of the dentist, which makes me think of novocaine, which leads me to Mable's pain medication and Mable and my mother and then, just as quickly as I started laughing, I cry. It takes a minute for my beloved college counselor-turned-shrink to realize I'm now on the other side of the bipolar express, but when she does, she hugs me. I can feel the candy cane points digging into my collarbone.

"I'm okay. I'm okay," I assure her—or myself. "It's just the stress of everything, that's all."

"You know what?" Mrs. Dandy-P says. "Can I let you in on a little secret?"

I nod. "Please."

"Now, I'd be out of a job if I said this too often, but"—she looks around her college-catalog-strewn room, at the piles of SIBOF score sheets and posters declaring the top-ten schools in the country—"none of this matters. Really. Wherever you go, it'll be fine."

And for some reason, right then, I believe her.

After my deranged emotional barfage, I find Chris at the student center, but rather than find solace with him, I'm faced with a new horror.

"I can't believe you said yes!"

"The plus side is, she'll look amazing," Chris says in defense of his saying yes to Lindsay Parrish's formal invite.

"But you're, like, betraying us," Arabella whines. "I thought you were supposed to be our escorts anyway."

"Can't your boy Toby fly in?" I ask Arabella.

"Could I explain yet again to you simpleton that he's otherwise engaged?" she quips back.

"He's not married or something, is he?" Chris asks her.

"No, fucker," she says in a firm but good-natured tone. "I'm adventurous, but not completely without morals."

"Anyway," I say, "bringing us back to the point, which I believe we deserted somewhere back there, Lindsay Parrish is your date?"

Chris smiles and fixes his hair. Since announcing his sexuality, he seems suddenly prettier, which maybe he is in his own mind. "It's all part of my master plan. To avenge the name of my girls. No one makes my friends run around a flagpole naked—not unless I want them to, anyway. And Jude Law you are not, my dear." He shakes a finger at Arabella. "No one—ever—should screw around with you." He pats my hand. "Especially not onstage. And particularly not on a stage with sets I have designed and painted myself. So there."

Mable comes for dinner, her bandages covered by a bulky gray sweater, save for the Band-Aid on her hand from numerous IV punctures. Her prognosis is good, and the doctors have told her she's okay—for now. All of this is, of course, a major league relief for me (oh, semi-sports anal-ogy, dad would be proud, even if annoyed that I'm wearing one of the shirts from the basement box), for all of us, but we don't discuss it at the dinner table, especially because there are no guarantees.

"Love's heading off to London," Dad announces during our salad. He takes a bite of beets and thinks a minute. "Didn't you spend some time there, Mable? Any suggestions that aren't tragically unhip?"

"Maybe a couple," Mable says and picks at her bread. She scoops out the middle part of the roll and eats it. "Any chance you can spare her before she leaves?"

They talk over my head as if I'm not there, or a toddler, which I guess I might be in their eyes. "For how long?" Dad asks.

"Long weekend? Can I pick her up Thursday night and bring her home on Sunday? I could use the help packing up in Edgartown."

"There's nothing going on right now," I say to my dad. "You know this time of year is futile."

"Fine," Dad says. "I think it's fine, but I also think, Mable, that you should take it easy. Just because you're better doesn't mean you're well. There's a distinction."

Mable nods to my dad in faux-seriousness and then smiles at me. "Pack warm—it's cold down there."

Fucking freezing is more apt. The Northeast wind hacks away at the lay-ers of fleece and wool I've put on, stings my ears until I think they're likely to drop off. Inside the cottage is marginally better, but not great. I sling log after log on the fire but need to stand within three feet of it to actually feel the heat.

"I just can't get warm," Mable says, shivering.

"You're kind of blue," I say.

"Blue like cerulean or blue like pukey baby outfit blue?"

"The first," I say. "You shouldn't sleep here. You're going to get sick and then I'll get in trouble."

"Yeah." Mable considers her options. "Should we stay at the Harborview?"

"Don't do it for me," I say. "I have to get ready for England and no central heating anyway, so you may as well let me bundle up here." I pat my extra sleeping bag and clap my gloved hands together. They make a muffled noise.

"Okay—but no visitors, got it? Otherwise I'll be the one in trouble," Mable says.

"Like I even have anyone to invite here," I scoff.

But of course, after I've carried Mable's small bag over to the hotel, I casually walk up Main Street and then over to the docks (casually = totally focused on finding Charlie, scanning each cold face for his beautiful one). But he's nowhere. The floats, empty of boats and boys, rock in the cold water. The gulls peck for nonexistant crumbs and the clam shack is boarded up, complete with a tattered sign reading *anks for a grea season*. I briefly consider going up to the Chappy ferry dock, but don't. Instead, I walk back by Lighthouse Beach, the night sky clear with star flecks and constellations I can't name.

"Jesus, slow down, will you?"

I whip around, slightly paranoid that I'm about to be jumped by a Vineyard villain. Facing me instead, is Charlie.

"Are you stalking me?" I ask.

"No, I bumped into your aunt at the hotel," he says seriously. "Also, you dropped this." He hands me my cell phone. I feel my pockets—with all the extra layers, the lump of familiar electronics had escaped without my knowing it.

"Oh," I say and feel mildly stupid. He wasn't flirting or following me for any reason other than being a good guy.

"But I could stalk you, if want me to," he says. Oh. Wait. Maybe we are flirting.

"I could, you know, let you know my schedule and where I'm staying and you could walk by at inappropriate hours and bother me—and you already had my phone . . ."

"So I could call multiple times and hang up . . ." He offers.

We stand there, the sand gritty under our boots. His are stained with paint and worn in at the toe. Mine are the blue ones, which he notices.

"Where'd you get those?" he asks.

"Uh, how much time you got?" I ask. "It's sort of a long story."

Which is how we get to be back at the cottage, sitting three feet from the fire, eating ice cream cones (Mad Martha's was the only place open and I had a massive sugar craving), and discussing our family histories. I tell him about being raised only by my dad, but how Mable's been in the picture forever; how I've not only never met my mother, but know virtually nothing about her.

"That's a lot to deal with," he says when I've gone through the past till now version of my life.

"Everyone's got a past, right?" I say and lick my black raspberry cone. "I should've gotten chocolate. There's something too summery about this flavor."

Without hesitating, Charlie swaps my cone for his double chocolate caramel. "Better?"

"Much," I say, aware that I now have one of those brown rings around my mouth that seem to instantly appear when I'm near chocolate. "So what's your story, then?"

He sniffs and finishes the ice cream. It's warm enough to take off his Carhartt jacket, and he throws it back, where it lands on the couch with a soft thud. Underneath, he's got on a black sweater, and peeking out from under that, I can see a waffled gray long underwear shirt. He stretches out his legs and, in doing so, inadvertently (inadvertently =

maybe intentionally?) moves his hands nearer to mine. "What did Leo Tolstoy say? 'All happy families are alike . . .' "

I complete his thought. " 'All unhappy ones are unhappy in their own way.' So which are yours?"

"Oh, mine's the unique, dysfunctional kind," he says.

"Care to elaborate?"

"Not really," he says and laughs. "It's too nice a night to ruin it with that stuff." He takes a deep breath. "Not that I'm fundamentally against hashing it out, but we have time."

"We do?" I look at him to see if he's looking at me or at the fire—oh, me.

"I think so," he says, then, without so much as a pause, puts his hand on my thigh, slides it up until it gets to my jacket. Various layers intervene until Charlie's cold hand finds my back. "You're nice and warm," he says.

"Well, you're freezing," I say. I reach for his hand and move it away from my bare back and onto my thigh, where, I have to say, I want to it to stay, if not forever, then for a long time.

"So warm me," he suggests and pulls me onto his lap so my back is to the fire and I'm spider-legged across him. He leans back onto the couch and—like something in a movie, but even better—takes my hair from its messy ponytail and tangles his fingers in it. "Can I just say that I've wanted to do that since the first time I saw you?"

"Mmm," I say. It's not terribly eloquent—okay, fine, totally mumbly—but it's all I can muster up until I remember something. "Not when I was being an inconsiderate asshole on a cell phone."

"No, pretty much then, too," he says. "What? I'm a guy. I can't help it. Sure, I thought you were being loud, and possibly running with—in my opinion—the wrong crowd. But there's just something about you that . . ." He doesn't finish. Instead, he put his hands on the back of my head and pulls my mouth onto his and we kiss for what feels like hours.

Actually, it has been hours and my face is stubble burned to prove it.

"I should go," he says and pulls me up toward the door. Then he looks at me. "Unless you want me to stay?"

Um, yes. Yes, a thousand times yes, but . . . "No. I mean, yes, of course, I do. But you can't. Or I can't."

He nods and leans in for one more kiss. "Want to have breakfast tomorrow?"

"Yes. That I definitely want to do."

"Meet me at the dock at six."

"Six a.m.?"

"Yes—that is an actual time," he says and shakes his head. "You city folk are so pampered."

"Oh, shut up, boat boy," I say and shove him—half heartedly—out the door.

I go to sleep under many layers, clothing, blankets, sleeping bag, and excitement. Then I try to think of his family, of what his story is—and picture him growing up on the island with a fisherman dad, struggling for money, how that would explain his disdain (a rhyme, no less) for the moneyed summer crew. In my dreams, there's ice cream being served from a boat that's just out of reach.

Charlie and I are back from fishing—yes, freezing, fun, ridiculous fishing— before the sun has come all the way up. Back at the cottage, Charlie fries up fish and makes home fries while I run to the store for muffins and bread and to get Mable.

"Here." Charlie hands me some cash when I come back with bags of baked goods.

"No." I brush him off. I don't want him thinking he has to buy me, or show that he's not penniless. "I got it this time."

He shrugs. "Okay, that's generous of you. Thanks."

We eat and talk and Charlie's home fries are so good that I notice

Mable even packs away more than I've seen her consume in ages, and when we're done, Mable and I go to the café while Charlie heads off to—yes, seriously—stack wood for the winter.

"Well, you've found yourself a man of the forest," Mable says while she takes inventory of her paper goods at Slave to the Grind II.

"I know!" I grin.

"How old is he, anyway? Don't get in over your head. I did that once, and it was terrible. I think I wound up crying for a solid month."

"I don't think Charlie's going to make me dissolve into a flood of tears, Mable. But I get your point. He's nineteen."

"Are you sure?"

I nod, and then in my head quickly do some math. "Um, maybe almost twenty," I say, correcting myself and acknowledge that I do, in fact, deserve a C+ for my numerical abilities. "But I'm seventeen," I remind her, just so she's not panicked. But instead she frowns.

"I missed your birthday." She puts her hand to her mouth, horrified. "I just completely forgot. How could I? I'm so so sorry."

I brush it off. "It was sort of a nonevent this year. Next year—my eighteenth . . ."

"We'll do something huge," she says.

Before meeting Charlie for dinner, I collect the papers Mable's asked me to gather and go to drop them off at the Realtor's office. I'm in la-la land, totally spacing on anything other than that incredible rush when you've thought about someone and have just discovered you are totally into this person—and he's totally into you. Which is why, when I get to the office and am standing face-to-face with Mr. Trip Randall III (aka Henry's dad, island property guru), I don't even notice Henry standing by the copy machine until his father barks at him to take my coat.

"Oh," I say, "I can't stay, but thank you. I just wanted to drop off the café's paperwork."

"Right." Mr. Randall takes the envelope from my hands.

Henry comes over and smiles, suddenly seeming like a floppy puppy (okay, a very cute, very rich puppy). "Hey, Love. Long time no see."

"Yeah, how are you?"

"Good. I wanted to see you, but when you didn't write back . . ."

"Huh? I didn't get another email."

"No—I stupidly tried to be romantic and sent you an old-fashioned letter by post, but maybe you never got it?" I shake my head. "I sent to it Brown University general mail and figured they'd pass it along. Oh well."

Ah, Brown. That's right. I'm midway through freshman year, according to Henry. "The campus mail system sucks." What is my problem? Why can't I just come clean? It would help if Henry's dad would stop eavesdropping.

"Well, maybe I'll drop by campus sometime?"

"Sure. Look, I gotta go," I say. Henry looks hurt, like I'm skipping out on some preplanned date we never had, and part of me feels guilty. He's so sweet, and he clears his throat like he's waiting for me to invite him to wherever I'm headed. Obviously, I can't. Or I won't.

"See you around?" Henry asks.

"Sure," I say, but scurry off to go to the diner to meet Charlie and Mable.

After sitting for a half hour, Mable and I go ahead and order. And after delaying eating another half hour, we eat lunch. And after dessert, and more waiting, it's clear I'm doing it in vain.

"Sorry," Mable says as if she had anything to do with Charlie's absence.

"I thought people only got stood up in movies," I say. "Isn't it kind of bullshit and lame? I mean, who does this?" I'm hit with flashbacks of the night before, of kissing. My face still hurts.

Mable pays the bill. "Maybe he has a good reason. Can you call him?"

"I don't have his number," I say. And I kick myself for it.

*   *   *

On the ferry back, I'm still kicking myself and the railing and my stupid suitcase and nearly the guy in front of me. Who just happens to move aside at the last minute. And who happens to be—

"Henry," I say. "Hi." I'm about to apologize for running out so fast on him, but then I remember the slap of being stood up and feel quiet. Henry somehow reads me well enough not to say anything, but turns instead to Mable.

"Hey," he says. "I'm Henry." He shakes Mable's hand. "I know I kind of met you before, but I'd like to be thought of separately from my father, if that's at all possible."

Mable smiles. "Enough said." She adjusts her scarf, and Henry doesn't turn away.

"Are you having treatment in Boston?" he asks matter-of-factly. I could get offended by his abrupt nature, but it comes off so nice, so honest, that it's just refreshing. I take one last look at the dock in case Charlie has come to say good-bye, to explain his no-show, to beg me to stay on the island with him, but he's nowhere to be seen.

"I am—at Mass General," Mable says. "The care's been really good there."

"My aunt is a nurse oncologist there. I should introduce you. Not that you hope to be spending much time there or anything, but she's really great. Her name's Margaret."

"I'll look for her," Mable says. "That's really nice of you." She nudges me. "Isn't that nice of your friend?"

I nod. "Yeah," I say. "It is."

Henry smiles at me and as we head back toward Woods Hole, leaving the island behind, I smile back.

CHAPTER SIXTEEN

A cross-campus buzz: My Dad (aka Principal Headmaster Bukowski) has announced a case of "serious faculty misconduct," which of course makes rumors circulate faster than Internet viruses. Some suggestions as to what: The German PE teacher was caught in a tryst with Eileen Finch, the very out sophomore, or that Ms. Gabovitch tried to buy pot from stoner Dean Hadjinow, and so on.

"I heard Lucy Fischer had an affair with Mr. Kaplan," someone says in the student center.

"No way," another counters. "Lucy Fischer's just spreading that rumor herself—to raise her desire factor."

And so on. Arabella did say she'd witnessed a "rather odd hand-holding session between Lana Gabovitch and some freshman guy," but then again, Arabella can find drama in the most innocent of situations. I make an attempt to garner more info from my dad, but despite the paternal connection, he won't divulge anything—"For legal reasons, I'm not at liberty to say." I look forward to using the same excuse the next time I get caught doing something I shouldn't and he pesters me.

All of this holds my attention for a solid ten minutes until Lindsay Parrish appears at the double glass doors that lead from the student center to the lower quad. She stands with her arms raised above her head like a deranged Gucci-Pucci-clad cheerleader, waiting for a reaction from underclassmen, which she gets in the form of admiring glances and shy hellos. The underlings aside, Lindsay proceeds to catwalk over to where I'm scribbling in my journal.

"I would never bring my journals to campus," Arabella says and reads over my shoulder until I push her away.

"I'm not that concerned with the paparazzi," I say without looking up. I've nearly completed my entry on the long and fairly ambiguous *Questions I'd ask my Mother* (I have tried to get beyond the simple *why, why, why* and move on to more productive, in my opinion, things, like *Where and how did you meet Dad?* and *Are your parents still alive?* This last one freaks the shit out of me. I could have relatives scattered all over the world—a grandmother or cousins I've sat next to on a train and never even realized).

"I've just had too many incidents with the printed word." Arabella coughs and sounds like she means it. Every once in a while she seems a lot older than I do. It could be the foreign thing, or it could be the possible wealth (of money and experiences)—at this point I'm just not sure. "So I think it's best not to put things onto paper that you wouldn't want falling into the wrong hands."

"Oh my God, you sound like a B-movie paranoid heroine." Chris rolls his eyes.

Then Lindsay Parrish worms her way into the conversation (and by worm I mean with the grace of a bulldozer and yet the sliminess of a— whatever category of animal/insect worms fall into. I'm annoyed that I don't know this off the top of my head and must remember to look it up later).

"Hey, sweetie," Lindsay says to Chris, oblivious to me and Arabella (oblivious = just rude in this case).

"Bonjour," Chris says and hugs her.

"Dance with me?" Lindsay asks. The only thing worse than her queen bitch role is her little-girl-lost voice she uses around Chris. I wonder if she talked like this with Robinson Hall—actually, no I don't want to wonder this; it's too icky.

Chris obliges her and they cha-cha (can she seriously be unaware of his royal gayness?) until Chris dips her and she blushes the blush you can only blush when you're around a huge crush, which is obvious now.

"She is so into you," I say when Lindsay momentarily vanishes to the snack bar to get a bag of Cape Cod chips she won't eat. She buys food but never seems to consume it.

"It's wonderfully sad, isn't it?" Chris says in the voice of Dr. Evil.

"Shh," Arabella says when Lindsay's within earshot.

"I have to run," Chris says and puts his hat on. It's a cashmere fisherman style hat that makes his very blue eyes even bluer. Lindsay whisks it off his head. "Give it back."

"Please," she begs, but it sounds more like *pweeaaase,* which makes me experience all the nausea of a stop-and-go cab ride in the rain.

"Gross," I say. "Just let her have it."

Chris smiles and shrugs, then walks away, leaving Lindsay holding the knitwear like she's caught a bridal bouquet. She smiles dreamily at the thing, puts it on her head.

"You look like a J.Crew castoff," Arabella says.

"Just because you make phone love to your pretend boyfriend," Lindsay says to Arabella, "and you" —she points to me with one tastefully French-manicured nail—"you're in love with my boyfriend . . ."

"Excuse me?" I laugh. "I'm neither in love with your boyfriend nor aware that you actually have one."

"Well, Chris is mine—and, well, I don't have to remind you about Robinson."

That's my cue to leave, which I do, linking arms with Arabella and going to the pillow pit to unwind from Lindsay's unpleasantries.

The pillow pit is a campus ode to the sixties, when the new wing of the library was put on to make room for the millions of books Hadley buys each year. As some research back then showed (research = pot smoking?) students could generate brilliant ideas when in a state of total relaxation. In other words, the pillow room was built for napping, which is just about all I've seen anyone do in here (except the odd fondle now and then, and the senior spring sleepover, when a pajama-clad bunch brings sleeping bags into the pillow pit and stays awake until dawn).

"No boarding school in England would ever have this kind of room," Arabella says and pounces on a marshmallowy cushion.

"No? Not traditional enough?"

"Not even close—even though the pillows are tartan," she says.

"How come you don't go to prep school, like a regular private school?" I ask, suddenly aware that I've never asked her before.

"This kind of school is called public school in England—as opposed to a state school." Arabella tilts her head up to the skylighted geodesic ceiling. "That would be an impossibility. My parents wouldn't stand for it." She rolls her head so she's facing mine. "Anything conventional is off limits for them."

"Them?"

"Yes, *them,* my parents. They eschew tradition—unless it's one of the bizarre ones they've created. And prep school—uniforms, rules, all of that crap—it's"—she sits up and speaks loudly, very BBC—"very establishment!"

"Oh," I say. "How confusing and liberating and backward. Well, not backward—but you know what I'm saying."

"Yep," she says. Then she counts. "Eighteen days and counting."

She means until we leave for London. Online yesterday I booked an e-ticket returning on January 2nd (enough time for the revelry of New Year's to semi-wear off) and I showed her (for the fifth time) that my passport was valid and I was ready. Last night at dinner, I'd asked my dad if Arabella could just stay for another term at Hadley. He very rationally explained that the way the exchange program was set up prohibited two terms in a row. How nonpresidential. This, of course, made me think maybe she could go home for a term, then come back, since that wouldn't be two consecutive terms. Dad sighed and did a parental *maybe,* which as Jack Johnson so aptly sang, *pretty much always means no.*

"I need to pack soon," I say and jump from the edge of the pit onto a giant red-and-green plaid cushion. The thing looks like a ball of Christmas ribbons.

"Yeah, you do," Arabella says, "seriously."

"What's that supposed to imply?"

Arabella props herself up as best she can amid the squish. "All I'm saying is that you need to pack up—emotionally."

I can't refute her, because I know damn well she's right. And for the rest of the afternoon, until I go home and find a package waiting for me on the mail table, I'm certain I won't be able to fit all my emotional baggage under the seat in front of me or in the overhead compartment to go away even for two weeks.

Back home, the international postmarks make me want to shriek, but I keep mime quiet until I'm sure my dad is not in his study and that he hasn't seen the mail pile in the communal entryway. Squirreling my goods upstairs, I head up to the safety and sanctuary of my green room and drop my various outergarments on the floor next to my 1985 bag.

My IKEA scissors—a very cool shade of orange and yet totally dysfunctional in terms of their actual ability to cut—prove useless against the tough padding of the package, so I wind up using a combo of my teeth (floss will be required to exhume the paper lint now embedded in my molars) and a small serrated knife leftover from my breakfast (whole-grain bread and soy butter, which I know from past culinary exploits is . . . well, let's just say crumbs and a three-hundred-count sheet—gift from Mable—don't mix). Finally, the damn thing opens. As well as scattering a snow of gray and white paper shreds on my floor, the package also reveals what I'd hoped.

Dear Miss Bukowski,

   With pleasure, we inform you of a provisional acceptance into the London Adacemdy of Drama and music for upcoming term. As an interview has been impossible to arrange due to geographic circumstances, we will assign your course schedule without your final approval. Please be advised that the provision requires parental signatures and in loco parentis as you are under the age of eighteen.

And blah blah blah. But I'm in—I'm in! I call Arabella's cell phone and am put immediately through to her voice mail, which is totally frustrating, but not as bad as the fact that I will have to tell my father (and by tell I mean actually ask if I can go) tonight, since his signature is required in five days, which means I need to overnight Global Express it tomorrow (and ask Arabella if her parents—the eccentric ones—will be my local ones). But any doubts I had about doing the application as a whim are gone. I'm the first to admit that I filled the thing out as more of a slap in the face to another term at Hadley, a gut reaction to the blue boots incident, but now I'm just plain excited. And nervous—if my dad says no, I have no recourse.

Which is why I make sure to ask him at a very vulnerable time—during Monday Night Football, with the Patriots ahead by one field goal.

"Daddy?" Oh, she brings out the *daddy* in times of great need!

"Hmm," Dad says, intent on the television screen. "How can I help?" It's his stock phrase for when students appear in his office at school. It's both a good sign (he considers me one of the flock and therefore might not react to my preposterous idea of going away for an entire term) and an annoying sign (he considers me one of the flock and yet I am not—I am his flock).

"I have some news," I say and sit next to him on the couch but avoid tapping him or distracting him further from the game.

"You got a date for the formal?" he asks without irony.

"No, but thanks for rubbing my singularity in," I say. "Actually, I did something without telling you and I . . ."

Dad immediately leaves his view of the TV and turns to me. "What happened?"

"It's nothing bad . . ." I say and briefly consider that technique where you list really bad things you could have done, like had unprotected sex or tried heroin "just to see what it's like" so that when you actually reveal the (in comparison mellow) thing you've done, it seems like nothing short of a godsend (i.e., "You failed chemistry but never dropped acid? Fine—we all make mistakes.").

"Are you in trouble?"

I pat his shoulder. "No, but I'm going to England."

"I know that," Dad says and sneaks a score check. "So what's the issue?"

"I'm going—or I'd like to go—for longer than I planned."

"How long exactly? I feel like hot chocolate," he says during a commercial. "Can I get you some?"

I shake my head. "No, Dad. Wait—I mean go abroad for a long time. A term." He stops in the doorway, his large frame filling up the rectangle of space.

"Is this because of what I said about Arabella Piece staying on here? It's not my decision—it's school policy."

"This has nothing to do with that," I say and stand up, too, just to make it so I'm standing—if not equal, then in front of him for impact. "I applied to LAMAD—London Academy of . . ."

He cuts me off. "I know what LAMAD stands for, Love. And presumably you've been accepted?"

"Yes. As of today."

He walks off without saying anything and I can hear him making hot cocoa noises in the kitchen, clanking the pot around, opening the fridge to get out the milk, and so on, until he reappears in the living room with a steamy mug in hand. The crowd cheers from the television.

"Well?" I ask.

"Well, I think you should go," he says. "But I wish you felt you could have told me you were applying."

Dad gives me a rather solemn hug, quiet except for his big sigh, which I interpret as a father-letting-go-of-kid embrace, like a movie bus or train station scene when the girl has the luggage at her feet and the parents let her go off into the distance, knowing it's for the best.

CHAPTER SEVENTEEN

♡

A heap of clothing, piles of old Hadley Hall yearbooks, and a tray of still-warm brownies are the backdrop in our preformal afternoon. The dance is tomorrow night, the Friday before the Monday before we get out of school, a couple weeks before I embark on my next misadventure.

"The funny thing about these books," I say and hold out a yearbook so that one of the *candid* spreads is showing, "is that they're all the same. You can, like, change how deep the part on someone's hair is or tweak the bootleg-slash-bell-bottom-slash-pencil-tight cut of the pants, but aside from that, look at how little changes."

"Ah, yes, the timelessness of prep school." Chris thumbs through 1987 and then grabs for a 1970s one. "Nice paisley. Dig it."

"You're right, though, Love. It's all bright autumn leaves and dogs and healthy white kids . . ."

"Now, don't let the diversity committee hear you say that," I say mock sternly.

"Yeah," Chris adds. "There are plenty of black, Asian, Hispanic, and Latino students—but they're all rich. Diversity just doesn't mean economic diversity."

"Hey—check us out—future politicos of America," I say.

"Speak for yourselves," Arabella says. "Well, it's more diverse here than at home—I'll grant you that."

"Oh—hot boy alert," Chris announces and points at a bright blond guy with typical prepster hair (i.e., once a normal boy cut but now grown out so the bangs cover the eyes). He checks the date on the yearbook. "Not so long ago."

"He could be familiar—or not." Arabella checks out the guy. "He is good-looking, though. You have swell taste in men, Chris." She pokes him and smiles.

I lean over to take a closer look, but what catches my eye is not the guy Chris pointed to, but one farther down on the page. As seniors, you're allotted half a page to do with whatever you see fit—mainly people band together with their cliques or two best friends and do the black and white snapshot thing: arms around each other outside on the swings (girls); casually leaning on someone's car with Led Zeppelin quoted on the bottom of the page (boys); downtown Boston shot under street sign or business that says something vaguely suggestive like "how many boxes have you had?"; or the ever-popular Lichter Street (boys); or the vacation shot/moody beach photo (rich girls); or a humorous one, such as the two buddies sitting under hair dryers at a beauty shop next to random old ladies. It's in one of these last categories that I spot a guy that makes me look twice.

"That guy is the spitting image of Charlie," I say.

"God, you're not going to relay that tragic story again, are you?" Arabella says, only half kidding. It's true. I have been plaguing her and Chris (and Mable and my journal) with a wide variety of interpretations of why he possibly didn't show up for dinner on the Vineyard, why he's disappeared, if he ever really existed.

"No, I'm not—it's just . . . look at this guy. You met him, Bels. Does he, or does he not, resemble Charlie?" I display the photo for them. Chris raises his eyebrows and nods, a silent *yes he's hot.*

"To be honest, I don't have the clearest memory of him," Arabella says. "Henry, however . . ."

"Okay, okay," I say. "Well, trust me. This guy—Nicolas Addison— looks a ton like Charlie." I close the yearbook, but dog-ear the page for no good reason except maybe so I can torment myself later by staring at the guy and wondering what became of my penniless fisher boy.

Then Chris insists on showing Arabella last year's yearbook, with my overeager face in miniature (only seniors get the half pages—all the underclassmen are grouped by dorm and year and made so small the snaps resemble Serrat paintings, all tiny dots with vague facial characteristics).

"This was my first crush," Chris says and points out a former senior I never knew.

"Really?" Arabella asks.

Chris turns to her. "Why, does that shock you?"

"Not shocking. He's good-looking and everything, but . . . interesting choice of trousers." She runs a finger along the very plaid pants.

"I think he pulls off the look. What do you think, Love?"

I smile and stand up, going to the closet to reconsider various items for the formal. "What do I think? I think that somewhere a golf bag is naked."

Chris shakes his head. "You both lack taste." Arabella pummels him with a balled-up shirt. Chris defends himself with his hands. "Fine. I retreat. You're both fashion mavens with impeccable taste."

"Speaking of taste," I say and hold out a dress I've had since eighth grade. It still fits, albeit snug in different places than it used to be. And boring. "Is this terrible?"

Nods from both friends. "I can't wait to take you to Et Vous in London," Arabella says. "The cut will be perfect for you."

"Well, until then, any suggestions?"

Chris pouts. "I can't believe you guys are leaving me here alone for an entire term. What am I supposed to do?"

"You'll survive," I say.

"Yeah," Arabella says and comes to survey my closet jumble. "Get yourself a man."

"I wish," Chris says. "By the way, I'm planning on outing myself tomorrow morning, just so you're aware."

My mouth drops open. "What about your plan for secrecy and self-loathing? Isn't that a bit psychologically healthy for you?"

"I know. I just figure I may as well do it before someone does it to me. Besides, what better way to liven up a dull prevacation assembly?"

Arabella shoves the swirly dress she found in the basement—namely, my mother's—and makes me take it. "Why don't you just wear this to the formal?"

I take it, considering its colors, then slipping into nostalgia. "Where do you think she wore this? Wouldn't that be so cool to know the stories behind it?" I slip it on over my onion-skin-thin blue T-shirt. "I think this could work."

"It'll be perfect," Chris says.

At morning assembly, no one's paying attention, just rambling about vacation plans, ordering taxis to pick them up as early as possible tomorrow without bagging class (Hadley avoids the preholiday class cutting by having the last one before vacations count as three cuts—an automatic detention—if you miss it). Mine's supposed to be Chaucer's class, but he is—quite notably—absent, which, of course, leads to further speculation about his possible involvement in the "faculty misconduct" case but could just mean he Pricelined a fare and had to bolt.

Then, suddenly, the doors swing open and the formal crew comes in. This is the group of students in charge of planning and organizing the dances, proms, and other festive fun for the year—basically, they're the girls who would be cheerleaders at a normal school, but Hadley doesn't have cheerleaders, never has, never will. Reasons being 1) it's too degrading/sexualizing of females and Hadley was originally a boys' school so it's semi-taboo, 2) cheerleading, while physically challenging and acrobatic, doesn't testify to intellectual prowess, which is what the prep school world is built on, and 3) the football games—which is pretty much where the cheerleaders would display said acrobatic wonder—suck. In fact, the football team is notoriously bad, made up primarily of boys who would be very cool at public school but somehow fall between the preppy cracks (heh) here. Hadley Hall's sporting strengths are the "social sports," the ones that will come in handy at country clubs later in life. A quick rundown (quick rundown = gross generalization) on the back story of each sport: tennis (read: *I'm bright, beautiful, and either in one of the pseudo-student marriages or away most weekends visiting my real friends*), golf (read: *I'm stoned, but have really good hand-eye coordination and at least one whale belt/anchor tie*), skiing (read: *want to have sex with me in the boot closet?*), squash (read: *I'm from the city, but summer in the Hamptons*), baseball (read: *I'm a day student going to an Ivy League no matter what*), lacrosse (read: *I'm hot and destined to be an investment banker/date rapist/binge drinker*), track (read: *I'm a mixture of every other generalization but can run fast*).

So the noncheerleaders (aka the party squad) come in to do some skit about the formal and how the decorative theme is "a lava lamp" —not sure what this means exactly, except maybe it's hot, retro, and possibly goopy, but it sounds fun anyway. Then, at the very end, Chris—who is in the skit as a sort of stone statue, is told to choose a female who will unmelt his heart (or unbreak it if you're into soft-rock faves) and he whispers something to Vanessa Hickey (yes, her real name), who weaves her way among the desks until she gets to Lindsay Parrish and pulls her up to the front so she can be the fire starter Chris's organ needs (or, um, something to that effect). Of course, Lindsay is all proud and coy, bursting with *see how much he likes me* and leaning into Chris in the hopes he'll plant one firmly on her mouth (um, it is an assembly—you'd think she could at least make it semi-open rather than full-fledged French). But he doesn't. Chris leans in, then suddenly says, "We interrupt this kiss with the following information." He turns to the whole school and says, "The formal begins at eight o'clock tonight, and also, I'm gay!"

Then he takes a bow, as do the party squad, who could care less what he's announced as long as he's done it cheerfully. They leave the stage, all except Lindsay, who pauses in the post-sexual orientation aura. She finds my face with her eyes, and I blow her a kiss and wave—*buh-bye baby*. All at once her face changes from shock to revenge, and Arabella leans in and whispers, "Uh-oh—the wound is seeping."

"I can take it," I say, and hope that I mean it. I can't wait to put three thousand miles between me and Lindsay Parrish. I spend the rest of the day wandering around saying good-bye (in my head) to the campus, the students, Harriet Walters (who gives me a list of things to do—a typed list no less—in London).

When I get home, my dad's not there, which isn't unusual save for the fact that he specifically mentioned wanting a preformal photograph of me, Chris, and Arabella (we figured we'd take turns doing the typical guy-behind-the-girl, hands-double-clasped-in-front prom style). But since he's not there, I change into my mother's old dress. I can't figure out what to do with my hair, so I pile it into a messy bun that Arabella can fix later, and wait for my friends to pick me up. (Pick me up = ring my doorbell so I can drive us all to the French library downtown, where the formal is being held amid the twinkling Newbury Street lights, the elegant wreaths that dot the doors of the Back Bay).

A final check of my email reveals that Jacob has written—I expect a big long entry since I haven't heard from him in a while (with a certain dread I realize I haven't told him about London yet either), but he's written a one-sentence message.

Did you check your mail yet?—J.

Ah, the enigma continues. I don't even have time to consider what Jacob's talking about before the doorbell sounds and I go downstairs to twirl for Chris and Arabella. They look polished and posh while I still feel like a preball Cinderella (minus the soot, I guess).

"You look great. What's the deal with the hair, though?" Chris asks.

"That's me—America's Next Slop Model," I respond. Arabella undoes my bun and manages to do a complicated twist and tuck under that I could never replicate. I look much more together as we head into the car. We blare cheesy but oh-so-singable songs from the likes of Spice Girls and DeBarge and Kool and the Gang until we reach the French library and head inside.

The decor is an odd mix of tradition (sparkling chandeliers, brass sconces, polished wood) and lava lamp add-ons (a black-lighted room, Donovan music, and Pucci-esque prints on the walls).

"Well if it isn't Queer Eye himself," Lindsay says, calmly as an airline attendant.

"Hello, Queenie," Chris says and eyes Lindsay's outfit—she's perfected the liquid eyeliner, teased but elegant hair with a wide pink band, and has elbow-length gloves on. In short, she's a tall drink of expensive water.

"Oh, Love," Lindsay says, and I notice she's slurring slightly. No doubt she made a stop at one of the hotel bars before coming here, running the tab up on her credit card. "I have a surprise for you."

Before I can even think of something cutting, clever, or kind to say, Lindsay gives some dog signal and produces none other than Robinson Hall. Robinson whom I haven't seen since last year. Robinson who still looks incredible but inspires instant heart pounding in that seeing-the-ex-boyfriend way, especially as we didn't end on the best of terms. At least not in my mind.

"Robinson was kind enough to fly in as my *date*." Lindsay emphasizes the last word and also manages to get across the idea that Robinson would fly worldwide to reach her if she wanted.

"How kind," Chris says.

"Hi, Robinson," I say.

"Hey, Love Budowski! How are ya?"

"Bukowski," I correct. I can't fucking believe he got my name wrong. I pray to the gods of bad-relationship decisions that Lindsay instructed him to say that, but I can't be sure. I don't know what else to say, and it's so awkward, with even Arabella—the chitchat master—standing there saying nothing, so I volunteer, "It's good to see you" in the hopes that this squelches Lindsay's plans for social humiliation.

"Yeah," Robinson says and lets out a worrying belch. "Lindsay said you still have a thing for me." Huh?

"I was just being polite," I say. Arabella and Chris take a giant step backward, wanting to let me fight my own battles.

"Polite? Oh, yeah . . ." I'm wondering if Robinson was always this dumb sounding or if he's just wasted. Just as I'm wondering this very deep thought, an even deeper belch comes from Robinson's mouth, the kind of burp that can only precede one thing. "Fucking hell!" I say as the vomit spews across my dress. Swirling into the swirls, Robinson's hurlage makes me want to heave myself.

Lindsay cracks up, one gloved hand to her mouth, eyes watering (and yet her makeup stays immaculate). "Payback time," she says. "Puke-owski."

By the time I'm home, showered, and in bed (the dress kindly rinsed by Chris and Arabella and hung over the railing outside to air out), I'm exhausted. I roll onto my left side (my preferred side for sleeping) and then remember I haven't brushed my teeth. Normally, I'd just leave it for morning—I have a good excuse for poor dental hygiene tonight—but then I already feel the tooth fuzz starting so I get up and run the water in the bathroom. I like to brush with warm water, which I know is slightly bizarre, but my teeth are really sensitive and the cold water stings. I have a mouth full of Tom's toothpaste (gotta love the fennel flavor) when my dad appears at the door.

"Hi, Dad," I say, but it comes out like *hmmi, ad* with the froth. I spit.

He cuts to the chase before I even know there is one. "Mable's sick, Love. I've been at the hospital all day."

I wipe my mouth on the back of my hand and feel the familiar chill run the course from neck to arms. "Again?" I sigh. If I'm this tired, this drained from hearing about it, I can only half imagine what Mable's feeling. "I thought she was better."

"It's spread to the other breast." Dad swallows. His voice is shaky. We don't even bother saying *cancer* anymore, just *IT*. Like it's some monster, which I guess is fairly apt. "So she needs more chemo, possibly a mastectomy."

"Oh my God."

Dad and I stand in the hallway for a half hour, making plans for seeing Mable—I'll go tomorrow after the half day lets out, and then we'll take it from there.

"At this point," Dad says, "it's a day-by-day thing. We'll just have to see."

The next morning, it's snowing. Tiny flakes shake from the sky, quilting the athletic fields, making me rummage around for suitable footwear. Unable to find anything upstairs, I head to the kitchen, grab a yogurt and a spoon (I'll shovel it in on the way to class), and go to the front entryway to see if my fleece-lined boots are there. Which they are. Also present is a pile of Christmas cards, which threatens to commit postal suicide, so I straighten it out before it careens to the floor and, once it's upright, I notice a letter addressed to me.

It's Jacob's handwriting, and the bulky size lets me know it's a long one, which I ordinarily would tear into without a moment's pause, but after last night's news, and juggling my dairy products and bag, I decide to save it for a calmer moment. I walk to campus, leaving a trail in the snow, finish the Yoplait and leave it and the letter in my desk in the assembly room until after my last meeting of the year with Mrs. Dandy-Patinko.

"Please send a postcard," she says when we're wrapping up. She's baked enormous gingersnap cookies and thrusts one, cloaked in a holly-print paper napkin, in my direction.

"I will," I say and accept her baked goodness, but I have a sinking feeling I won't. Not because I won't remember, but because London is feeling far away now, and I'm having serious doubts about disappearing for months when Mable may or may not be around when I get back.

"And just think," Mrs. Dandy-P, ever the enthusiast says. "When you return home it'll be time for your college tour!"

"Right," I say. I'll have to take the SATs in London with all the other ex-pat kids, and I picture filling in bubbles while looking at the Thames or Big Ben—presumably they have number two pencils there.

She hands me a packet of college materials, including the handout most juniors receive in the spring but I—lucky soul that I am—get the pleasure of skimming now (skimming now = obsessing over later).

I read part of it, knowing it's not meant for right now.

As Hadley heads into the final days of the term, we wish you all a happy and relaxing summer. (Um, relaxing except for everything we're about to tell you—plus it feels weird to read about stuff that's six months away.) I shove the thing into my bag to look at several months from now.

Back in the assembly room, Arabella closes her cell phone and rolls her eyes. "He is so sweet!"

"Toby?"

"Of course, Toby," Arabella says. "I can't wait to have you meet him." Then, when she notices my face (I have a bad habit of biting the side of my lip when I'm sad or anxious), she says, "Oh, what's wrong?"

I tell her, and without a word, accepting the cuts she'll get (which, come to think of it, may or may not matter to her and her transcript and won't show up since Chaucer's not there to mark us absent from his class) for skipping her last Hadley class, we pile stuff into our bags and head to the hospital. Only when we're on Storrow Drive do I say, "Wait—did you see my letter?"

"What letter?" Arabella automatically reaches into the backseat for my book bag and begins looking through my papers, the gym clothes shoved inside, the *Guys and Dolls* script I still haven't shelved, to see if she can help.

"I got this letter from Jacob this morning—well, presumably it arrived yesterday, but I didn't see it under the mass of holiday cheer that's overtaking the mail table."

"Sorry to say, I don't see it in here. Did you leave it in your desk?"

I feel my coat in case I pocketed it. "No, it's definitely not in my desk. I emptied that out." I sigh. "Par for the course." Oh, golfing analogy.

"You must really be upset."

"I am," I say and turn to look at her while we're paused at the red light. I click my indicator on for the left turn into the hospital area.

"No—wait—you're not . . . You're still coming, aren't you?"

Biting the inside of my cheek until it hurts, I half shrug and open my mouth. "I don't know, Bels—I just don't know if I can."

Arabella nods and sighs. "Okay. Just do what you have to do. If it's meant to be, it'll be." She's amazing that way—just allowing life to flow without trying to steer it one direction or another. I'm so not like that. Even if I try to be mellow or of the *whatever happens happens* mindset, it doesn't work for me.

Arabella says hi to Mable but then gives us a moment alone (alone = one medical student, an intern, and a nurse all in the room).

"Well," Mable says in her burned-the-eggs voice, "this sucks."

I give a small laugh. "How are you not just falling apart?"

"I'm past that, I think. I'm just getting on with it—what choice do I have?" She takes my hand and gives it a squeeze. "Plus, I kind of like my Sinead O'Connor look—you do know who she is, right?"

"Yeah, yeah, the crying video and, yes, I'm aware that Prince wrote that song."

"Good. Anyway, I'll be all through with this shit by the time the Avon Walk comes around which you'll fly home for, and we'll be back in business for the summer. In the meantime, eat some roasted chest-nuts for me."

"What?" I can't help but stare at the dripping IVs, the way Mable has one arm draped protectively over her chest.

"Rooooaaaasstted cheeesstnuttsss," Mable says ridiculously slowly. "In England—like *My Fair Lady*?" She sings a line from "Wouldn't it Be Loverly."

"That's chocolates, not chestnuts," I say, automatically correcting her.

"Fine. My point being—eat some for me. They're really yummy." Then she watches my face, waiting for me to respond. "Oh—no—no nonononononono. You are going. Going."

I protest. "I don't know. Actually, I'm thinking it'd be better for me to just . . ."

"What, stay?" I nod. She points at me. "No way, Love. This"—she ges-tures to her body—"is not about you. It's not about you postponing your life, your semester abroad. It's just—cells. Shitty, sickening cells. And I'm going to poison them."

"Are you sure? I'd be much more comfortable staying here with you."

"Right," Mable says. "And you need to not be comfortable. I think you'll benefit from getting out of this so-called comfort zone and living it up in the land of kings and queens." Mable presses the call button on her bed and a nurse mumbles something.

"Can I get you anything?" I ask. "Water? Cookies? *Us Weekly*?"

"Definitely some trashy reading material. Hey, did I tell you who my nurse is?" As if on cue, a tall woman with deep-set brown eyes and a mousy bob comes in. "Love, this is Margaret. Margaret Randall. As in Henry Randall's aunt."

I stand up and shake her hand. "Hi," I say.

"Hello," she says, "Henry's told me so much about you. And don't worry about Mable here, she's in good hands."

I don't know how much Henry could have told his aunt, but I'm not displeased that he's had me on his mind—and I'm more than happy to have Margaret looking after Mable.

"Do you want turkey?" Arabella asks in the cafeteria. We had to vacate Mable's room so she could have an exam of some kind and get some sleep.

"Sure—and here." I hand her a wad of cash. "Get a roast beef for my dad? With Boursin." Arabella nods and I go find a table for us.

Dad's already in the back corner, reading a pamphlet. "To top it all off," he says as if we've just been talking, "I'm supposed to have a date next weekend."

"Conveniently scheduled for when I leave?" I raise my eyebrows at him in mock hanky-panky suggestion.

"I wonder if she'll like hospital food," Dad ponders and then reimburses me for the sandwich when Arabella returns with the food.

"This is for you," he says and hands me a ticket. "It's an open one—good for whenever. You just keep it somewhere safe, and know that you can come back at a moment's notice."

I'm hoping he doesn't mean for this to be in case there's a medical crisis, but I say thanks and accept it. "And speaking of keeping things safe, you didn't, by some chance, see a letter of mine—an unopened one?"

Dad shakes his head. "Anything important?" he asks and brushes his just-beginning-to-turn-shingle-gray hair back from his eyes.

"Not really," I say, but of course I have no idea. Probably, the tome was just another one of Jacob's ethical missives, another set of questions that are supposed to reveal to him who I really am. But there's a slight chance he turned the mirror on himself and told me what he's thinking about coming back to Hadley, or about me. Anyway, now the letter is as good as unsent since I'll never know (never = not until I ask him) what the pages said.

We leave the hospital and head back to the house, dropping Arabella at the dorm so she can load up (and by load up I mean neatly pack her stylish old-school trunk with the few books, clothes, and photographs she brought here) and wait for us to collect her later. I can't think about my good-bye to Mable because we decided not to say it, just to give a hug, a kiss, and say *more soon. More soon,* I think. The phrase echoes with each stair I climb to my room to finish packing.

Computer screen glaring at me, I write, then erase, then rewrite an email to Jacob and set my mail function to send it after I'm already on the plane (i.e., where he can't reach me, at least not for a while, since Arabella has told me her parents' house has only one phone, a rotary, and no Internet capabilities—ah, wilderness!). Maybe it's a shack in the woods. I'm torn between truth and terror, the bareness of telling Jacob that I still think of him romantically, even though we're not supposed to, even though he clearly had a Beatrice and I had a—well, fine, I didn't exactly have anybody, but I damn near had Charlie and Henry (one kind of, plus one almost = real boyfriend? The math never stops). And so I tell him—I write a short but honest note:

Jacob—
    By the time you get this, I'll be three thousand miles away—and the flip-flop of our geographic positions won't help with the ongoing push pull of this whole situation. But

I want you to know that I'm okay with whatever you did (or didn't do) in Switzerland, that I know you have a life that doesn't always include me, but that I welcome the chance to be a central part of your days (and nights) again. I feel like we started something and it never really finished—so I'll leave this note open ended, too.

-Love

CHAPTER EIGHTEEN

♡

nd then, later, Arabella's trunk is in my dad's car and she's waiting for us. With the help of my dad, I shut my suitcase (suitcase = one suitcase, one lumpy duffel bag, one bright red backpack and a two-toned Chapelier bag for a carry-on—*gracias* Señora Mable for that last one) and join my friend.

"I wish we were flying together," I say to Arabella for probably the eighteenth time.

"Again—I am more than happy to cancel my ticket and come on your flight," she offers from the backseat.

"No, that's such a waste," I say, thinking of the vocal funds I had to set aside for my own ticket. "But you'll wait for me at Heathrow?"

"Yes, yes, a thousand times, yes. And if for some reason I'm not there, just look for a sign with your name on it."

"Oh, you mean my fan club will send a representative to welcome me to your fine land?"

Arabella kicks the back of my seat, which she knows bugs me. "No. Dream on. I meant the driver will be there."

"You have a driver?" I ask, like she's hidden a third arm from me this whole time. "What else haven't you told me?"

Arabella quickly shrugs off my question and thanks my dad for the ride, assuring him she'll take good care of me. Then her bloody (see, I am getting her lingo already—note to self: do not try to sound English, as even I find that annoying) cell phone blares and she retreats to the corner of the car for a quick gabfest.

"I'm nervous about leaving," I say to my dad.

"You mean you're nervous about leaving Mable," he corrects. We exit toward Logan International and I check my paper confirmation again, just to see that the time is right (not for dancing in the streets, but for checking in twelve hours early).

"Yes, Mable. It's just—what if . . ."

"There are so many what ifs. It's best just to go ahead, I think. At this stage . . . well, I'll call you back if I think you need to be here. Would that make you feel better?"

"Definitely. Even if you think there's a chance of—just tell me what's going on. Don't hide her condition or anything."

"I won't. But by the same token, I want you—now that you know and trust I'll keep you informed—I want you to really enjoy yourself there. Let go, and don't think so much about what's happening here."

I nod. I look at my blue boots and wonder if my father notices I'm wearing them, if he remembers his reaction to them.

When we unload curbside onto two trolleys, Dad does take a look at my feet and wraps his arms around me. "I love you—call when you get there."

"I will," I say, my breath gray in the cold air.

"And you know what? The boots look good on you." We look groundward at my mother's old footwear and I wish I knew what images float through my father's brain. "I'm actually kind of glad they're being put to some good. They're one of the last things I ever bought her." This is more than he's said about my mother ever, really, and it makes me think of something I learned in my oral histories class at Hadley. We had to write about superstitions and stories passed down and one kid wrote about how her grandma told her never to buy shoes for a man "because he'll only use them to walk away from you." I think this but don't relay it to my father because he's well aware of what happened, even if I'm only just figuring it out.

"Keep warm—and tell me what happens on your date!" I say when Arabella and I are nearly through the automatic doors.

"Wish me luck!" he says, and Arabella and I say "luck" back to him at the same time. He's got some date, not from his personals ad, but through the Von Tausigs (aka the dorm parents who busted me). All Dad knows about her is that her name is Louisa and she owns a bookstore in Cambridge.

After we unload our bags at separate check-in stations, Arabella and I meet at Dunkin' Donuts for a final glazed cruller and extra milky coffee.

"I'm not ready to be tea focused," I say.

"Come on, we drink coffee, too," she says. "And speaking of consuming too many caffeinated beverages, I need the loo."

She disappears to the bathroom and leaves me to guard her bag. I open the side pocket of it to check for gum, but find none, just her passport and tickets. We leave from the same area—both flying Virgin Atlantic (though only I have the distinct honor of being at one with the name)—but not the same gate, and since I'm paranoid about missing my flight, I want to head down there when she emerges. Casually, I check out her passport—a million stamps from a billion countries, visas for Nepal and India, old ticket stubs from flights to Australia and Fiji come sprinkling out. I pick them up from the grubby linoleum floor and then two photographs fall out. One is of Hadley, the front entrance to the main building, with the crest in full view. Instant nostalgia. Then, just as I'm about to flick through mental images of the campus and all the stuff I'll miss when I'm away, I flip over the other photograph.

Hulking in the background, a stone building so large and carefully crafted I'd hesitate to call it anything other than a castle. Not a palace (though what's the distinction, exactly?), but a turreted, arched-doorwayed, mammoth structure—and the kicker: the guy standing in front of said building. Tobias. Better known as Toby—though perhaps best known as teen idol/English royal, the one who's constantly in *People* magazine and *Us Weekly,* the one who plays polo and heads up charities and whose shy grin is familiar to everyone—even in this country. "Toby" is Lord Tobias Wentworth-Jones. I take a quick look at the back of the photo again before placing the passport and its contents back in Arabella's bag. On the back, in her handwriting, it says, "Toby at Bracker's Common."

Arabella's back and sips her drink and shoves the last bite of doughnut in before announcing, "We should head to the gates, no?"

"Yeah," I say and stand up, slinging my bag over my shoulder and taking my boarding pass from my back pocket. "By the way, what's Bracker's Common?"

Arabella looks at me with her eyes all squinty, lips in a mock pout. "What have you been doing?" We hug, then part ways. She trots down the corridor toward gates twenty-three through forty and turns back. "Bracker's is my house, which, I might remind you, you'll see soon enough."

I'm agog at the idea that Arabella is not only dating a semi-royal but also lives—apparently—in a manor or a castle or whatever you call it (um, a fucking huge house, for lack of a better phrase). Arabella's flight takes off an hour before mine, so I have time to kill after she's gone through the door and onto her plane.

I eat a twelve-dollar tuna sandwich that's gone soggy around the edges and then wander around and look at the magazines on offer in the newsstand. I see a father and daughter together (I assume they're dad and daughter, but they could be slimy older man/bimbo combo—you never know) and I go to the pay phones (so antiquated! I have to drop real coins in the slot rather than just using a cell phone, which I've had to leave behind) to call home.

"Hi, Daddy," I say, and it's only slightly whiny.

"Hey, Love. I'm just heading out to play squash," he says. I can hear the front door squeak open in the background. It's so weird—when I'm away from home everything sounds fun—like *Oh, squash. I so want to play that right now,* or *Oh, laundry—I like laundry!* But then I know it's just distance-induced nostalgia for normalcy, which, based on the few things I've just learned about Arabella, I'm not sure I'm about to have much of.

"Listen—someone called and left a message . . ." Cue sound of papers and Dad searching for whatever message he took. "And . . . I seem to have not written it down—"

"Specifics? Dad, anything resembling a person or reason for the call?"

"I think it was Lindsay Parrish," Dad says, and even his tone suggests this would be out of the ordinary.

"Really?" Doubtful, but possible I suppose. "Are you sure?"

"Yes, I'm pretty sure it was. She's with your friend Cordelia." I love how parents add phrases like *your friend* as if they have any clue about the subtext of the relationships. I would never define my interaction with Cordelia (at least as of this term) as friendship—fauxship, maybe. "And—wait here's call waiting."

I tap my feet and watch the shoeshine guy while I wait for my dad to come back on the line. "That was actually Lindsay again. I told her to call your cell phone."

"Which I don't have," I say, annoyed. I need to leave this country and go eat scones or something. Go be discovered in a London record shop and suddenly be catapulted to international singing sensation stardom. Not deal with this petty shit.

"I'm aware you are without your phone. It's sitting on the table in front of me, waiting to be sent back," Dad says. "But the voice mail is still active, so I told her to leave a message on it. Now—safe flight. Love you."

I use my last quarters to call my voice mail and, indeed, there's one from Lindsay, which I can hear only part of before the operator asks for two dollars more. Who carries that much change with them when flying internationally?

"Hell-o, Love. It's me. Just wanted to wish you well"—drips of sarcasm—"and say that we'll miss you next term"—floods of sarcasm—"and, hey, just in case you were wondering, you don't have to worry about your boy Jacob. Suffice to say he's in"—(insert giggle from Lindsay, snort from Cordelia)—good hands—and so is the precious little letter he sent."

You've got to be kidding me. With only twenty minutes until my plane boards and nothing left to lose, I call the number the annoying redheaded comic on TV tells you to, and once connected to an operator, call Cordelia collect. It's an automated thing and you have to insert the caller's name so the person can decide whether or not to accept the charges.

Cordelia answers, "Hello?"

Automated voice, "This is the operator with a reverse charge call from *answer the goddamn phone.* Do you accept the call? If so, say *yes.* If not speak the word *no* clearly."

"No, bitch," Cordelia cough giggles. And I can hear—at least I swear I can—the all-too-familiar chords of acoustic guitar in the background.

"I didn't understand you," the automated operator says cheerfully.

Again the music. This time Cordelia confirms my fears. "Jacob can't come to the phone right now," she says. "He's otherwise . . . engaged."

I hang up and stare at the pay phone as if the plastic handset and twisty silver cord will explain what just happened.

Looking out the tiny circle of window, I watch the ground crew load the luggage on to the plane, and I take out my journal for later and swig water from my large Evian bottle. Would Jacob really go for Lindsay? I have to hope no, but then again—oh crap! My email. There's no way to cancel it now, so within a couple of days, Jacob will know what I feel. Felt. Feel. Whatever.

We taxi down the runway and I'm securely buckled into my seat, secure, too, with the knowledge that I don't have the answers to any of these questions. I write them in my journal, knowing at some point in the future I'll be able to look back on them with the understanding of what happened: Will Mable be okay? Will Jacob and I ever get together? Will he like Lindsay (and if so, under false pretenses?)? Will London change my life? Does LAMAD end up furthering my singing? Who will my next kiss be from? Is Dad going to find love in the personals?

We take off, my ears popping despite my Trident bubble gum, and I look at the shrinking land below. The water is slate blue, and I can see the coastline, the tiny islands. Somewhere out there is Martha's Vineyard— and Henry and Charlie and Slave to the Grind II and Charlie and Henry and . . .

The captain gives a welcome speech and announces we've got six hours and twenty-five minutes until we touch down at London's Heathrow Airport. Until we land. Until I find Arabella and she shows me her world. Until I see whatever happens next.

Dear Mable,
    It's true what you
said about Christmas
in London, but what
about Spring Break in
Nevis?
    More soon, Love

Dad –
 I'm stuck in the squalor of my
LAMAD digs – picture (dated,
yucky but somewhat true to life)
on front. Classes are harder
than I expected – not Hadley
heavy, but trying in their own
way. Not to mention the language barrier! How's winter back
home?
 XO L

Lindsay –
This is my house. Turn
to page 142 of this
week's Us Weekly to see
the crowd I'm hanging
with.
– Love

Dear Mrs. Dandy P – As promised,
a postcard of Big Ben. It's a very
large clock, as you know. Give my
best to Hadley and my fellow sec-
ond-term juniors, and reserve a
place for me at the college planning seminar next summer. (I
haven't totally forgotten college
and life back in the states, but it
does feel far away.) In the meantime, London's a blast. – Love

Chris – We miss you! Will you come
visit (and bring your new "friend")?
Have you seen Jacob? (Not that there
aren't plenty of guys here to make me
forget him – okay not plenty, just
one...). Life in the UK is eye-opening,
to say the least. Keep me (and by
me I mean Arabella, too) posted on
the latest and greatest (or lamest).
And know that I'm sending lots of —

Love from London
Read. Coming in March 2006

Read on for a sneak peek at the next addictive book in the
Principles of Love series . . .

LOVE FROM LONDON

Coming in March 2006

My tray table is in its upright and locked position, carry-on luggage
safely tucked under the seat in front of me, and my seat belt is securely fastened; but my emotions (and my hair, for that matter) are not.

I'm sitting here in my little seat feeling like a total mess—and, judging from the looks I've gotten from the woman sitting next to me—
looking like a total slob, too. Crumbs from the long-ago digested cheese
crackers have amassed on my chest, wrinkles abound from top to pants
from sitting in the same position. Granted, seven hours of flying does not
make for beauty queens.

"It's okay, dear," the granny-type lady to my left says and pats my
hand. She's pruny, tiny and so sweet I could cry.

"Do you think I made the right choice?" I ask her even though she
knows nothing about my life, my upcoming months in the UK, my aunt
sick back home, my father pacing until I call to say I've landed, my near-
miss boys left stateside, my transcript waiting for good London grades.

Pruny Lady looks at me and tilts her head, seriously considering. A
total *What if God were one of us?* moment. I suddenly think—maybe She
would come in the form of an elderly plane passenger!

"You know, I do think you made the right decision," Pruny says. "Just
keep your eyes open and your heart will fill up."

Prophecy or purely pointless drivel, who can tell. We land with a bounce and bump and I keep my fingers poised on the belt buckle until we've taxied to the gate. So far, out the tiny window, nothing looks that different.

Inside, however, it's another story.

I've been to Europe (albeit not in the jet-set way of most oh the Hadley Hall crew)—a two-week vacation in France before sophomore year at Hadley, and an entire summer in Berlin with my dad when I was eight years old, so it's not like I've been completely holed up in the land of Americana, but Heathrow is itself a blender of races, languages, and emotions. Accents, smells, green fluorescent lighting—it's all a bit much right after landing, but it's a thrill anyway. My thoughts are battling against each other—half longing for sleep and the comfort of known things, and half wanting to go exploring right away.

I stand with the last of the other Virgin Atlantic passengers, waiting at the carousel for my final duffel. At last, the machine coughs out my stuff and I pile it onto my little trolley. Lopsided, the thing is determined to wheel to the left, so I have to lean my (very tired) body into it to get it to follow the green line through customs and out to the international arrivals where I'm supposed to meet Arabella.

With a silly smile plastered on my mouth, I scan the crowd for Arabella's face.

The semi-familiar faces from my fellow passengers disperse, heading home with their friends and family, touristy hotels, leaving me sitting on my trolley, wondering what to do next. Before that thought grabs hold of me, someone's hand grabs hold of my arm.

"What the—"

"Miss Bukowski, welcome," says a tweedy man dressed as a chauffer circa 1940, cap, gloves, jackets, the works.

"Hi?" I say (note to self: stop speaking in questions—it's annoying and way too teenage girly insecure. I may as well just walk around with my hands tucked into my sleeves a la every teenage girl on TV who tries to look coy).

"Miss Piece arrived earlier and has gone ahead," the man says. "I'm Lundgren Shrum—the driver."

"Oh—right. I kind of remember Arabella mentioning you. Thanks." Lundgren pushes the trolley for me and walks me to the parking garage where I wait for him to pick me up.

I wonder if he's going to drive me in a limo—or a regular car—instead, Lundgren Shrum (will everyone I meet have interesting-bizzaro names?) pulls up in an antique Volvo. It's purple, kind of like the car in *Pretty in Pink* (minus Ducky).

"Your cases are in the boot," he says.

"What?"

"Sorry—the trunk," Lundgren explains and opens the door for me. At least I can sit in the front and not feel totally Hiltoned-out by riding in the back. Inside, the car is outfitted with modern amenities—a phone, a GPS (just where does Lundgren drive to that he needs one of those?), and custom fabric seats in burgundy and purple stripes.

We leave the airport environs and Lundgren gestures for me to open the glove compartment.

"I thought you could use a little something," he says when I've un-latched the small door and revealed a silver thermos shaped like a large bullet.

I pause for a second, unsure what to say. "I don't really drink."

He laughs. "It's not liquor—it's espresso."

"Oh—right. Thanks—I am so in need of that right now."

"Sugar's in the small pot just there."

We speed along the M4 (the motorway) as I sip my highly charged drink and then, despite wanting to look around at the billboards, the row houses, the funny shaped street lights, I nod off. Screw the fun of driving—I could so get used to having my own chauffeur.

"Here we are," Lundren says, "at Bracker's Common." I wake up from my freakish dream in which I am trying to find Jacob in some huge body of water but Lindsay Parrish (the pariah and piranha) is holding me back, while Arabella sings "Midnight Train to Georgia" and I have an illegible note from Charlie saying he's waiting for me on the Vineyard. Man, even my dreams are exhausting.

"Miss Bukowski?"

I shake off my nap and rub my eyes, then do a double-take. "Whoa." Bracker's Un-Common. Not eloquent, but an honest reaction to what I see in front of me.

Marked by two large, marble dolphins on either side, the driveway curves through flat still-green fields. We drive under a canopy of umbrella pines, the kind I remember from *Winnie the Pooh* books. To the left, a lake that shimmers with morning sunshine, the steam rising from it. To the right, sculpted topiary, formal gardens. Oh my god, I'm in *Dangerous Liasons* or one of those English historical movies where everyone skulks around and has nothing to do all day but write love letters and carry parasols. Sign me up. It's all so beautiful and historic—except for the security cameras.

"I'll take you to the front of the house and bring your bags round the back," Lundgren says.

"Thanks—and thanks for getting me at the airport. Sorry I fell asleep."

Outside, the cold air feels good—a refreshing wake up call to the amazing sights and wealth around me. It's so weird to suddenly have another side of Arabella, to know where she grew up, to fit her into the context of this place. I can't imagine what her parents are like—possibly they sit on thrones and wait for their servants to fetch them arcane items like wigs and dusting powder. And just think—they're supposed to be my local parents while I'm here. An enormous (and by enormous I mean seriously bigger than waist-high) Russian Wolf Hound bolts from the bushes and over to where I am, nearly knocking me over.

"Don't worry—that's just Mouse," says the woman at the massive entryway to the house. "She won't bite." She motions for me to come in and I walk with Mouse following me up four shallow stone steps.

"I'm Love," I say and shake the woman's hand.

"I'm Shalimar de Montesse," she says. "Better known as Monti—or, as you might know me—Arabella's mum." The handshake turns into a huge hug and Monti welcomes me into the museum-like front room. "Of course you can show yourself around later," she says and flails her hands to a hallway to the left, a flight of ridiculously large stairs to the right. "Up that way's the billiards room and guest suites, Arabella's loft is that way—library's to the back. Let's just go to the kitchen and get you something to eat. You must be starved."

Monti is totally familiar to me—her eyes, in particular are breathtaking and it suddenly dawns on me that she's *that* Shalimar. Shalimar de Montesse—Monti—*the* Shalimar. As in that woman whose face is always done in Wharhol-type art (the pink and green cartoon sort of things), the woman who ran (still runs? Jogs?) with the Jerry Hall Mick Jagger totally cool crowd from way back when. The woman who broke Bowie's heart (prior to his finding solace with Iman), who led Clapton astray, who revived the club scene in post-punk London. Who posed half-clad with a cheetah in those black and white photos. Just as I'm thinking this, Monti turns around from her position under a blue and white chandelier, looking like some glacial goddess in her pencil-cut jeans and bat-wing cream-colored sweater.

"Yes, I'm that Shalimar—formerly—now I go by Monti," she smirks. "Didn't Arabella say?" I'm unsure whether she means the name change or the fact that her mother's a major icon in the fashion-rock world.

"No." I shake my head. "She kept . . . pretty quiet about her—your—family."

And so begins my uncommon stay at Bracker's Common.

For more information go to www.emilyfranklin.com Sign up for Love Letters, the Principles of Love *newsletter, and find out how you can have your own name mentioned in a future* Principles of Love *book!*